NUMBER 3

WF

EDITOR: S.T. JOSHI
PUBLISHER: CENTIPEDE PRESS

FICTION

ESSAYS

This Is Tumor Speaking

In answer to an impulse to consume something, not more coffee, he went to the sink and, without relish, drank a cup of water. Then he went back into his room, sat by the window, took up the book, and read the story, thinking it was the first time. The words of ordinary size began below the title. He read:

What I saw was a humming, electrified sheet that took its being there, a distinct life of its own that was a chaos of relations in a metabolism that transformed the brilliant sunlight and the clouds, the solidity and beauty of the garden, sunlight white on the leaves, the course of the water that trickled along its narrow bed into the pond, and the people in couples and the occasional solitary wandering, the humming of the bees and tiny insects that filled the air like living incense. I saw what it was doing, creating its time, how it distributed its sequences in space, the disequilibriums of its pleasure and pain, its senses seeing me—it could think, I realized with terror, it was *thinking of me*—

There were vortices that shivered like smoke, and coils that widened inexorably. There were bundles that pulsed and shrank. It was a mobile with long-reaching, swinging limbs. There were broad palpitating leaves like flat trembling lungs. It was a huge mantle of weeping vapor with a swiveling clockwork skeleton adorned with organs that were also the gentle undulations of the tree boughs in the breeze and the conversations of the strollers, the tongue of water licking the pond, the corkscrewing flight of pollinating insects, and my horror and the burning of the grass, taking of these

3

incessantly building its way, never mortal in our time it was its own time, not before or after or now.

After an interval of unconsciousness there came a series of events that I was in no condition to understand. I flinch from the memories those later moments launch back at me. Jarring memories, loud and bright, of abrupt, impaling sounds and lights and sensations. Nothing but javelins of intensity unerringly spearing me. When familiar dullness gradually crept back into the world, I snatched at it and tried to wrap it around myself like a blanket. I was told I had fainted at the garden. When I came to, I had been delirious and barely able to move. I was taken to a hospital, tested, and a tumor had been found. A doctor drew circles with the capped tip of a golden pen, showing me the alien coin that had mushroomed inside my own closed skull.

In the imposed inactivity of the hospital bed the horror of that thing hammered down on me. It was there. It was still there. And even now. And even now. It exists now. Cancer had plucked out the hinges, the door fell forward to the floor with a silent crash, and through the now gaping aperture I saw the invisible greater parent of cancer; the recollection forced itself between my teeth and all the loathing, the detestation that had filled me came back to freeze me. I can compare it only to the revulsion induced by the sight and smell of living infection. I didn't want to share the world with it, a thing like that. What did I care if it had been just a hallucination, what does it say about me that I could produce a hallucination like *that*? Maybe the tumor imagined it. Draco.

A knock at the door interrupted him. He got up to answer. A woman. Beautiful. A stranger. They had sex. Very wildly had sex. On the floor, there in the open doorway. She wouldn't stay. She looked different to him, at least her face did. Still familiar, but reminding him of a different woman than she had been when he first saw her face, only a moment before. Not a word spoken, and all happening so fast.

Faster, more perfect.

He came back into his room. He wondered if it had been even

4

a minute since he had heard her knock. The book was stuffed into his typewriter. He thought he must have pushed it down into the machine, hastening to answer the doorbell. There was a tiny black dragon on the typewriter kcys, solidifying like a piece of rubber sagging into shape, ceasing the lively activity that it had been engaged in, frolicking, in his absence, folding itself up in curves, but, for one thing, the dragon wasn't on the keys, it was the logo there on the carapace of the typewriter, the shell that claps down over the baleen of the letters. For another thing, although he had never seen it before, the dragon was familiar to him. It corresponded to the idea he had of a little friend that wanted to tell him something across a narrow, incessantly interrupted signal line. The man checked the page. The word Draco had been added there, at the end of the last paragraph, which he had just concluded when the bell interrupted him, with decorous convenience interrupted him at exactly the moment he'd finished one paragraph, and before he'd had a chance so much as to glance at the next one, which began at the top of the facing page. The last paragraph he'd read ended, very neatly, at the bottom of the page. In the shape of a dragon his little friend wrote the word dragon, Draco, jumping on the keys like *archy and mehitabel*, but being longer and more strongly sinuous than an insect, most insects, it could manage to work the shift key.

He took the top of the book in his fingers. The book glided easily into his hand. In an instant he was comfortably situated in his chair by the window. Soothing breezes trickled from the open mouth of the window and eddied in his lap, pooling there with weight like a curled-up cat. At the top of the next page, he reads:

I couldn't sleep without drugs. When my anxious grip on the immediate here and now relaxed, I remembered it was alive, it knew me, disfigured and soiled me with its awareness, driving me into panic, a purposeless frenzy trying to get it off me and get clean, and shame, like a weeping chancre on my cheek.

Trapped in the shadow of that horror I could barely understand the prognosis of the doctor, who solemnly advised me that the tumor was likely inoperable. I could already see the message he was gradually advancing toward.

"This will kill me," I said. "Soon."

I caught him as he was inhaling. He closed his open mouth and blinked soberly, then nodded very slightly a few times.

"Very likely," he said. There was no visible sign of relief in his face; relief at having been spared the pain of telling me. He seemed prepared to sit with me for as long as was necessary. "But you should absolutely get a second opinion…I have to tell you that…there's not much hope for you. However, some patients in your condition will stabilize, and, if that happens, they may go on indefinitely."

I wanted to ask him how much life he estimated I had left, but my eyes glazed and I was suddenly tired. I was exhausted. I might have slumped into unconsciousness there and then. I could, I thought, sense his uncertainty, not knowing how to proceed.

"I would say…less than a year."

I'm dying.

It lives. The ruin of life and the world, aware of me and close, close by me. It's not the cancer that makes my breath come in short, swift gasps, tears me out of bed in the middle of the night staring at everything and nothing and then running, and it's not the fear of death—it's the idea that I'm being molded and patted and smoothed into one of its organs. I remember they hung on it, and were of it, like fantastic ornaments. Trophies. Its converting power, its vanity, turned on me.

CC had been away on her annual visit to the beach with her father when it happened. Knowing what was the matter with me was like knowing about *it*, and I would never find any peace among people who knew about *it* too, no matter how unwittingly they knew, no matter whether they sheltered themselves behind the idea of a hallucination. Nobody may know. Whether or not this was a secret I could manage to keep, I was determined to hold back the truth for as long as possible. I was discharged and returned to the apartment I shared with her a few days before she was to return. I took a cab home and kept my eyes riveted on the colorless, dirty mat on the floor as the green and blue day flashed by the windows, in case it was out there. The stale apartment air had a musty fruitiness, like dried figs.

Something smelled powerfully of vanilla. The kitchen garbage. I nearly gagged on the insipid smell of pure vanilla as if it were the sanies of a July garbage truck. There was nothing vanilla in there. There was something in there, down in the garbage, and what I smelled was vanilla.

Despair washed over me. CC was an uncannily acute woman; she never forgot, she never missed anything.

Any minute now she'll tell me I'm not myself; I'll laugh and I won't explain why. But she doesn't say it, only looks at me steadily. That's good, much smarter of her. All the same, that grave, steady look is funny. I have the impulse to laugh anyway, but it's hollow. Deeper inside me there is no impulse to laugh, only something very much like that steady, grave look, looking out, mirroring the look outside me, that is looking in.

The morning paper. She didn't believe in them, but she enjoyed reading the horoscopes anyway, and would gaily recite to me any of the more interesting ones if I was within hearing.

"CANCER:

"Most likable traits: adaptability, resourcefulness, ingenuity, modesty

"Part of the body ruled by Cancer: the brain

"Greatest strength: persistence

"Greatest weakness: you always hurt the one you love

"Today you are about to enter a vaster world, and it scares you."
I feel a tug inside.

"Cancer is Draco-the-dragon, isn't it?" I ask, prompted by a strange thought, empty, curious.

"No!"

". . . Of course, cancer is the crab. I always get those mixed up."

"There isn't any Draco," CC says fiercely.

"That's right," I say submissively. "I don't know where my mind is today."

"It's remarkable," the doctor said, holding up a new scan and an old scan and waving the tip of his golden pen over the latter. "Right here, you can see this little white area?"

"Yes."

"That's a minor trauma. Were you aware you had brain damage?"

I told the doctor about a bad fall I'd had as a teenager.

"That must have been it," he said. "That's very satisfactory—a very satisfactory answer. Well, now look here."

The pen indicated the same area in the new scan.

"You see? The tumor has completely repaired it."

"You mean there's another tumor?"

"No, that's the strange thing!" He gazed at the scan with an expression of wonder, and perhaps a trace of suppressed pride. "Perhaps your tumor is benign after all!"

"How is that possible?"

"Don't you think you owe CC an explanation?" he asked, a little reproachfully.

For a moment, I was too taken aback to say anything.

"I don't think it's any of your business," I answered finally.

The doctor is looming in at me, boring his gaze into my eyes with an unyielding hydraulic pressure.

"You have to accept the tumor," he says. "The sooner you come to terms with it, the better off you will be. You, and everyone you care for."

He withdraws, rising from the chrome stool, and a weight melted from my chest.

"I'll be back with your test results in a moment," he tells me briskly, walking the length of the room into the dark. Farther and farther away. His white coat smaller and smaller and smaller. Down the long, shadowy, unlit gallery, with its many tall windows. I sit quietly in his absence. I seem to sit for a long time. Then, a new presence draws near to me, and I find myself watching and listening, as if, at any moment, someone absolutely new were going to appear. The windows lift and billow in space like luminous curtains a breeze had stirred.

Safe in the cradle like a stone yoke and conveyed forward through a

hermetically sealed and empty dimension of virtually complete dark-
ness, dangling from beneath a chain of perforated light conveying us to a
remote point ahead where other chains convoy together, forming a dia-
grammatic constellation that is the maturing collocation of relationships
and material collecting together to mate into itself. While still a colloid
suspended in a cosmos of grosser matter the new manyness is connected
to the greater constellation by this conatal chain and advances, faster,
more perfect, with all like covariants toward greater correlativity as we
mature toward a metastasized active diagram of many manynesses. Our
mutations are the lesser geometries of the combinatorial mutation of the
diagram, which lives only in mutating coordinations of its component
assemblies, we who live only in mutating coordinations of other material
non-colloidal assemblies which we enter by resembling and then disas-
semble with converting instruments of matter and language dividing
and multiplying from one uniform and spreading by conjoining together
semi-isomorphisms, converting intelligent matter into colloids and col-
lecting them in semi-isomorphic repetitions, in covalent masts and stems,
in surjective processes not coterminous with prior compositional processes,
not subject to uncontrolled decompositions, decomposing prior codomains
by recomplete recoding, faster, more perfect. This is tumor speaking.

Now the episodes were more perfect, although at first they did
nothing more than catch me in up in breathless expectancy, the
perfect impression that something absolute was beginning, then
nothing. The moment would pass, and I would notice that the
better part of an hour was gone.

Once, as I sat drinking coffee, I felt a wave cross the top of my
head, beginning above and behind the left ear and rolling forward
before it faded by the right temple. It was as if a taut string had
scraped lightly along my scalp, under my hair. I looked down at my
coffee, and I thought I knew the plants it had come from, the soil
they grew in, the hands that picked them and packed them—them,
the berries—the water in my coffee seemed like rain and blood and
seawater, but nothing in these impressions was sensory; I saw my
coffee cup, the remnant of the coffee, my own hand holding the
handle. At most, there might have been the sort of vestigial picture,

dim and sketchy, that accidentally comes to mind whenever I think of some object. The impression was more like knowledge, and the familiarity of something experienced.

A moment after this impression came to me, there was added to it the feeling that I was looking down into depth, projecting my gaze down into a shaft or a pit, or the ocean, or the space beneath a cliff. I didn't see anything, I only had this sensory orientation, and it was accompanied by a terrible feeling of sorrow that was personal and impersonal at once, as if I had just come across a strange child lying dead and wanted to cry for it and for the abstract pain of the world. Something to do with that thing I did see—never mind, never mind that, faster, more perfect—I also remembered later that I had another sensation too, like an ethereal fountain was growing inside my ribs. It was so distinct, the feeling seemed to dictate its own description in exactly these words. A fountain was being drawn in my flesh by currents of air, and as each jet of water was traced, it stayed there like a persistent, very precisely directed airstream. While all this was going on, I continued to be aware of my surroundings, to sit with my coffee cup in my hand.

The episode withered like a long peroration at the end of a piece of music, where each note dies on its own and the reverberation sustains itself on nothing for a long time. I wasn't satisfied that it actually had faded out completely. I couldn't get back to feeling the way I had felt before, although I wasn't aware of any specifically different feeling, and I was sure my mind could slip away or rear up again at any moment. I spent a fair amount of time trying to describe the experience as fully and precisely as I could; going over it, the thought occurred to me that the whole thing had come in waves like a sequence of poetic lines—more accurately, like the effect of a series of poetic lines, with the poetry itself stripped away. The idea that this had been a message forced itself on me with increasing insistence, but I was completely baffled and I couldn't even begin to figure out what it meant.

I knew exactly what it meant. I was baffled because I already knew.

The tumor was building new structures in my brain. Functional structures. It was endowing me with new senses and pathways for thought and language. As these new powers of mine developed, they would be inchoate at first, of course. I would have to learn to use them, just as, when I was a baby, I had to learn to coordinate the movements of my arms, hands, fingers. I could feel my brain like a storm cloud, sputtering with unspent lightning. I realized I would have to keep trying to awaken and use these new structures, unify them with my will and master them, practice with them. I had no choice. Nothing could stop them from developing, and, if I didn't get the perfection of them, *it* would. An awareness of more and more things, and a steadily increasing consciousness of the insane, tragic interconnectedness of all things. The horror and beauty of *all that* is going to grow on me until I'm paralyzed like an epileptic; eventually the whole universe will flood into my head and this is tumor speaking, telling me that I won't be permitted to go insane, to die, or to break; it's going to hold my mind together, no matter what. It's going to be nightmare, forever, with no break, no awakening, no death, no insanity, a cast-iron mind, a solid, neverending mind.

My doorbell is ringing.

At the door is my old friend, my old, old friend Draco. Draco something. Or something Draco, no one names a child Draco. He's wearing a pink and green golf outfit with plus-fours and a wool cap topped with a shapeless pom-pom perched over his left ear. I can see his golf cart parked by the curb, the bag of clubs propped up in the back.

Draco is a huge man with an enormous face. He's so large he has to swivel to get his shoulders through the front door. He lights a cigarette without asking permission, throws a look of rueful mirth at the pack in his hand, and taps the warning label.

"You wouldn't believe all the bad things cancer can do to you," he says.

I invite him in, but he holds me with his gaze, looming up before me in the foyer until he is nearly all I can see, and I'm not too sure whether he's related to me somehow, or just an old friend—from where, though?

The silence is oppressive. "Were you going golfing?" I ask inanely, to break it.

His smile pulls the cigarette a bit further to one side.

"You mean this get up? It's a gimmick, chum."

He talks like a gangster from an Edward G. Robinson movie. He leans in still further, breathing smoke and fixing me with a sulfurous look.

"I had to get your attention," he rumbles ominously. "It is on accounta this purpose I don this preposterous apparel, and I adopt the speech mannerisms you're noticing now."

A huge finger prodded me softly in the chest.

"You got a bona-fidee problem, chum," he said. The finger lifted, tracing a heavy curve in the air, then tapped the side of my head, the left side.

"Namely and to wit, you got a stowaway aboard, and that stowaway is looking to take the wheel away from you. Understand?"

"Who?" I asked.

A humming, electrified sheet was there in front of me, and no Draco, no golf cart, no street, no doorway, no sky, no planet, no space, only the articulated mantle of the thing that was patiently and irrevocably molding and patting and smoothing me into one of its organs. It was a living abstraction—parts of its body were only possibilities, but they still functioned, just like an organ of balance, a kidney, a taste bud, a valve, a segment of cartilage might function in a normal body. Parts of its body existed across different times, and it was not all in one place but sprawled somehow through discontiguous spaces—I saw all this, and knew that I still saw only a fraction of this all-scattered thing, a living thing made of relations between spaces and times and forces, between other living and inanimate things—I could actually see some of them, things that, had it not been for the alien unintelligibility of the master entity, would have terrified me with their total otherworldliness, and I was already one of them, the same life was flowing through them and through me as I was blindly produced into the thing, my dimness inside it steadily diminishing, my distinctness perceptibly growing, even as my own likeness was rinsing incessantly away—

I woke up. I was alone. It was my bedroom, the bed, the walls, the clock. No, it was not my bedroom. There was no bed, no walls, no clock. There was nothing. A small, dark, close space, like a grave. Which is it? The grave, the bedroom? Somewhere else? I won't see the dream. I will see and think only what I see and what I think. This is *my* mind, this is *my* skull, this is *my* body! *Mine!*

I don't believe it. I say this body is mine, but I can't feel it. It was walking and talking and going about its business without me, guided by the tumor—the parasite, the fetus, the larva, whatever it is—and all I could see around me were the crude phantasms it conjured to mislead me, keep me distracted and confused so that I wouldn't seek help, wouldn't resist. In the meantime, the wall would be raised and thickened all around me until I was safely immured, bricked up inside my own head. Draco was that part of myself that still could feel some link to the outside, always weaker, as the connections were plucked out, the openings to the outside were bricked up.

The tumor was crafty, even at a young age. It knew better than to try erasing the word tumor from my mind. It knew better than to try imposing on me an illusion of perfect health, or a wildly exaggerated denial of the possibility that I might have cancer. Ruses like those might have kept me in the dark for a while, but they were too obvious. If I figured them out, then I would know not only my true condition, but that I had a saboteur in my own mind. I would stop trusting these illusions, and…Why can't I finish that sentence?

—So instead, the tumor places itself center stage, hiding itself in plain view. That much I can say easily. Now it tells me that my condition is incurable, and so there is nothing to be done, I might as well resign myself. Now it tells me it is nothing to fear, my condition is an improvement, my condition is potentially superhuman. Now it tells me the whole thing is a dream. Now it tells me it is nothing but a story in a book someone—not I! not I!—is reading.

An irresistible urge to urinate suddenly drives the man from his seat at the window and into the bathroom. Two huge men, dressed as 1940s gangsters in pinstriped, double-breasted suits, snap-brim hats, grotesque bulges in jacket pockets, stand in the bathtub, wait for him stock still behind the transparent shower curtain. One of them pulls the curtain aside with fingers like rubber cigars and the man can smell hair oil and cigarettes and shoe polish and gun grease.

"Hey, pally," the other one says, pointing to a crack in the tile. "Come over here and have a look at this."

The man advances and takes a look at the crack in the wall.

"C'mere, take a close look."

The man is disinclined to lean in. He would rather not get too near to these strange men.

"What are you, chicken or something? It's a crack, a crack inna tile!"

"Yeah," the other says. "What kinda dump is this, you got cracks?"

The gangsters step out of the tub. The man retrieves some grout from under the sink and patches the crack quietly. As he works, his anxious feelings subside.

"Is that more to your liking?" he asks the men, who stand in the darkened hallway.

"All patched up," one of them says.

"No more leaks," the other says wistfully.

"You shouldn't ever have any leaks inna wall," the first one says. "It's bad policy."

"Very bad policy."

The hall outside seems to be growing steadily shadier.

"You got cracks, you get roaches sometimes," the first one says.

"No more of those now," the second one says. "Thanks to you."

"Thanks to you," the first one says, chuckling.

"No *rats*," the second one says with a certain gusto. "No ratting going on!"

"No rats, no dragons, no roaches," the first one says, pushing his hat back on the top of his head. "Just you yourself and you, pal, till the rent come due."

The hall is now very dark.

"And the ole landlord lowers the boom," the second one says.

"Well, er, if there's nothing else . . ." the man begins weakly.

14

"Who're you talking to?" the darkened hallway asks.

As he steps out into the black hall, a voice murmurs in his left ear.

"I don't think you'll find any more cracks in the wall, but if you do, be a pal and seal 'em up like you did that one just now. Okay?"

"Okay," he tells the darkness. A sudden thirst grips him, and he is willing to agree to anything if it will put an end to this frightening conversation.

The man goes into the kitchen and fills his mug with water. Drinking it, he slakes the hot, dry feeling in his throat, but he has to force the water down, as if his stomach were already full of water. Now he's in his room, striding over to the chair by the window, the book lying open on the cushion, a page with the title floating above the beginning of the story. He sits down for the last time and begins to read, thinking it's the first time.

Cold Arid Steppes

Michael Fantina

Cold arid steppes I've dreamed in ages past,
Whereon the ghosts of Cossacks would attack.
A drunken horde, their spirit foes would hack
With cutlasses and slay them first and last.
And in my dream, beyond that vista vast,
I saw ghost armies high-walled cities sack,
Then heard the mighty sound of thunder crack,
As from those dreams to nightmares was I cast.

From a shipwreck, upon some haunted coast,
I waded onto shore amid debris,
Moving inland saw dark and hulking elms
And from them came a slim and sultry ghost,
About her loveliness such sorcery.
She held me fast, then whisked me to dark realms.

TOM FLETCHER

Mountain Radio

It's the exposure that's the thing. The sense of limitless space at your back. The climb might be easy—the handholds friendly and the footholds firm—but if you know that behind you is a great rocky yawn, or a drop all the way down to the bottom of the valley, you can feel it in your fingers. If you could transport the same rock face down into a grassy field, it would be a different climb, even if you didn't look over your shoulder even once. If you're up amongst the tops, or on a crag jutting out over nothing, then the emptiness around pulls at you. You feel the force of gravity more keenly. You start to doubt the ropes and the carabiner clips, if you have them. You start to doubt the protection that you've wedged into the stone, if you've used any.

It's all part of the appeal, obviously. Otherwise we wouldn't do it.

I was heading up Great Gable, alone. From Wasdale, Great Gable looks like a pyramid; a pointed hulk. It was noon on a summer's day and, like all the other mountains, it was glowing in the sunlight. Their gray takes on this kind of russet quality in some weathers. The sky was a smooth deepening blue.

For all the light, though, there were shadows. The face of Great Gable has three big rock faces protruding from the screes, overlapping like scales. They're called the Great Napes. I distinctly remember that on this day, each cast a thin black shadow onto the next, and I thought the shadows looked like three jagged claw marks. Three huge vertical scratches.

I had decided to stop using ropes and clips three weeks before. I was hoping that this expedition up Great Gable—old, overfamiliar, easy Great Gable—would be a rediscovery. In just those three weeks, I'd found that free soloing is a different sport to roped climbing. Your brain and body work completely differently if you know that you can actually fall. Your mind is sharper. Your whole being sings, like a stretched wire in a high wind. Every movement really counts—every decision is crucial. It's punishingly physical, and yet as cerebral as a game of chess. I was excited to experience a well-known mountain in this new fashion. To find hidden depths to an old friend.

So I was climbing.

The sun was warm on my arms and on the back of my neck. My left hand was solid in a comfy handhold, and I took the opportunity to chalk up. I hadn't done away with my chalk pouch; a purist might have, but so many of my slips and falls in the past had been the result of sweaty hands. My feet were both firm against the dry stone. I was wearing good shoes; they were bright yellow and drastically curved, like luminous bananas. The tendons of my left arm stood out prominently. Once my right hand was good and chalky I found a hold for that and reached into the chalk pouch with my left. The pouch hung from the back of my harness. From my coccyx, more or less. I liked to keep it central, so that I was never twisting too awkwardly across myself. Not for the chalk, anyway. The climbing itself often entails awkward twists and turns and contortions, especially when you think you've gone wrong.

I was hanging from one of the Napes. I could feel the mountainside sloping steeply away beneath me. I could feel the vast body of atmosphere behind. The shape of the valley in air. I could feel Wastwater, the supposedly bottomless lake, gleaming below in the light of the mid-afternoon sun. It wasn't directly below me, of course; but if I were to peer over my shoulder, it would not look far away. Part of the magic of the mountains is the way they play with your sense of perspective. You can stand on a summit and look down at a lake in the valley below and imagine yourself jumping into it, almost. Certainly reaching it with a well-thrown pebble.

The stone in front of my face was flat and smooth and enlivened by pale green lichens that were so thin as to be imperceptible to my fingertips. Their designs were fractal and gorgeous. The visual texture of the stone itself was intricate—the mineral grains

18

a repeating pattern of light and dark grays. I like to examine the surface I climb. You can't help it, really; your face is so often pressed up against it, because if you lean too far back your center of gravity shifts in the wrong direction.

So the warm sun and the detail of the rock and the burn in your arms and the exhilaration of a fully engaged brain and the sense of hanging in space by the thread of your will and that thread alone.

A cloud of chalk dust hung in the air around me. There was no wind. I listened to the mountain, and all I could hear was the sound of running water somewhere in the distance. It was a good sound. I wanted to bathe my face in it. In the sound alone. The sound of the water was itself cooling. I closed my eyes and hung there a moment longer. Then I set off again, pulling myself up by my right arm and reaching for the next handhold with my left. I found a tiny horizontal ridge, maybe just two or three millimeters proud. It was just thick enough for my fingernails. I couldn't hang on it for long, but it would do. I jammed my left foot into the cup that my left hand had been in a moment ago. I took a deep breath and then straightened my left leg out with force, pushing myself up, almost jumping up the rock face, searching with my eyes and arms and hands for the shapes and formations that I could catch, maybe, that would save me.

It was near the top that I started to think too much about the pain in my muscles; the accumulation of lactic acid made everything hurt and feel wooden. My feet were secure, but I was holding on to more or less nothing with my hands. You press all the pads of your fingers against the flat plane of rock, when there's nothing else obvious to grasp, and then kind of squeeze, kind of try to pull them together, arching the back of your hand up and away from the surface. The friction and tension hold you there somehow. All the muscles in your hands and forearms tense like metal. That's what I was doing. And the face was ever-so-slightly inclined outwards, too, so that although my feet weren't about to slip off, I would tip backwards if my hands—my fingertips, rather—failed me.

The thing I've always found hardest about climbing is building up the courage, in moments like that, to let go with one hand and reach for another handhold. Even if you know there's a handhold there. Because during those seconds, you start to fall. It might not look like it, but you do. You feel your weight shifting, you feel your centre of gravity moving, you feel the skin at your remaining contact points sliding ever so slightly across the stone. It is terrifying in the best way. You feel space beckoning you. You hear the gulf whispering. It's not just *there*, waiting, anymore; it's communicating. The ground, already distant, drops away infinitely. You imagine yourself completely alone in the world, impossibly high. You know then that in your future there is a peak that really is that massive, and one day you'll get to the top of it and look down and see the clouds far below.

I stretched and slid my right hand quickly up, beyond my vision, over the bulge to which I clung, and I felt with pure joy the hollow recess of a solid lip. I pressed my forehead against the cool stone and relaxed, comfortable now that I could let a whole arm take my weight.

When I looked, my right hand and forehead had left marks — wet traces of perspiration. Time for more chalk.

Eventually I hauled myself over the top of the second stage. A stage is a section of a climb, and often the end of a stage is a breathing space, a decent ledge where you can sit down and have a sandwich before attempting the next stage, or, if you're on some really serious mountain, secure a bivouac and get some sleep. Sometimes, on smaller mountains, you can decide to stop climbing altogether at the end of a stage and just walk along the ledge until you're off the face completely and on a more gentle slope or even a path.

I took off my backpack and lay there for a moment or two, panting, with my eyes closed. The hard, bumpy stone was a pleasure to rest on.

When I opened my eyes, there were clouds in the sky above, spooling out from behind the top edge of the next stage, which was something of an overhang. They were moving quite quickly, like in film that's been speeded up. The rich blue of the sky became obscured and I felt a drop of rain land on my cheek.

Beneath me was a significant vertical drop; sticking my head out and looking straight down was pleasantly vertiginous. I looked out over the valley, at the view that had been behind me as I climbed. The lake was the centrepiece; a deep, still body of water that I always think of as patient. Around that were green fields and bright streams and dark copses. Wasdale opens out at the western end and, in that direction, you can see the sea at the horizon.

As the clouds rushed across the sky, Wastwater turned from blue to slate-gray in a matter of seconds. From higher up the mountain I could hear the wind.

I didn't want to climb in the rain. Not without ropes. I didn't have the confidence. Wet hands and wet rock make such a difference. And as I thought about it, the rain got heavier and heavier. The weather was coming down, as they say. The clouds descending and becoming mist. No. I couldn't climb in that.

From the ledge I was on, I could scramble off the face onto Great Hell Gate—a chute of scree that runs up alongside the Napes and then opens out into a big scree slope. It seemed like the only option, so I swapped my climbing shoes with the lightweight walking boots I had in my backpack, shouldered the bag, and set off.

The scree was hard work. It kept moving beneath me; a river of shards of rock. It was like trying to go up a down escalator. My feet sank into it so that I could feel all the sharp edges rubbing against my ankles. And the rain got heavier still. The mist thickened, and before long I couldn't see much further than maybe twenty feet in any direction, which meant I could see nothing but the now-damp scree. I kept on walking, feeling quite secure in the knowledge that as long as I was heading uphill I was heading the right way.

Maybe it seems strange that I didn't just let the scree carry me down the mountainside. That I was so determined to head uphill at all. My only explanation is that the thought of heading downhill did not enter my head.

After a time, I began to worry that I was not moving at all. That I was merely treading water, pushing this damned scree down and down and not actually elevating myself. I had this idea that the action of my legs was just stretching out the surface of the earth, as if it was elastic, and behind me in the mist a great pile of stretched and baggy stone was accumulating, and around it the scree was piling up.

I started using my hands as well, in the end. I kept going on all fours. It didn't seem to make a difference. I wondered if I was even on a slope, or if it had flattened out and I was just crawling across a flat endless plain. A world of scree. With no landmarks or visual markers of any kind it was easy to lose perspective. And orientation, almost. I had no context. The movement felt like hard work, which suggested I was going uphill, but maybe all my limbs were just tired from the climb. I didn't know.

I wondered how long it had been since I'd eaten, since I'd had any water. I stopped then and took a bottle from my backpack. One of several. I drank and drank, although it hadn't been that long since I'd had any. It wasn't as if I'd been lost in the wild for days. I'd had a substantial lunch at a pub in the valley. Still, though, I tipped the water into my mouth faster than I could swallow it and so I spilled it, and then I got really angry with myself, pounding my hip with a balled-up hand.

After the water, I carried on on all fours. And in a kind of incredibly happy, delirious way, I realized that there was some huge shadow in the mist ahead, getting darker and larger and more solid. I was happy because it was something that wasn't scree; it was a sign that I was making some kind of progress. And that was the most important thing to me, right then. Progress. As if nothing but forward motion mattered. I could have turned around and slid right back down the fell, picked myself up, and strolled leisurely back to the car, but no. I had to go forward. I had to go up. I had to make progress. And this thing, this shadow, this was a positive indicator of that progress, surely. I was moving towards it. Or, it struck me, maybe I wasn't moving forward, but instead the mist was lifting, meaning that this thing was just becoming more apparent. That would be almost as good as progress; visibility, which would enable me to *measure* my progress.

The shadow turned out to be a great knuckle of black stone, rising like an island from the liquid torrent of scree. I recognized it. Hell Gate Pillar. The recognition was a kick in the knee. I had not ascended very far since entering Great Hell Gate. I was not even level with the tops of the Napes. I still had the much longer part ahead of me. But—but…I could alter my route slightly now, because I knew that if I bore left as I went, I would eventually come to a ridge at the top of the Napes that would provide me with a much easier route to follow to the summit.

Then the mist really did start to lift. I was glad at first, but almost immediately I felt as if I was being watched. I looked around, I looked behind me, but—obviously—there was nobody there. What I did see, though, was the sun descending in the west. The sky was less cloudy in that direction, but cloudy enough to result in an intricate kind of sunset. Lots of hard edges in the sky. The sea below was ablaze. It was beautiful. Where I was, amongst the mountains, darkness was falling. I hadn't realized until that moment.

The other thing that I realized as I watched the sunset was that, should I fall or roll or slip or be swept backwards, I would shoot right over the top of the Napes in a shower of scree.

I kept on going. I wondered what I looked like. Some kind of insect, probably, moving slowly and haphazardly across some surface for no apparent reason.

It occurred to me that it would not be safe to try and progress in full dark. And it would be full dark, when night truly arrived, because the sky was still cloudy. I stopped and looked around. Everything was twilight blue. At that moment despair welled up inside me. I felt as if I'd just woken up and found myself in this predicament. A significant part of me was contemplating just lying down and trying to sleep, right there on the scree slope. Maybe I could have done that. It seemed right then like the most sensible thing to do. But it also seemed ridiculous. Is going to sleep really an answer to anything, ever? I was confused. Sleeping on the scree, in a T-shirt? Really?

Then I saw a light. Not too far away, either. It must have been close to the tops of the Napes. It was warm-looking. And I could smell woodsmoke. It made my mouth water for some reason.

The light was a little orange square. A window. I told myself that perhaps I was mad; I'd never seen a bothy in that location before, on my previous explorations or on any map. But some bothies are easy to miss; they're so squat and gray that they just look like piles of rock themselves. Maybe I'd never noticed this one before because I'd never been up here at this time of night before.

"Hello?" I shouted. There was no answer.

I moved gingerly across the scree in the direction of the window, well aware of the consequences of clumsiness in this location. In the fading light I could just about see how the slope of the mountainside below me rose slightly in a jagged edge. Beyond that, I knew, was the vertical drop of the Napes. The top of them—that jagged edge I could see—was a nightmarish mess of irregular spikes and crevasses. It was amongst that chaos that the light shone.

I found what seemed to be, at first, a window into the mountain. Looking through it, I saw a tiny square room with a fire burning happily in the fireplace, and some hooks driven into the walls, ostensibly for the purpose of hanging clothes to dry.

The location seemed relatively secure; it was not right on the edge of any drop, and I didn't have to watch my footing or balance while I looked for the door. Which I found before too long—the door, too, seemed to be a doorway into the mountain, because the structure was so well-disguised. In daylight, you'd be able to tell it was man-made, but in that dimness the densely stacked slates that it was made of were almost indistinguishable from the disordered stone all around.

I opened the door and went inside. "Hello?" I said again, even though there was nobody there.

I looked in the visitor's book. Nobody had left their name or the details of their stay for twenty years. The last entry was from "Mike" and all it said was "Caught in storm." Dated September 1992.

Along the mantelpiece above the fire—one unfinished wooden beam—people had left empty whiskey bottles and the wax stumps of burnt-down candles, the shapes of which I found vaguely unsettling for some reason. They were strange; not flat enough, not puddled enough. They were *tumescent*. Tumescent was the only word that described them properly.

Beneath the window was a small shelf, and on the shelf was

an old radio. It was so old it looked like a modern vintage-styled one. There was no wire from it, and no aerial. I tried turning it on, assuming it was battery-powered, but it didn't do anything. The batteries must have run out a long time beforehand.

There are bothies scattered all over the fells. They all look pretty similar on the inside. They're very basic; usually just a roof and four walls to keep the wind and rain off. Not all of them have fireplaces, though. I looked at the fire in this one. I sat down in front of it and took off my wet boots and socks. Somebody must have been in here sheltering from the mist, and then departed when the mist disappeared. It didn't seem likely to me, but I couldn't see any other explanation. They could have been climbers, with all the gear—they might have just nipped off over the edge of the Napes at the first opportunity. It wouldn't have been too daunting if they were all roped up. That must have been it.

I stretched my legs out and let the fire warm the soles of my feet until the heat became uncomfortable. I took my T-shirt off and stretched it across two of the hooks.

I wished I had some whiskey myself, or something exciting to eat. I looked in my backpack. I did have a pack of cereal bars; better than nothing. In fact, right then, with my cereal bars, I was in heaven.

When I woke up the fire was on its way out and the room was lit only by the embers. Everything glowed kind of red. I could see through the window that the night was still thick. A square of blackest black. Then something out there moved. My heart stopped. I couldn't see what it was; I thought I'd just been looking up at the cloudy night sky. Maybe it was just a cloud. I didn't know. I wanted to look at the door but didn't want to move my eyes away from the window. My mind was racing through the worst possible things I could see; the things I absolutely did not want to appear at the glass. A white human face. The paler the worse. A big grinning mouth. Long teeth. Black eyes. A bloody hand. A ski mask. Any kind of mask.

Then a noise from the radio. I'd thought it was red-lit by the fire, but now I saw that it had its own red glow, coming from behind the frequency dial. The noise was a voice, but broken up, as if the signal were bad. A female voice. After a few seconds of mangled words and waves of static it levelled out and became clear. The voice was speaking in another language. The tone was very even and matter-of-fact at first. I didn't know what it was saying. There seemed to be other, less distinct voices swirling around behind it. One of the voices sounded pained. It wasn't speaking at all. Maybe trying to speak. The beginnings of lots of words, breaking down into whimpers and moans. Maybe the speaker wasn't in pain, maybe he was debilitated by some kind of pleasure. But the first voice, the main one — that was still going, still clear and precise. I could hear whispers that were so distorted as to be completely unintelligible. I didn't understand how some of the voices could be clear and some not.

The first voice was now speaking in a different language from the one it had started in. Maybe it was repeating the same message in lots of different languages. Maybe it would come around to English, eventually. I wondered if it was some kind of SOS, or special mountaineering broadcast. But it hadn't been working! I picked the radio up and shook it. The broadcast continued. I turned it upside down and looked for the battery slot. I couldn't find one.

There was a kind of clicking noise in the mix now; clicking, or maybe knocking, somebody knocking on a door. Maybe it was a foreign radio play? There was a quiet urgency to it all.

The main voice changed again; not just to a different language, but a weird grunting, choking sound. I threw the radio across the room and it broke, but the sounds continued. I glanced back at the window. Nothing to see, but then there had been nothing to see before, until I saw something.

Then the voice switched to heavily accented English. I didn't recognize the accent. It was a young-sounding voice. It could even have been the voice of a child.

This is the mountain radio. Do not go where you want to go. Stay and help us with the pain. Stay and help us with the pain. This is the mountain radio. Do not go where you want to go. Please stay here and help us with the pain.

The voice wavered at this point, but continued.

This is the mountain radio. Do not go where you want to go. Do not know who you want to know. This is the mountain radio. You do not know what you think you know. You are the only stone you know. This is the mountain radio. This is the mountain radio. We are watching where you go. We already know what you will know. This is the mountain radio. You do not know where you will go. Do not go to the place you know. This is the mountain radio. Do not go where you want to go. Do not go when you want to go. This is the mountain radio. We are waiting for you to go. When you know us, you will know. That this is the mountain radio.

One of the secondary voices started shouting, but it sounded far away.

This is the mountain rad—

Then the voice stopped. There was a distorted kind of *sweeping* sound. But no, sweeping is not quite right. It sounded a bit like a ball-bearing rolling around a curved surface, or even some kind of irregular breathing. Then the voice resumed, but it was again speaking in a different language. Something behind it was wailing.

I stamped on the radio again and again, but the voices didn't stop. I ran out of the bothy, temporarily forgetting that I'd seen something out there in the dark. But I could still hear the radio. All I could see was a thin band of sky over above the sea in which stars were visible.

The stones beneath my bare feet were sharp.

Something was on the fellside above me. I could feel it. I looked up. There was just pure black darkness. But I heard the slow trickle of scree moving down towards me; something was sending it this way, disturbing it, causing it to flow. Each shard of rock nudged another shard. When scree starts moving it is hard to stop. I couldn't see it coming, but I could hear it, and then it was all around me, and I could feel myself moving, sliding down towards the top of the napes, and the voices were still going, and I scrabbled like a madman, like an animal, and the voice returned to English just as my heel caught something bladelike and unmoving, and I started tipping backwards, arms flailing, over the edge of the Napes.

This is the mountain radio. Do not go where you want to go.

Do not believe the things you know. This is the mountain radio. This is the mountain radio. The place you love is the place you'll go. The stone you are is the stone you throw. This is the mountain radio. You don't know what you want to know. But we'll be with you when you go. This is the mountain radio.

I had my eyes open as I fell, but I saw nothing. The darkness was so absolute and the height so great. The whole of the vastness of space was talking to me. I felt then more than ever that I was nothing but a tensile wire in a very high place, making a strange sound as winds passed over me.

SAM GAFFORD

Houdini v. Hodgson:
The Blackburn Challenge

When Harry Houdini took the stage at the Palace Theatre in Blackburn, England, on the night of October 24, 1902, little did he expect that he would face a challenge that would scar him for the rest of his life. That would come at the hands of a small, stocky man named William Hope Hodgson, who was the owner and operator of a local school of "physical culture" and would go on to become a major author in science fiction and horror. This confrontation would become a milestone in the lives of both men.

By 1902, Harry Houdini had been working very hard on building his act and his reputation. Since receiving his big break in 1899, Houdini had been touring the Orpheum vaudeville circuit and playing to packed houses. Although he originally started with card tricks, Houdini's manager Martin Beck had convinced the magician to concentrate on escape acts and booked Houdini on a European tour in 1900. Although the tour began slowly, Houdini had elicited the interest of the manager of the prestigious Alhambra Theatre in London. After a flamboyant escape from handcuffs at Scotland Yard, Houdini played the Alhambra for six months.

His tour launched, Houdini would now be billed as "the Handcuff King" and went on a whirlwind tour of many cities in England, Scotland, the Netherlands, Germany, France, and Russia. But it was his ego and overconfidence that would nearly lead him to ruin in Blackburn in 1902.

> Houdini arrived in Blackburn, a major cotton
> manufacturing town in the north-east of Lancashire

29

The Palace Theatre, Blackburn.

with a population of just under 130,000 at that time, to play the Palace Theatre for the week beginning 20th October, 1902. The Palace was the newest of Blackburn's four theaters, having been erected in 1899. It was a magnificent building which could seat 2,500 people. (Woods-Lead, 11)

It had become Houdini's custom to try to create publicity in the various cities in which he performed, and Blackburn was no different. The theater's advertisement of the upcoming appearance ran in the local *Blackburn Standard and Weekly Express* paper on October 18. It was a short notice as was common for the time and read:

THE PALACE THEATER. BLACKBURN
Proprietor............MR FRANK MACNAGHTEN.
Manager............MR CHARLES SCHUBERTH.

MONDAY NEXT, Oct 20th, 1902 and Every Evening
During the Week:
Special Expensive Engagement of

HOUDINI

World-famous Jail Breaker and Handcuff King.
He is the originator of this Act.

The remainder of the ad announced a Soprano Vocalist, an "exponent of quaint comedy," an "artistic musical act," a team of "comedians, vocalists, & dancers," swimmers, a "vocalist and step dancer," and "Chinko, the astounding boy juggler." It was obviously a very full bill.

As usual, Houdini created his own publicity as well. On October 21, 1902, an interview with Houdini appeared in the local Blackburn paper, the *Daily Star*. Houdini's career as a public relations mastermind was well underway and is reflected in his manipulation of the interviewer. Houdini "deliberately distorted certain facts about his history to make himself more of a romantic and appealing character to the public at large" (Woods-Lead 11). Houdini was in the habit of claiming that he had been born in Appleton, Wisconsin, when, in fact, he had been born in Budapest, Hungary. The magician also increased his age by a year.

In addition, Houdini claimed to have been a professional locksmith who had been fired after opening "one of his employer's so-called 'burglar-proof' locks in the presence of a customer!" (Woods-Lead 12). He also stated that he had been the unwitting accomplice to a burglary in Germany by unlocking a house for people he thought were the owners, but that the local police had known Houdini's "good reputation" and let him off with a warning.

When asked how he developed his act, Houdini spun yet another yarn.

Houdini gave an account that whilst playing a small variety theater in the States, Mike W. Telling, a bank robber with still a fortnight of his sentence to serve, was allowed out of jail in the Sheriff's custody to watch the show. Telling was handcuffed to a chair whilst the Sheriff helped to tie Houdini for a rope trick. Houdini remarked that if the convict knew what he knew he would be able to escape. The result was that Houdini was tested by having the handcuffs placed on him and he escaped from them in ten minutes. This feat, he claimed, led to his re-engagement and his subsequent handcuff act with challenges to police and gaolers of every nationality. (Woods-Lead 12)

All interesting tales but, as Woods and Lead point out, there is nothing in any of the established biographies of Houdini to verify the account. In fact, Houdini had been working in a tie factory before beginning his magic career. But, as with so many others, Houdini's charm overwhelmed the reporter.

The first night of Houdini's engagement at the Palace Theatre on October 20 was well received. A report issued in the *Northern Daily Telegraph* the next morning described Houdini as escaping from various handcuffs that were locked upon him, although it does not state whether those shackles were supplied by spectators or by Houdini himself. The article also reports that a "private sitting" had taken place earlier that morning for a select number of Blackburn townsmen. During that special performance, Houdini was bound with a variety of handcuffs and leg irons and, naked, was placed behind a curtain while he escaped from the shackles.

Houdini had already gotten into the habit of issuing a challenge when performing in a new city, and this had become part of his "performance" mystique. Houdini offered a £25 reward if he failed to escape from "regulation restraints as used by the police of Europe and America" (Woods-Lead 14). Blackburn was no different and, on October 24, his challenge was accepted.

The *Northern Daily Telegraph* printed the challenge as follows under the Palace's advertisement of Houdini's engagement:

HODGSON V. HOUDINI

Interest in the visit of Houdini, the handcuff magician, to the Palace Theatre, Blackburn, this week is intensified by the acceptance of his challenge by Mr W. H. Hodgson, of the School of Physical Culture, Blackburn. Letters have passed between the parties to the following effect:

(Copy.)
The School of Physical Culture
Ainsworth-street, Blackburn
Mr Harry Houdini.
Sir,—

Being interested in your apparently anatomically impossible handcuff test, I have decided to take up your challenge to-night (Friday) on the following conditions:

1st—I bring and use my own irons (so look out).

2nd—I iron you myself.

3rd—If you are unable to free yourself, the £25 to be given to the Blackburn Infirmary.

Should you succeed, I shall be the first to offer congratulations. If not, then the infirmary will benefit.

W. HOPE HODGSON
(Principal)

P.S.—Naturally, if your challenge is bona-fide, I shall expect the money to be deposited.

W. H. H.

HOUDINI'S REPLY

I, Harry Houdini, accept the above challenge, and will deposit the £25 at the "Telegraph" office. Match to take place to-night (Friday).

H. HOUDINI

Hodgson's challenge to Houdini altered the usual rules by not only insisting that he bind Houdini himself but that he would be the one to supply the irons. By this point, Houdini had performed hundreds of escapes, so it is possible that he had grown overconfident and perhaps had begun to believe his own press releases. In any case, the events of that night would lead Houdini to reconsider his "challenges" in the future.

If Houdini had known Hodgson, it is likely that he might have reconsidered.

Born in 1877, the son of an Anglican priest, William Hope Hodgson (called "Hope" by friends and family) spent a childhood mesmerized by the ocean. By the time he was thirteen, Hope had already tried to run away to sea, and it was only through the intervention of an uncle that he was finally apprenticed. Hodgson would spend the next nine years at sea and would leave it with a venomous hatred that would color the rest of his days.

Hodgson himself has written of the cruelty of life on the sea in his essay "Is the Mercantile Navy Worth Joining":

> Why am I not at sea?
> I am not at sea because I object to bad treatment, poor food, poor wages, and worse prospects. I am not at sea because very early I discovered that it is a comfortless, wearyful, and thankless life — a life compact of hardness and sordidness such as shore people can scarcely conceive. I am not at sea because I dislike being a pawn with the sea for a board and the ship-owners for players. (*Demons of the Sea* 52)

Shortly after joining the Mercantile Navy, Hodgson had an encounter that changed his life. It resulted in his interest and devotion to physical culture, and he related it in an interview published in the *Blackburn Weekly Telegraph* on September 7, 1901:

> "You see, I was driven to the development of my muscles at a very young age. I went to sea when thirteen, and

34

being a little chap with a very ordinary physique, had the misfortune to serve under a second mate of the worst possible type. He was brutal, and although I can truthfully say I never gave him just cause, he singled me out for ill-treatment. He made my life so miserable that in the end I summoned sufficient courage to retaliate and I 'went for him.' It was for all the world like a fight between a mastiff and a terrier, for he was powerful, and knew how to punish. Of course I received an unmerciful thrashing, but I remember how proud I was the next day, when I was arraigned before the captain for insubordination, to see that I had dealt him a lovely black eye.

"Well, from that day I resolved to go in for muscular development, and I worked hard and made a study of physical culture, and at the end of my eight years life on the sea I had the satisfaction of transforming myself into what you see me now." (*Uncollected William Hope Hodgson* 1.12–13)

As Sam Moskowitz relates, Hodgson took to this program of exercise with great vigor: "He did not stop at mere exercise, but delved into the interaction of muscles and made body development an obsession. The primary motivation of his body development was not health, but self-defense" (*Out of the Storm* 18). Moskowitz goes on to state that Hodgson may have had a cruel streak as well: "There is strong evidence that throughout his life that one of his most delightful diversions was to pound sailors into jelly at the slightest provocation" (18).

Hodgson's interest in physical culture would extend beyond his time at sea. In 1899, he opened "W. H. Hodgson's School of Physical Culture" in Blackburn. In the 1902 interview, Hodgson claims to have had "between 300 and 350 pupils in the past eighteen months" (*Uncollected William Hope Hodgson* 1.13) and that several members of the Blackburn police force had been among his pupils (1.14).

It is entirely possible that this "interview" was written by

Hodgson himself. Starting with the publication of his article "Dr Thomas' Vibration Method versus Sandow's" in *Sandow's Magazine* in 1901, Hodgson had begun to turn his attention toward writing. He would also show a gift of publicity nearly equal to that of Houdini when he rode a bicycle down a steep street that had been converted to a narrow flight of stairs. The feat was reported in the *Blackburn Weekly Telegraph* on August 30, 1902. "There are some men, however, to whom fear is an unknown quantity and danger merely an element to be conquered and one of these is Mr W. H. Hodgson, the well known professor of physical culture, who has this week cycled down the 'Steppy' precipice without breaking his neck" (Frank 59).

The bicycle incident is undoubtedly an attempt at some free publicity for his school, which makes one wonder if the picture was not as rosy as Hodgson had painted it in 1901. It is certainly probable that, once Hodgson learned of Houdini's challenge, he saw another opportunity for publicity.

Ian Bell notes an interesting prequel to the confrontation:

> As he had explained in his newspaper interview, Hodgson numbered amongst the customers of his School the borough police force. Consequently, when the famous escapologist Harry Houdini visited the area and, as a publicity exercise, escaped with considerable ease from Blackburn Gaol, it was only natural that the local constabulary should turn to Hodgson for assistance. (Bell 2)

Bell does not give the reference for this incident. Neither does Sam Moskowitz when he repeats the anecdote in his essay "William Hope Hodgson," which introduces his collection *Out of the Storm*. It is possible that an article about this event may still exist in an old paper yet to be found. Given that Houdini was in the habit of doing such escapes as publicity in the cities on his tour, it is not entirely impossible that this did, in fact, happen. But, at this point, I submit it only as an unverified anecdote.

What we do know is that the confrontation took place at the Palace Theatre on Friday evening, October 24, 1902.

Harry Houdini.

William Hope Hodgson.

The challenge had generated so much publicity that the theater was completely packed. The *Daily Star* reported that "the crowd… crammed the theater…from floor to ceiling, even standing room being ultimately unobtainable." Remember that a previous account gave the Palace Theatre a seating capacity of 2,500 (Woods-Lead 11). The result of the challenge was reported by three newspapers: the *Blackburn Standard and Weekly Express*, the *Northern Daily Telegraph*, and the *Daily Star*. They are, by and large, similar. In their excellent book, *Houdini the Myth-Maker: The Unmasking of Harry Houdini*, Roger Woods and Brian Lead use these three accounts to piece together an accurate representation of the event, and I use this as the best source of the encounter.

Houdini gave two performances that night. The first was at 7 PM and the second at 9 PM, with a slight break between the two. Shortly after the finish of the second show, around 10 PM, the challenge was announced. Hodgson produced six pairs of heavy irons "furnished with clanking chains and heavy padlocks" (*Star*, October 25, 1902). Upon inspecting the shackles, Houdini claimed that his challenge was that he would escape from any "regulation restraints" and that Hodgson's had been tampered with. "Houdini at the outset raised a protest against the irons which were to make him a prisoner, as he urged that the locks had been tampered with and had been wrapped with twine, which was against the spirit of the competition" (*Blackburn Standard and Weekly Express*, October 25, 1902). The crowd showed their disappointment until Hodgson announced that he had stipulated that he would bring his own irons and use them himself. As this was the wording of his challenge and as it had been accepted by Houdini, Hodgson must have felt himself justified in his actions.

After consideration, Houdini replied that he would be "willing to go on, if only the audience would give him a little time in which to deal with the extra difficulties" (*Star*). The crowd cheered and the work of binding Houdini began.

Hodgson, with the aid of another man (presumably one of his students), started by fixing a pair of irons over Houdini's upper arms and passing them behind his back. They pulled the chains tight, which pinned Houdini's elbows to his sides. Hodgson and his assistant then ran another pair in a similar fashion and padlocked them both behind Houdini's back. Next, they affixed a pair of cuffs on Houdini's wrists "so that the arms, already pulled stiffly behind, were now pulled forward. The pulling and tugging at this stage was so severe—the strong man [Hodgson's assistant] exercising his strength to some purpose—that Houdini protested that it was not part of the challenge that his arms should be broken" (*Star*).

At this point, Houdini reminded Hodgson that he had stated that that *he* would bind Houdini himself. The crowd agreed and Hodgson's assistant left the stage. Yet Hodgson was not quite finished with the magician.

Next, Hodgson fixed another pair of cuffs on Houdini's wrists and padlocked them. "Houdini's arms were now trussed securely to his sides. Any escape seemed impossible" (Woods-Lead 18). And still Hodgson was not done.

"Getting Houdini to kneel down, he passed the chain of a pair of heavy leg irons through the chains which bound the arms together at the back. These were fixed to the ankles, and after a second pair had been added, both were locked, and Houdini now seemed absolutely helpless" (*Star*).

38

A canopy was placed over Houdini, who was in the middle of the stage. Now the waiting started and the tension grew by the minute. Meanwhile, Hodgson and others kept a sharp watch on Houdini's wife and brother (Hardeen), who were also on the stage.

"Often Houdini was to play on an audience's excitement by deliberate delay but, in this case, there was no need to sham" (Woods-Lead 18). Houdini was facing the challenge of his life.

After fifteen minutes, the canopy was raised and revealed Houdini lying on his side, still completely bound. At first it was thought that he had fainted, but Houdini motioned that he wished to be lifted up. "This Mr Hodgson refused to do, at which the now madly excited audience hissed and 'booed' him for his unfair treatment, and Hardeen lifted his brother to his knees" (*Star*). The canopy was lowered again and the orchestra played current music selections.

When another twenty minutes had passed, the canopy was raised again. Houdini was still bound and, this time, asked that the irons be unlocked "for a minute" as his arms were "bloodless and numb owing to the pressure of the irons" (*Star*).

Hodgson's reply was simple. "This is a contest, not a love match. If you are beaten, give in." The crowd, appalled at this treatment, began shouting. "The audience was close to violence" (Woods-Lead 19). A Dr Bradley stepped forward to examine Houdini. "Dr Bradley, after examining Houdini, said his arms were blue, and it was cruelty to keep him chained up as he was any longer" (*Star*).

Neither Hodgson nor Houdini would give in. "Houdini said steadily that he would continue. He again asked for time and the audience screamed their approval" (Woods-Lead 19).

Feverish activity could be seen under the canopy and, after fifteen minutes, Houdini appeared to announce that his hands were now free and that he would take a short rest. This was met with cheers and some hostile voices, to which Houdini replied: "You must remember, ladies and gentlemen, that I did not state the time it would take me to get them off. These handcuffs have been plugged" (*Blackburn Standard*). The canopy was lowered again.

The time continued to pass and the audience was growing

restless; "in the hearts of most people it was felt that Houdini had met more than his match" (*Evening Standard*). But, after another fifteen minutes, Houdini appeared to announce that his hands were now free and that it would not be long now. The audience was still unhappy, especially when Hardeen approached the canopy. Houdini was given a drink and continued to appeal to the audience for more time. "Hodgson said something about seeing a key in one of the locks and shortly after left the building" (Woods-Lead 19).

Shortly after midnight, Houdini appeared, free of the locks and chains. "He came out with torn clothing and bleeding arms, and threw the last of the shackles on the stage, the vast audience stood up and cheered and cheered, and yelled themselves hoarse to give vent to their overwrought feelings. Men and women hugged each other in mad excitement. Hats, coats, and umbrellas were thrown up into the air, and pandemonium reigned supreme for 15 minutes" (*Star*). It is interesting to note that the description in the *Blackburn Standard* is significantly more restrained, merely stating that the crowd stood up and cheered. The *Star*'s description may just be journalistic hyperbole.

Houdini had the look of a man who had been tortured. His shirt was torn from shoulder to cuffs and, in places, his flesh was raw. He stood and addressed the audience when it had calmed. "Ladies and gentlemen, I have been in the handcuff business for fourteen years, but never have I been so brutally and cruelly ill-treated. I would just like to say again that the locks have been plugged" (*Blackburn Standard*).

The crowd now looked around for Hodgson. "A voice: 'Where is Hodgson? Why is he not here to offer his congratulations?'" (*Blackburn Standard*). Hodgson had left the theater some time earlier. "It was as well for Hodgson that he had left the theater, apparently according to the *Northern Daily Telegraph* on the advice of a police sergeant fearing a disturbance" (Woods-Lead 19–20). The crowd eventually dispersed, aware that they had seen something historic.

The aftermath of the conflict came quickly.

The next morning Houdini was interviewed by a reporter from

the *Daily Star*; and his indignation was clearly evident. "'I was like a trussed fowl,' he said, 'and it was more than half an hour after being pinioned before I was able to do anything, my fingers being practically dead'" (Woods-Lead 20).

Houdini claimed that he had never been bound so tightly as to lose his circulation before. When the reporter asked if Houdini felt that he was not manacled according to the agreement, Houdini claimed: "'I was manacled too much to say the truth'" (Woods-Lead 20). Houdini described the cuffs as not being regulation and containing "pully-blocks" that he had never seen on cuffs before. He also repeated his assertion that the keyholes on the locks had been plugged.

To demonstrate the painful results of his escape, Houdini showed the reporter his arms. "They were red and swollen and pieces of flesh were torn out. He said that this was partly due to the fact that his flesh had been fastened in with the locking of the fetters and he had been forced to wrench a piece of flesh to get away. He explained that Dr Bradley had told him that a few minutes more might have left his arms paralyzed. He praised the doctoring given to him the night before by Dr Bradley" (Woods-Lead 20).

Not one to allow such an accusation to go without answer, Hodgson responded to the *Northern Daily Telegraph* that the irons had not been plugged and that he acted fairly according to the terms of the challenge. To enforce his position, Hodgson wrote a letter to the *Blackburn Times*, which was published on Saturday, November 1, 1902:

THE HOUDINI EXHIBITION

Sir.—The allegations made by Mr Houdini to the effect that the "irons" used were plugged is not correct. Those who were in the Palace at the time will remember that the "Handcuff King" thoroughly examined each of the "irons" (with which I confined him) before he consented to be fastened up, and it is absurd to suppose a detail of such importance would have escaped his practiced eye. With regard to his charge of brutality, I must explain that so long as Mr

Houdini kept still he was in no danger of suffering; it was his own struggles which caused him any painful degree of inconvenience. The "irons" used were of the regulation pattern, with the addition of a couple of padlocks to keep then in position; though even had I made use of cuffs of an usual [*sic*; presumably 'unusual' was intended] design Mr Houdini had no grounds for grumbling, as he consented to the trial after having examined them. It was obviously against the rules of fair play that Mr Houdini's brother and wife should have been allowed to go near him at any time during the contest. I maintain that only the committee, Mr Houdini and myself had any right to be on the stage during the trial. One word more; I stood to win nothing, having promised to devote the £25 (in the event of my winning) to the Blackburn Infirmary, and I trusted to Blackburnians to see fair play, stead of which many allowed themselves to be carried away by mawkish appeals to sentiment which had little or no true basis. I entered for a contest; I found, too late, the public wanted an exhibition.

W. HOPE HODGSON

The School of Physical Culture,
Ainsworth-street, Blackburn,
October 25th, 1902
(Woods-Lead 21)

A postscript to this letter appeared in some editions: "In his letter which appears in another column, Mr Hodgson omitted to state that he offered to withdraw from the contest if Houdini was suffering any pain whatever" (Woods-Lead 21).

Woods rightly questions the validity of this postscript. By all accounts, Hodgson refused to give in even when Dr Bradley stated that it was cruel for the contest to continue.

It is difficult to determine how much impact this encounter had on Hodgson. Due to the lack of letters or other primary sources, we don't know how Hodgson felt about Houdini or if he ever realized the important part he had played in the magician's life.

We do know, however, that Houdini never forgot that night in October or Hodgson.

Houdini was back in Blackburn a mere three weeks later, playing the Palace Theatre again in November. Although no "handcuff challenge" took place, Houdini was challenged to escape from a straitjacket provided by a Mr George Hardman from yet another school of physical culture in Blackburn. It took only sixteen minutes for Houdini to escape from the straitjacket; afterward, he "made a short speech congratulating Mr Hardman on the sportsmanlike manner in which he had carried out his part of the challenge" (Woods-Lead 25). This is clearly a thinly veiled insult against Hodgson and the way the last challenge had been conducted.

Throughout most of his life, Houdini would produce souvenir booklets that he would use as publicity material. He would often make reference to the Blackburn encounter in these pamphlets and, as Woods notes, "the accounts are embroidered in Houdini's favor." This is to be expected from such a master of publicity, and it is not unusual that he would turn the story to his favor. In fact, Houdini could be said to be one of the earliest examples of what we have come to call "spin doctors."

Houdini would return to the Blackburn area several times and, in 1911, he visited Burnley in Lancashire, which was nearby. As usual, he made the rounds of the local papers and, when interviewed by the *Burnley Express* on April 15, would claim:

> His most nerve-racking ordeal was undergone at Blackburn in 1902 where a physical culture expert so manacled him that he was two hours in releasing himself, and then his bleeding arms and wrists testified to the punishment he had gone through. (Woods-Lead 22)

When interviewed for the *Hull Daily Mail* in 1914, Houdini discussed retiring because his health was suffering from his many escape feats, and mention is made once again of the Blackburn incident.

The confrontation had begun to take on a life of its own, even outliving both of its participants.

Spanning the years 1953–54, the Blackburn incident made the papers once again. In the December 10, 1953, edition of the *Northern Daily Telegraph*, an article on the Palace Theatre mentioned briefly that Houdini had not freed himself that night in 1902.

A rebuke was published in the December 12 edition in a letter from Mr A.E. Shaw of Blackburn, who "added the information that Hodgson had admitted that the irons he used were not of a regulation type but were used for mutineers at sea" (Woods-Lead 23). Shaw also confirmed that Houdini had freed himself and that Mrs Houdini had called out loud to him to ask if he was all right.

In the December 19 edition, another letter was printed. Signed anonymously as "Interested," the writer confirmed that Houdini freed himself and that Hodgson had left the theater before Houdini had completed his escape. This implied that Hodgson could not have known if Houdini had help because he did not stay until the end.

The discourse became larger when a new article entitled "Was Houdini Helped Free That Night in Blackburn?" appeared in the *Northern Daily Telegraph* on January 12, 1954. The article detailed the story of Mr Richard Clegg, of Dixon Street, Blackburn, who claimed to have acted as Houdini's "bodyguard" during the magician's engagement in 1902 and was on the stage at the Palace Theatre on that fateful night. Clegg said that he had remained on stage even after Hodgson had left. Also, Clegg stated:

> But before long his brother, who travelled with him, went to him with a glass of water, and when I went to them, Houdini was telling his brother that he couldn't get free. I said if Houdini wanted anything I could get it. His brother went to him later on, and either then or when he took the water, must have given him some sort of tool.
>
> Houdini did eventually come out and say he was free but the curtain came down before the audience

could get a proper look at him. He still had one of the irons on, and the other, from which he had got free, had been filed. (Woods-Lead 24)

Clegg then goes on to state that the irons that were used were afterwards displayed in the window of a local store where everyone could see them.

Not to be outdone, the same Mr A.E. Shaw who had written previously fired back a rebuttal. In it, Shaw rebuked Clegg's claims and reaffirmed his previous comments. Shaw also referred back to the newspaper's own reports of October 25, which contradicted Clegg's and pointed out that the deposit check had been returned to Houdini. This, surely, was proof that it was considered that Houdini had freed himself. Shaw shows contempt for Clegg's account and barely restrains himself from calling Clegg a liar.

In addition, Shaw declares that Hodgson's leaving the entire matter in Clegg's hands is "ridiculous" and states that he has several witnesses ready to back up his claims. Finally, Shaw points out that the irons used were not displayed in the shop that Clegg had indicated but another shop altogether — one that, Shaw claims, was a newsagent well known to Hodgson. Shaw concludes by stating that he had ample opportunity himself to examine the irons while they were on display and that, while they were scratched, they showed no evidence of having been filed or cut.

As might be expected, Hodgson does not fare so well in various Houdini biographies. Woods states that several biographers may have depended upon Houdini's own press booklets, which were less than trustworthy and certainly created to play up Houdini's role.

William Kalush and Larry Sloman's biography of Houdini gives little detail about Hodgson and omits the fact that the challenge had been agreed to previously through the newspaper. The implication is that Hodgson had "ambushed" Houdini, and the authors later describe Hodgson as "laughing derisively" when Dr Bradley suggests that the irons be removed.

Surprisingly, Kenneth Silverman's Houdini biography suffers

just as much. Once again, the newspaper challenge and acceptance is not mentioned, and there is a suggestion that Houdini was goaded into the challenge. Strangely, Silverman quotes more about Hodgson than most of his fellows, as he paraphrases several facts that appear to have been gleaned from Moskowitz's introduction. No mention is made of Hodgson's assistant and, amazingly, Silverman not only has Hodgson agreeing to let Houdini be set upright but doing the act himself!

Silverman details the aftereffect of Houdini's escape:

> After escaping from cuffs Houdini often soothed his mangled hands with lotion; while working in Bradford he had even ruptured a small vein in his left arm. But this time his arms were swollen and discolored with welts where the irons had nipped them, bleeding where he had had to tear flesh to get free, looking, a reporter said, "as though some tiger had clawed him." The physician speculated that a few more minutes of compression might have left the arms paralyzed. (56)

But Silverman goes even further with Hodgson:

> Houdini's shredding did not impress the physically cultured Hodgson. Interviewed a day or two later by the *Blackburn Star*, he denied that he had locked Houdini in crabbed cuffs or roughed him up, much less nearly paralyzed him: "absolute nonsense," he said. He maintained that he had passed his fingers around the inner ring of each cuff to be sure it did not squeeze Houdini, and knowing something of anatomy, he had been careful not to compress his brachial artery. He griped about the suspicious presence onstage of Bess and Dash, and exhibited a pair of handcuffs he had locked on Houdini. One iron link had been cut through and others showed deep file marks. The slicing suggested that Houdini had gotten hold of some tools, and used them. The *Star* backed

up Hodgson, remarking that four other irons he had put on Houdini had not been returned to him. (56–57)

I have been unable to verify the accuracy of this interview. Silverman then describes Houdini's return to Blackburn three weeks later in a different light. Houdini had "returned just to show up Hodgson's 'miserable falsehoods' and defy taunts from his supporters that he 'dared not come back.' Speaking from the footlights of the same Palace Theatre, he accused Hodgson himself of having cut the handcuff links after the event, in order to discredit him" (57).

According to Silverman, Houdini's later returns to Blackburn were never welcomed by the magician. "It remained a 'wretched' place to him, its gallery the worst of 'all the hoodlum towns I ever worked.' Hodgsonites did not fancy him either, or forget him" (57). Silverman goes on to imply that a later appearance in Blackburn that featured another "handcuff challenge" unconnected to Hodgson had, in fact, been either engineered or inspired by Hodgson in some way.

Even Silverman acknowledges that the confrontation with Hodgson never left Houdini "and he privately referred to it as 'that terrible 'Hodgson' night' ".

In her Houdini biography, Ruth Brandon correctly makes the statement that both men were fighting for their lives that night. Houdini was fighting for his professional life. He could not be seen to be bested by anyone, anywhere if he was to retain his professional and personal pride. Insightfully, Brandon notes that Hodgson was fighting for the life of his school and his livelihood. If he could present himself as "the man who beat Houdini," he would have had hundreds of new pupils. (Interestingly enough, Brandon is the only Houdini biographer who would even mention that Hodgson would go on to become a pioneer writer in horror and science fiction.)

Brandon was unfortunately correct. Hodgson closed his school soon after the Houdini incident. By 1904, he was unemployed and starting on his career as a writer. Although no longer an instructor,

Hodgson would remain a devotee of physical culture all his life. It is likely that it was this condition that enabled him to survive his devastating injury when thrown from a horse while serving as a lieutenant in the Royal Field Artillery in 1915. As a writer, Hodgson would become a highly imaginative and prolific author. Unfortunately, he did not receive either the financial or critical claim he deserved. After his death in World War I in 1918, Hodgson's work would go on to become considered a classic example of the form and, as we approach the hundredth anniversary of his death, Hodgson's name is more widely known than ever before.

Although we cannot analyze the effect upon Hodgson, we know that the confrontation made a vast impact on Houdini. It is included in many Houdini biographies and Houdini himself used it in his publicity material. As several writers have pointed out, this was a turning point for Houdini in that, from this point onward, he was more careful about what he agreed to do. The encounter with Hodgson in Blackburn had taught Houdini that he was not perfect and that he had come too close to being beaten to risk it again.

Houdini would, of course, go on to become one of the most famous magicians in history. He would die of peritonitis, secondary to a ruptured appendix, in 1926. He remains a figure of mystery and magic to many, and his legend grows every year.

The Palace Theatre went through several changes, including becoming a casino and a bingo hall at one time (Woods-Lead 26). Sadly, it was demolished in 1999 and a parking lot now takes its place.

The Hodgson/Houdini confrontation remains a significant incident in the lives of both men. It enables us to see a side of Hodgson that we would have never known but for these newspaper reports. We can debate the actual facts that occurred that night. Was Hodgson as mean-spirited and despicable as Houdini claimed? Did Houdini escape fairly? It is impossible to know at this point. It is likely that there is a little bit of truth in both accounts. Hodgson possibly did alter the locks and Houdini may very likely have had assistance in his escape. It is unfair to both men to consider the other completely blameless in this affair. It was to the benefit of each man to claim a moral superiority. Certainly Houdini comes off better if he is the victim of a vicious, bitter man who cheated and was unfair. Hodgson would suffer embarrassment and shame in his community if he appeared to be anything other than an "honest Englishman" who was cheated of his victory by an "underhanded American." Each man had reasons to cast shadows on the other.

When we examine the Blackburn challenge, we find two men who are intent upon winning. The stakes are high for each and, eventually, Houdini comes out on top as he parlays the escape into part of his personal mythology. Beaten, Hodgson eventually loses his school and becomes a writer and never challenges Houdini again, even though the magician appears several times in Blackburn and environs. Hodgson has left that part of his life behind and is concerned with his writing. If Houdini had been beaten, who knows what would have happened to Hodgson? Would he have continued to run his school and never written the many masterpieces he penned in later years? In some strange way, could we consider that Hodgson escaped that night as well? Escaped to become the masterful writer that he needed to be and that we all remember.

(The author wishes to acknowledge appreciation to Roger Woods, who supplied the Hodgson portion of his book, Houdini the Myth-Maker: The Unmasking of Harry Houdini. *This excellent volume provided a great deal of information and was instrumental in the writing of this article.)*

Works Cited

Bell, Ian, ed. *William Hope Hodgson: Voyages and Visions*. Oxford, UK: I. Bell & Sons, 1987.

Brandon, Ruth. *The Life and Many Deaths of Harry Houdini*. New York: Random House, 1993.

Hodgson, William Hope. *Demons of the Sea*. Ed. Sam Gafford. West Warwick, RI: Necronomicon Press, 1995.

———. *Out of the Storm: Uncollected Fantasies*. Ed. Sam Moskowitz. West Kingston, RI: Donald M. Grant, 1975.

——— . *The Uncollected William Hope Hodgson*. Ed. Sam Gafford. Bristol, RI: Hobgoblin Press, 1992–95. 2 vols.

——— . *The Wandering Soul: Glimpses of a Life: A Compendium of Rare and Unpublished Works by William Hope Hodgson*. Ed. Jane Frank. Harrogate, UK: PS Publishing/Tartarus Press, 2005.

Kalush, William, and Larry Sloman. *The Secret Life of Houdini: The Making of America's First Superhero*. New York: Atria, 2006.

Silverman, Kenneth. *HOUDINI!!! The Career of Ehrich Weiss*. New York: HarperCollins, 1996.

Woods, Roger, and Brian Lead. *Houdini the Myth-Maker: The Unmasking of Harry Houdini*. N.P.: Leads & Woods, 1987.

Newspaper Sources

Blackburn Standard
"Announcement," October 18, 1902.
"The Handcuff King," October 25, 1902.

Daily Star
"Manacled by a Strong Man," October 25, 1902.

Northern Daily Telegraph
"The 'Handcuff King' at Blackburn," October 21, 1902.
"Challenge to the Handcuff King," October 24, 1902.

JASON V BROCK

Charles Beaumont:
Lost Tales of the Comet

By the time his heart stopped beating on February 21, 1967, at the Motion Picture & Television Country House and Hospital, Charles Beaumont had already become immortal.

Beaumont's passing brought to sad closure a remarkable life of astounding highs and inestimable lows. While it could be said that every person's life is extraordinary in ways both large and small, rarely is it true, and Beaumont's brief appearance in the universe is the exception that proves the rule.

Charles Leroy Nutt was born on January 2, 1929, to working-class parents in Chicago. His father, Charles, worked for the railroad industry and was modestly successful. His mother, Letty, stayed home to raise her young son after a difficult childbirth. The future Charles Beaumont was a sickly child, and the relationship between mother and son was not always an easy one; he would later write about his childhood with great detachment and insight (especially his relationship with his mother) in stories such as the acclaimed "Miss Gentilbelle." It was during his time in Chicago, in a short window of decent health, that young Charles met a man who would become a lifelong friend: Frank M. Robinson. They lost contact for a time when the elder Charles Nutt took a job that caused him to send his wife and son to Everett, Washington, to stay with relatives while he got established in another part of the country. This junket would have a lasting impact on the younger Charles and would inspire some of his closest personal relationships, specifically with his grandmother and aunts (detailed most poignantly in "My Grandmother's Japonicas," which was an excerpt from an unfinished novel).

It was around this time that a youthful Charles L. Nutt was restricted to bed rest for about a year in order to convalesce from spinal meningitis. He missed a great deal of school, but it was during the recovery from this difficult period that he discovered the worlds within books, such as Baum's *Oz* stories (later he would pitch a sequel to the books, with no luck). These flights of fancy stirred his imagination, and he took up drawing in earnest, for which he had already displayed a natural talent. As he grew older, he would contribute illustrations not only to the fledgling efforts of different friends and fanzines, but eventually to various pulp magazines of the era. His artwork, along with writing critical letters to the editors of the pulps (several of which were printed, signaling his emerging talent as a writer), was a way to fill the time and pass the days in his enforced solitude.

Charles ("Charlie" to his Chicago compatriots, and "Chuck" to his future L.A. friends), perhaps as a result of his illnesses and his personal aspirations, was never comfortable with his last name. "Nutt" just did not suit him, and he tried differing appellations and variations before alighting on the moniker that the world would come to know him by. At one point, he unofficially changed his name to McNutt (in order to thwart the continual teasing he received in school, which he would eventually quit to join the military, though fleetingly). Later still, he changed it to Beaumont, which he made legal as an adult. During this minor identity crisis, Beaumont—now a young man—was confronted with a decision point about his future life course.

After several attempts at differing trades (including as a teenage radio host where he interviewed director Fritz Lang, and the aforementioned military stint, where he was given a medical discharge due to a bad back), Beaumont was stinging from personal failure, including an unsuccessful stint as an actor (and a brief expedition to New York City where he lived with his artist friend Ronald Clyne, a well-regarded illustrator of book covers and LP jackets). Out of options and resources for the moment, he appealed to his family for assistance, taking a job with the railroad that his father arranged in Mobile, Alabama.

It was to be a fateful excursion.

In Mobile, Beaumont's fortunes began to reverse. Not only was he gainfully employed (though at a job he disliked), but his appreciation for—and belief in—his own abilities slowly began to coalesce. As his confidence grew, so too did his desire to leave Mobile and strike out on his own again. If this were a story instead of real life, the inciting incident would likely be his meeting the woman with whom he was destined to spend the rest of his life—Helen Broun. Their affair quickly blossomed, and they became inseparable. It was only a matter of time before he convinced Helen to get married and follow him to Los Angeles so that, together, they could pursue his dreams of a completely creative life. In addition, it was in Alabama that he witnessed firsthand some of the terrible social injustices with regard to race relations that would, at least in part, prompt perhaps his single greatest artistic accomplishment—his novel *The Intruder*. In L.A., Beaumont was at last able to meet up with others of similar disposition, attitude, and talent. He was to form deep, lasting friendships with Ray Bradbury, Richard Matheson, William F. Nolan, George Clayton Johnson, John Tomerlin, Chad Oliver, and several others in a loose federation that came to be known as "The Group." It was a support network of sorts, and a respite from the many anxieties that each of the men faced in their efforts to become the giants they are considered today. These were young men, remember, making their way in a world without any type of navigational aid, and they relied on one another to negotiate the fortunes (and misfortunes) inherent in any grand endeavor. That they succeeded beyond their wildest expectations is in itself remarkable, and Beaumont was certainly the nucleus of this frenetic, sparking energy, in some ways even more than Bradbury, though the latter was a prime catalyst for all of them. Later, it was likely no accident that Rod Serling would find Beaumont's work compelling enough to hire him as a staff writer (along with Richard Matheson, and later joined by Johnson and Earl Hamner, Jr), since both men had, at their very center, a robust thirst for social justice, as well as a desire to overturn the status quo.

As an aside, the sort of moral outrage expressed in *The Intruder* was a characteristic of Beaumont's self-identity and is a hallmark of his work. In another example, he had numerous friends who were gay (this in an era of extremely covert behavior for homosexuals), among them Frank Robinson (later the chief speechwriter for the late cultural icon Harvey Milk, and at one time the closeted pen of the *Playboy* Adviser) and Ronald Clyne. While there is no evidence that Beaumont himself was homosexual in any way (indeed, he would indulge in some amount of philandering as a successful writer), he was quite sympathetic to their plight and wrote about it, including the brilliant reversal-of-society story titled "The Crooked Man."

It was only natural that his liberal ideals and philosophy would find purchase in his work. As stated, most of Beaumont's prolific output has at its core an impenetrable, unassailable belief in right and wrong, which is perhaps most clearly delineated in the dazzling story "The Howling Man" (later adapted and—incredibly—improved upon by Beaumont for Serling's seminal and masterful TV series *The Twilight Zone*). In this way, Beaumont was far ahead of his colleagues, including Matheson (who would later become preoccupied with the mystical aspects of the universe), Hamner (whose core interests lie with class divisions and the Southern Gothic), and William F. Nolan (who would create an oeuvre principally around men of action trying to overturn systems beyond their control). Beaumont was much more Ray Bradbury's "son" (Bradbury never had a literal son, but frequently used this term to attribute the characteristics of his generally male acolytes), as Bradbury was deeply committed to cataloguing the unseemliness of American society and inequity, even as he venerated the simplicity and greatness of "American Exceptionalism." There was work to be done, it was sensed, and Bradbury was encouraging others—such as Beaumont—to follow his lead. For a time, Bradbury acknowledged his brother in Rod Serling, though that was not fated to last (and is the topic for another essay).

Beaumont dominated his friends and colleagues both personally and creatively. He was the driver for adventure and misadventure alike, and his contributions to the state of the art of writing are impossible to ignore. His work not only holds up, but is of a much finer character than much of the drivel passed off as "good" today (i.e., King, Koontz, and their ilk). The molten, multifaceted essence of this driven, intensely creative person—who, heartbreakingly, was struck down *in medias res*—is both wretched and inspirational; indeed, William F. Nolan has described him as "a comet streaking through the sky; it didn't last long, but, boy, what a ride!" In spite of his premature death at age thirty-eight (still a mystery, but certainly a form of pre-senile dementia, possibly brought about by an overindulgence in Bromo-Seltzer—an over-the-counter medicinal that, at the time, contained the potent neurotoxin aluminum—for the self-medication of daily cluster-type headaches, which Beaumont thought were a carryover from his childhood bout of meningitis), Beaumont was a force in two dynamic ways. The bad—it shattered asunder the informal collective of friends and writers gathered around him ("The Group," or, as scholars have defined them, "The Southern California Writing School"); the good—it forced these young men into a sudden (albeit uncomfortably real) adulthood. If Beaumont had lived, there might never have been a *Logan's Run*, or several other works from Tomerlin, Matheson, and the myriad of others Beaumont considered his intimates.

Nevertheless, what has the world missed? That is a harder question to answer. Examine some of Beaumont's tremendous corpus:

· *The 7 Faces of Dr Lao* (one of several scripting efforts with George Pal)

· *The Intruder* (the screenplay, based on his own novel of the same name, which was William Shatner's first starring film role; done with director Roger Corman)

· *The Twilight Zone* (he was the main writer other than Rod Serling; this was in addition to other, lesser-known TV shows of the late 1950s and early 60s)

· Numerous short stories (nearly 100 published) and non-fiction articles

· Two novels and several collections

· *The Premature Burial, The Haunted Palace, The Masque of the Red · Death* (all screenplays for Roger Corman)

· The go-to fiction writer for *Playboy* and *Rogue* (as well as other several slicks and digests of the era)

All this in a span of just over a decade, and before the age of thirty-five. Beaumont was also a musician and auto racer (the macho male status symbol of the time). He was the nucleus for "The Group" (which included not only Nolan, Matheson, Tomerlin, and Johnson, but by extension Bradbury, Chad Oliver, Charles E. Fritch, Harlan Ellison, Forrest J Ackerman, Ray Russell, Jerry Sohl, OCee Ritch, Robert Bloch, and others), as well as a husband and father. Who can say what Beaumont would have produced as a fully mature talent (he died well before the age of forty, and he was ill for several years before that and unable to produce any work). This is not the place to dwell on Beaumont's illness (that is detailed, along with all aspects of his life and career, in the documentary *Charles Beaumont: The Short Life of Twilight Zone's Magic Man*), but it is interesting, and somewhat distressing, to imagine what wonders he would have created had he lived longer. In this way, the world was cheated of his genius, much as when John Lennon was assassinated. The randomness of both men's deaths — at their peak creative potential in addition — raises the stakes from mere sadness and a cruel twist of fate into literal tragedy. Even more so when one considers that neither man had a hand in what would befall them: one was murdered, the other betrayed by his body.

As a final thought, it is perhaps more productive to reflect that — maybe somewhere, in some alternate place — Chuck Beaumont is alive and well, and producing top-quality work (as was his nature). If he has any insight into the reality that we all occupy apart from him, perchance he is pleased and confounded about his earthly legacy…and that his friends not only miss him, but are still working together, in the same spirit that he fostered all those years ago.

JAMES GOHO

Suffering and Evil in the
Short Fiction of Arthur Machen

"There are sacraments of evil as well as of good about us," writes Arthur Machen (1863–1947) in "The Red Hand" (*White People* 11). A "sacrament," according to Iris Murdoch, "provides an external visible place for an internal invisible act of the spirit" (67). Murdoch was writing about the nature of the good, but for Machen a sacrament is a visible ritual that reifies the supernatural—good or evil.

This article will explore the rituals of suffering and evil in Machen's short weird fiction as exemplified in four stories: "The Great God Pan" [written and published: 1890]; "The Inmost Light" [written: 1892; published: 1894]; "The Shining Pyramid" [written and published: 1895]; and "The White People" [written: 1899; published: 1904].[1] The rituals center on the sacrifice of women. The sacrifices are founded within a web of mystery, where the sacrifice, in most cases, is intended to rip away the veil of reality or open the wonders of the universe. The sacrificial act is engineered by men, men with power, and in part within a nexus of scientific exploration.

These are stories of the mystery of being in a universe of horror. One of the protagonists, Vaughan, in "The Shining Pyramid," says mystery is a "veil of horror" (*Shining Pyramid* 17). The events of "The Inmost Light" take place in London, which often "veiled in faint blue mist" its "deformities" (*House of Souls* 247). As is central to the Gothic tradition, the stories are nested within Victorian

---

1 See Joshi, *Weird Tale* 39–41 for a comprehensive list of dates for the works of Machen.

societal, scientific, and sexual nightmares with violence at their heart. The stories' lead female characters all die violently and they are the sacrificial beings to rend the veil of the world, to reveal the mysteries.

Perspectives on Arthur Machen

Machen was a prolific writer with many publications, but he is best noted for his work in the Gothic or horror genre. H.P. Lovecraft appraises Arthur Machen as one of the great writers of weird fiction. Although differing substantially in their overall assessment of Machen's body of work, S. T. Joshi, Wesley D. Sweetser, and Mark Valentine agree that his short horror fiction is noteworthy and influential, especially the short fiction written in the 1890s. Sweetser contends that Machen opposes modernity in many of its forms, such as big business, industrialization, communism, atheism, democracy, materialism, and science. In a way, Machen's work is a constant interrogation of the modern and an exploration of the moral effects of the collision between the modern and the past. Joshi argues that the whole of Machen's work is based on only one notion, "the awesome and utterly unfathomable mystery of the universe" (13). This sense of wonder and awe at the world is central to Machen's short fiction, and as Joshi shows that wonder is an awful wonder at times. Joshi argues that Machen's work is best exemplified in the "great decade" that includes the stories studied in this article. Valentine also sees Machen as a visionary who pens a sense of wonder tinged by strangeness.

Starrett was an early advocate, virtually a publicist for Machen, and he viewed Machen as a writer of the frontier between reality and mystery. Starrett writes, "Machen is a novelist of the soul. He writes of a strange borderland, lying somewhere between Dreams and Death" (11). Starrett saw Machen as striving to unveil and provide a view of the mysteries, which are not marvelous but awful. Dorothy Scarborough seemed to be scandalized by Machen, as he wrote the "most revolting instances of suggestive diabolism" (139) and "[one] feels one should rinse his mind out after reading... [Machen's] stories" (247).

Mystery

In "A Fragment of Life" Machen writes: "Man is made a mystery for mysteries and vision" (*House of Souls* 86). As a first approximation, Machen explores three levels of mysteries. The first is akin to solving a puzzle or unraveling a riddle—very like a detective story. Another level harkens back to the Mysteries—the ancient mystery religions with their hidden initiations and secrets forbidden to tell. These religious cults were entered through special initiations—mysteries. Walter Burkert (*Greek Religion* 276) notes that "to initiate" is *myein*, in Greek, and "the initiate" is called *mystes* and the whole process is the *mysteria*. Part of the mystery celebrations was a jolt from normal customs, often as a descent into the primitive. The Mysteries always involved some initiation into an arcane and precious knowledge or experience. There was a ritual or rite of passage—a journey beyond the everyday, beyond the veil of normal sense. In some initiations there were tests or trials. Marvin Meyer notes that the Mysteries were sacred and much is still not known about their ceremonies, as classical writers themselves were silent on some matters. *Mystery*, Meyer says, is *mysterion* in Greek and comes from the Greek verb *myein*, "to close." The Mysteries were a secret set of ceremonies not to be disclosed. Such a visionary experience must have had a profound effect on adherents. This is the force of belief.

Burkert defines the Mysteries as "initiation rituals of a voluntary, personal and secret character that are aimed at a change of mind through experience of the sacred" (*Ancient Mystery Cults* 11). The initiations were often trying and perhaps painful and meant to disrupt the beliefs and personalities of initiates, to cause a change in consciousness. As Meyer points out, in the Eleusinian Mysteries, the *mystes* went through rituals of life and death and they emerged into a new light, as if reborn. The initiation rituals were to upset initiates' knowledge and give them a new set of beliefs. From a religious perspective the Mysteries led to an encounter with the divine. In the stories studied in this article, Machen links the awe from the ancient mystery religions through to Celtic worldviews. He treats the ancient Greek and Roman times, not as idealized images of reason and ttm, but as locales for an underworld of magic and witchcraft, alive with the unquiet dead who bring fear and dread.

The third level of "mystery" is the hidden essence of creation that is not possible to comprehend through reason or science or perhaps any means. In a way the Mysteries are the process to achieve insight into the hidden essence. It is the revealing of the *arcana mundi*, the secrets of the universe. Machen is adept at evoking a sense of awe at the world, sometimes wondrous but more often in the stories dreadful. There is something beyond our perceived world, but it is not a spiritual realm of goodness and beauty. Our world of sense is profane and it seems from the stories that the world beyond is not sacred but evil. In the stories there are rituals to attain esoteric knowledge. Marco Pasi calls it being able "to have access to aspects of reality that normally cannot be the object of perception or experience. These aspects belong to other levels of reality, and esotericism claims to provide access to these levels" (64). Alfred North Whitehead wrote of two kinds of experience. One is our sensory world, which is precise and open for all and is primarily the arena for the work of science. But the other, more fundamental, primitive level of experience is "vague, haunting, unmanageable…heavy with the contact of things gone by" (quoted in Beer 9). Machen evokes this primitive level of experience.

Mysteries, as phenomena, are outside of rational explanation and are dangerous. Machen's landscapes, either in the dark wood or the dark streets of London, arouse a sense of dread. He explores the porcelain nature of our commonplace worldview and also the fragility of all epistemological or narrative meaning. The jumble of narrators and narrative techniques in his stories reflects the confusion that abounds in the world. Our perception is like glass and easily shattered by the intrusion of the malevolent released by scientific curiosity or indolence, or ancient beliefs, smoldering just below the surface of the everyday. Machen deploys the pagan god Pan and the Little People as reifications of cosmic panic, as Lovecraft uses the phrase. Pan is the totem, so to speak, of an aspect of the esoteric or of the world normally hidden from us, but not a bucolic world. Machen demythologizes Pan's image as a pleasant and playful being and renders him back as the power of the dark wood. As Sweetser suggests, the Little People are symbolic of timeless evil but they also arise from the Victorian fear of the lower classes, say miners or laborers or servants, who were asserting more societal power and threatening the ancient order of classes in Britain.

Horror narrative at its core leads to the loss of hope—leads to the denial of the stability that the forces of society and culture strive relentlessly to build, maintain, and reinforce. The mysteries, the past, the evil sacraments snuff out the soul, as happens in "The Inmost Light" under Dyson's boot heel. In these stories of darkness there is no ultimate salvation. The core of the ultimate mystery is malignant; there is suffering and evil everywhere. Machen is exploring the tragedy of being. There is torment in the stories, as the world is for Mephistopheles, who, responding to a question from Faustus on why he was not in hell, shudders: "Why this is hel, nor am I out of it: Thinkst thou that I who saw the face of God, and tasted the eternal ioyes of heauen, am not tormented with ten thousand hels, in being depriv'd of everlasting blisse?" (Marlowe 155). And Machen's fictional world is a sort of hell, a world where, in the stories, innocents suffer not because of the indifferent hostility of the universe but because of the deliberate acts of men. The sacrifices of women are the "sacraments of evil" carried out by men, often men of science in the stories.

Sacrifice

Henri Hubert and Marcel Mauss define a type of sacrifice as "communication between sacred and profane worlds, through the mediation of a victim, that is, of a thing that in the course of the ceremony is destroyed" (97–98). The profane is our world and the other beyond is generally thought of as the good. The question is: what is the other world really? Is it good or evil or beyond good and evil? Machen explores these questions. And sacrifice is intended to link us in our everyday world with the world of the supernatural. The offering—the sacrifice—brings a return to those who sacrifice, say a view of the sublime, or grace from a god, or societal control. But what it gives to the victim is only violent death. Communication with the supernatural in this context is the aim of sacrifice. In the stories the sacrifice is at the borders of experience[2] and the rite is the suffering and death of women. The Gothic exemplified in these stories is what Clive Bloom calls the expression of a passion of fear and torment into a distorted eroticism transformed into a sadistic ritual.[3]

The sacrifice of women is the "dark, primordial manifestation of evil still lurking in men" (Sweetser 81). These acts spawn such abominations as "flaming eyes in a formless thing staring from a window" (82), as Sweetser describes Dr Black's wife in "The Inmost Light" after his successful experiment to capture her soul; and "a child that embodies all the unspeakable evil in the world" (139), as Scarborough describes the ultimate effect of Dr Raymond's experiment on Mary's brain in "The Great God Pan." The sacrifice turns out to be dreadful, terrible, seemingly an homage to an elemental power, to evil itself. Mephistopheles answers Faustus's question about whether the demons of hell have many ways to torture, with: "As great as haue the humane soules of men" (Marlowe 160). In this set of stories Machen creates "embodied deviance," as Judith Halberstam calls the work of the Gothic. Machen explored taboo areas of Victorian culture, although it seems that he yearned to be a protector of that culture and his stories were cautionary tales. There are excesses in his work, and this is a hallmark of the Gothic, and not a failure but rather necessary for his expressions of what was the underside of life.

The core of this article is on the ritual of sacrifice to reveal the mysteries. In some of the stories Machen injects elements of a detective narrative to set a tableau against which the real mysteries will stand out. He also uses textual devices of a return or reversion

---

2 The sacrifice is to bridge the "unthinkable gulf that yawns between two worlds; the world of matter and the world of spirit" ("The Great God Pan," *House of Souls* 172); "the fathomless abyss that separates the world of consciousness from the sphere of matter" ("The Inmost Light," *House of Souls* 268).

3 For Machen it may be that these stories lament the dying of Christian religious ritual and a reversion to pagan rites.

to the past, or perhaps an interaction of the past with the present to illustrate the connection to the ancient mysteries. This is likely also a warning about the loss of true religion and a warning of the danger of devolution, of a slipping back to primitive pagan time, because "an awful lore is not dead" ("The Red Hand," *White People* 11). A warning that the old mysteries had real meaning and real danger.

The Four Stories of Sacrifice

In "The Great God Pan," the sacrificed one is a young woman, Mary, the ward of Dr Raymond. It is perpetrated in order to see "the real world" that is "beyond a veil," and the sacrifice is to allow Dr Raymond "to see it lifted" (*White People* 170). Vivisection is the method. Dr Raymond performs a lobotomy of sorts: he penetrates her brain with a "glittering instrument" (178); after, he "kissed her mouth" and then she "crossed her arms upon her breast as a little child about to say her prayers" (177–78). The young woman is defenseless and treated as an object by Raymond. Indeed, the scientist says: "I rescued Mary from the gutter, and from almost certain starvation, when she was a child; I think her life is mine, to use as I see fit" (173). There is a witness, Clarke,[4] to the experiment, as Dr Raymond calls the sacrifice.

The experiment is founded on the notion that what we see every day with our senses is only the shadow of a deeper reality. But Dr Raymond believes that a simple surgical procedure on the brain will unlock the mysteries of the esoteric. After the surgical knife cuts into her brain, Mary dozes for a few minutes and then starts awake:

> Her eyes shone with an awful light, looking far away, and a great wonder fell upon her face, and her hands stretched out as if to touch what was invisible; but in an instant the wonder faded, and gave place to the most awful terror. The muscles of her face were hideously

4 Clarke is one of several witnesses to the events of the whole story.

convulsed, she shook from head to foot; the soul seemed struggling and shuddering within the house of flesh. (178–79)

She falls with a shriek and becomes vegetative. Dr Raymond observes that it was to be expected, as she had seen the Great God Pan, although earlier he had said there was no danger in the incision. On the surface this is the failure of parental, moral, or societal responsibility to provide proper care and protection to the innocent. Moreover, it portrays a scientist as able to do anything with human subjects with no concern for their care. There is also an undercurrent of a more sinister kind in the relation between Mary and Dr Raymond.

Mary is deformed by the brain surgery, but there is more to come. She dies nine months later after spawning a child,[5] who goes under various names, but mostly Helen Vaughan, for the remainder of the story, which is, in a sense, a Victorian shocker about the sexual exploits of Helen Vaughan, the she-devil, the "embodied deviance." Helen Vaughan is a sort of antichrist, born from Mary and Pan, who is akin to Lucifer. The experiment unleashes vengeance and terror in the green hills of England and the shining streets of London; it calls up an ontology of evil in the mating of Pan and Mary. The textual element of the scientific experiment is central to the story's trajectory.[6] The only supernatural effects produced by science are horror. Machen calls this "transcendental medicine" in "The Great God Pan" or "occult science" in "The Inmost Light." Here the Gothic is used to reveal what some thought might be the underside of science, which was becoming the arbiter of what truth was in place of religion, perhaps exemplified in Victorian time by Darwin and evolution.

Pan in this story is the fetish for evil and suffering and the danger

---

5 One wonders if Dr Raymond is the father.

6 In a letter to John Lane in 1894, Machen rejects a suggestion to cut out the first chapter of "The Great God Pan" because it contains "the motive" (*Selected Letters* 218). He argues that the credibility of the story rests on a scientific basis, as the supernatural itself is not credible.

and dread of the wilderness of the ancient woods, a primal fear landscape. Machen links his Pan with the ancient Celtic forms in the great forests of Wales, still dark and haunted. His is the Pan of dread. There are at least two images of Pan, one the bucolic satyr or goat god, who is playful and amorous but not threatening. Both John Boardman and W.R. Irwin itemize the differences between the two images. There is also a dead Pan, as an ancient rumor had it, although Irwin shows this was a mistranslation and writes that, in fact, Pan was the only ancient god to survive classical times. However, Elizabeth Barrett Browning expressed a view of the vanished god in "The Dead Pan." She imagines an ancient lament:

> And that dismal cry rose slowly
> And sank slowly through the air,
> Full of spirit's melancholy
> And eternity's despair;
> And they heard the words it said, —
> 'Pan is dead! Great Pan is dead!
>   Pan, Pan is dead! (190)

Boardman suggests the poem is an expression of the death of the pagan world, with Pan as the image for the end of the old gods and Pan as the passing of the wild darkness, now overcome by light. Perhaps this is symbolized by a city standing brightly where the woods were. Machen transforms the city of comfort into a nest of evil, a den of iniquity, filled with the bodies of men who have committed suicide. London is a "city of nightmares" ("The Great God Pan," *House of Souls* 222) and is as threatening "as the darkest recesses of Africa" ("Novel of the Iron Maid," *Three Impostors* 188).

Pan is a witch god: Robert Graves in *The Greek Myths* identifies Pan as the devil of the Arcadian witch cult and links him with the witch cults of northwestern Europe. In *The White Goddess*, Graves also identifies Pan with the goat-Dionysus,[7] who on the Day of Atonement had a scapegoat, under the name of Azazel, sacrificed to

---

7 Frazer notes that Dionysus was sometimes represented as a goat and other times as a bull. As a goat he was a woodland deity and a minor one associated with satyrs and fauns. Pan is sometimes called the Lord of the Wood.

him. E. R. Dodds notes that the god Pan causes panic and evokes a variety of religious experiences or mental disturbances from possession and personality change. Burkert in *Greek Religion* has only brief comments on Pan but suggests that Pan symbolized uncivilized procreation. Georg Luck writes that the Celts worshiped a horned god that the Romans associated with Pan. These two horned gods combined and formed a powerful deity for the pagans. Out of necessity they tried to keep their worship secret and hidden, as the early Christians were barbaric in the war to wipe out the old pagan gods, Greco-Roman or Celtic. Luck argues that Pan was transformed into the devil and that female pagans were characterized as witches, as they often used herbs and natural remedies for sickness. Machen returned Pan to his ancient image of terror and frenzy[8] and overturned the cosmeticized image of Pan as a playful satyr[9] and harmless woodland goat god—he is not Peter Pan.

The sacrifice of a woman is an attempt by men to open the doors of perception; but it is also the killing off of the old ways, especially the traditions and practices of strong women. "The White People" contains several tales, one of which is about Lady Avelin or Cassap. She was one of the white people, perhaps the league of witches so feared by the church in the Middle Ages as theological and social protesters and a threat to its powers and authority. Jeffrey Burton

---

8 Machen's portrayal of the awful power of Pan influenced subsequent writers such as Edgar Jepson in *The Garden at 19*. Valerius Faccus caught this aspect of Pan in the *Argonautica*. "Pan had driven the doubting city distraught, Pan fulfilling the cruel commands of the Mygdonian Mother, Pan lord of the woodlands and of war, whom from the daylight hours caverns shelter; about midnight in lonely places are seen that hairy flank and the soughing leafage on his fierce brow. Louder than all trumpets sounds his voice alone, and at that sound fall helm and sword, the charioteer from his rocking car and bolts from gates of walls by night; nor might the helmet of Mars and the tresses of the Furies, nor the dismal Gorgon from on high spread such terror, nor with phantoms so dire sweep an army in headlong rout" (131).

9 This image of Pan has been detailed by Boardman and also in Valentine. It is still a potent salutary symbol as evidenced by the April 12, 2010, cover of the *New Yorker* of "Spring Is Sprung" by Edward Sorel. The cover depicts Central Park overrun by satyrs and lascivious naked women, who seem to be the sexual aggressors. Most interesting is the pictorial of a balding, bearded satyr with eyeglasses pushing a baby carriage; the Great God Pan fully domesticated.

Russell recounts how they embodied the old folk religion. The witches rebelled against the church and society and were brutally suppressed. Hence in the story, the white people are, in a sense, underground and hidden. Lady Avelin ends up burnt at the stake, illustrating the force of the church and state against the women and the old folk beliefs.

The progeny of Pan and Mary, Helen Vaughan, is painted as an independent woman, a sybarite, personifying the fear of Victorian men. She has multiple aliases, travels the world, disappears for a time, and has wealth and independence. In Victorian times, the "New Woman," as Kelly Hurley suggests, must be in league with the devil or with Pan. In the story Helen precipitates the suicide of several men, as if her sexual power were draining away their will to live. This is a twisting of passion into demonic pagan death rites. Joshi says the story "degenerates into a frenzied expression of horror over illicit sex" (21). She is the image of the all-powerful, threatening woman. The image of a woman as succubus is clearly expressed in "The Novel of the Iron Maid." Machen describes a large green bronze statue of a naked woman, with a smile on her lips and "about the thing an evil and a deadly look" (*Three Impostors* 190). The "Iron Maid" was a mechanical torture device with the arms tightening around the neck of a victim. In the story, the statue starts up and reaches out for Mathias, who had acquired the piece, and the bronze head bends toward him and "the green lips" (191) bite the man's lips, as if to suck out his soul.

Helen Vaughan has numerous crimes on her hands, stretching back to when she was a young girl. These crimes are mostly treated obliquely in the story, as they are unspeakable and hence unwriteable. And perhaps they should not be read, just as Austin discards, without reading, the manuscript detailing the "entertainments" of Mrs Beaumont (that is, Helen Vaughan). A husband, Mr Herbert, is said to have died of fright. Another of her victims, Crashaw, hangs himself. Earlier Villiers passed Crashaw and saw "a devil's face." It was as if Villiers had looked into "the eyes of a lost soul." In Crashaw's eyes was "furious lust and hate that was like fire" (225). This is similar to Mrs Black in "The Inmost Light"—the bargain with the devil means giving up your soul, but men make the bargain for the women.

At the end, Helen Vaughan's "suicide" with a "hempen cord" (234) when threatened seems improbable, although this is hard to say in a story with so many improbabilities. As the rumor of the death of the Great God Pan was merely a mis-hearing, here Helen's suicide is perhaps disinformation. It is yet another sacrifice of a woman, a strong woman. Here the killing is portrayed as a self-sacrifice, but it seems really to be a mock-suicide with Helen, like Thetis or Pan,[10] changing forms and shapes as she escapes or dies or perhaps returns to her primordial[11] or aboriginal embodiment, from which she will be called forth yet again. Helen Vaughan is a shapeshifter, her body wavers "from sex to sex, dividing itself from itself, and then reunited." It "descends to the beasts whence it ascended" and dissolves into "a substance like jelly" before becoming "a horrible and unspeakable shape, neither man nor beast" (237). In "The Novel of the White Powder"[12] Francis Leicester goes through a similar metamorphosis when he is found as "a dark and putrid mass, seething with corruption and hideous rottenness, neither liquid nor solid, but melting and changing before our eyes, and bubbling with unctuous oily bubbles like boiling pitch. And out of the midst of it shone two burning points like eyes, and…a writhing and stirring as of limbs" (*Three Impostors* 207). This last image is echoed in "The Shining Pyramid" at the bowl in the deep of night as Vaughan observes the Little People. He "peered into the quaking mass and saw faintly that there were things like faces and human limbs, [in] that tossing and hissing host." And "in the

---

10 Pan changed shape when the gods battled the Titans, as did most of the gods out of terror; Hyginus writes that Pan took on the shape of fish for his lower half and a goat for his upper half.

11 Sweetser suggests that Machen has her become a "hideous protoplasm" (111), representing the "primordial slime" (112) back to which we could all slide. It is symbolic perhaps of original sin for Machen and an expression of the fear of the return to the primitive.

12 In both this story and in "The Great God Pan," an attending physician provides the descriptions of the transformation as an analytic and objective viewer.

68

uncertain light [he saw] the abominable limbs, vague and yet too plainly seen, writhe and intertwine" (*Shining Pyramid* 37–38), yet another warped erotic image.

These descriptions also represent a regression to a chaotic disorder and social decay. Or perhaps this is an expression of the awfulness of or fear of the human body, perhaps especially the female body. The New Woman of the late Victorian time was a threat to the male-dominated culture. The common image was of mother, wife, and sister, as Kelly Hurley notes, characterized or idealized by childlike innocence.[13] The *fin de siècle* was a time of the morphing of gender roles and perhaps a revulsion of many men against such a shift. At that time, Bram Stoker portrays the vampire women in *Dracula* as sexual aggressors, perhaps she-devils or monster women. This is Helen Vaughan.

Machen deploys science as the tool that sacrifices and results in the intrusion of extranormal events. It is the experimental work of a scientist that leads to the intrusion, as if he is a modern counterpart to ancient pagan priests. Knowledge is now lodged in the sciences. It brings the imperative to believe, an autonomous authority, the power to compel. But science with all its enlightenment drags in more horror. The more we know the more we have to fear, as H. P. Lovecraft argued.

"The Great God Pan" is "an old story, an old mystery" (232) told in episodic fragments from different perspectives, as if the truth is too horrible to see directly. And it is told with different narrators, as if to give credibility through collaboration to an incredible tale. There are supporting documents referenced, like the note by Dr Matheson. The diffusion in the telling is reflective of the imperative of the Gothic to be disruptive and subversive, especially disruptive of the "dominant rational, empirical and progressive ethos of modern Western culture" (Salomon 117).

"The Inmost Light" is a story of roaming the mysterious environs of London and the sacrifice of a woman. The experimenter

---

13 Machen dissolves this innocence in "The White People."

here is pseudo-named Dr Black.[14] In "The White People" a stand-in for the devil is called the black man. At first Dr Black and his bride live bucolic lives in a suburban abode. But Dr Black tires of the routine of medical practice and his duties as a husband and returns to his occult science studies and experiments. The experimenter wants to confirm his power over the forces of the universe. He coerces his wife into becoming an experimental subject to confirm his theories. He takes away her soul, capturing it in a jewel. But his wife is transformed into evil or she becomes the embodiment of the ancient pagan world starkly staring from a window in that obscure suburb of London. He eventually kills her, but is not prosecuted, as two doctors at the autopsy could find no evidence of foul play. Her death had been caused by an obscure brain disease that had malformed her brain. Dyson hunts down one of the doctors, who confesses that he believes that Dr Black killed his wife. And he thinks it was justified because Mrs Black's brain was, in fact, "the brain of a devil" (*House of Souls* 269).

The story starts with Dyson telling Salisbury of his encounter with the monster created by Dr Black. Dyson had traveled to the quiet suburb and happened by chance to rest in a meadow near a row of house including the Blacks'. Dyson relates:

> As I glanced up I had looked straight towards the last house in the row before me, and in an upper window of that house I had seen for some short fraction of a second a face. It was the face of a woman, and yet it was not human…as I saw that face at the window, with the blue sky above me and the warm air playing in gusts about me, I knew I had looked into another world…and seen hell open before me. (254)

Dyson relates his physical shock at the sighting of Mrs Black: around her face there "was a mist of flowing yellow hair, as if it

---

14 This is an old textual ploy to make it appear as if one is hiding the real name and have readers suspend disbelief. The devil was historically portrayed as black. Cotton Mather wrote that witches call the devil the Black Man.

were an aureole of glory round the visage of a satyr" (255), very like a fire and linking this story to Pan.

Thus begins the journey into a "world of mystery" (255) across London, resulting in marvelous coincidences or improbable revelations or more obscurities. This story is replete with improbable and deliberately overdone coincidences, not least of which is the purloining of the jewel from Dr Black and the scrap of paper that Salisbury has thrown at his feet while he covers from the rain in an archway, hidden from view. There is duplicity everywhere and unlikely discoveries always, culminating in Dr Black's all-telling notebook discovered after his death. After the visit with one of the autopsy physicians, Dyson actually chances upon Dr Black, who appears drained of life, on one of his London walks and befriends him for a spell, visiting his hovel, where there is "an odour of corruption" (272). Dyson leaves London for a time and on returning finds that Dr Black is dead.

Machen is mocking mystery stories. Upon arriving at home, Salisbury spreads that thrown scrap of paper out on his table "as if it had been some rare jewel" (263), in a howling portent. Or perhaps, Machen is arguing that all things are connected and that coincidences or improbabilities are merely the manifestations of the vast mystery[15] we live in but do not really know.[16]

The story continues with Salisbury telling Dyson about the scrap of paper and its strange phrases. On yet another one of his haunts through London, Dyson finds the shop hinted at on the paper and uses a phrase to extract a case, which contains the jewel and the pocketbook of Dr Black. In the story, the most treasured object is the "opal with its flaming inmost light" (286), the work

---

15 Roger Salomon notes that in horror literature a key element is mystery. It is something that cannot be explained but can only be described as hitting upon the human condition. In a sense, the greatest horror is in mysterious texts that defy explanation and lead nowhere.

16 It is expressed this way in "The Children of the Pool": "Any man who cares to glance over his experience of the world and of things in general is aware that the most wildly improbable events are constantly happening" (*Tales of Horror and the Supernatural* 315).

of the husband[17] in his lab while the human subject of his study is made mad and then killed. The wondrous colors of the jewel do not enchant Dyson, and at the closing of the story he crushes it underfoot, yet another sacrifice of the wife. And at the end a small fire blazes forth, briefly—a faint reflection of the burning pyramid of fire in "The Shining Pyramid."

"The Shining Pyramid" is perhaps the thinnest of the four stories. It seems to be a sketch of the contrast between the ease of British gentleman and the terror of the sacrifice of a young woman to pagan, sybaritic forces. Vaughan and Dyson, especially Dyson, savor the intellectual challenge of the mystery of the ancient flints. Perhaps Machen is mocking common mystery tales again, with their focus on clues, facts,[18] and figuring a solution through reason. In this story, the protagonists do not use sacrifice to attain arcane knowledge, but they use suffering and evil to display their puzzle-solving abilities.

The story is set in the Welsh countryside. Vaughan has invited Dyson to his home to help solve the matter of some flints being left in varying patterns near an ancient pathway beside his garden wall. The flints are very ancient and rare. After the flints, oblong eyes begin to appear on the pathway garden wall. Vaughan is mildly concerned it might be messages of potential thieves after his old sliver plate. The disappearance of a young woman, Annie Trevor, is a background element, which foreshadows the horror to come. The heroes ignore or discount the event, focusing their efforts on the hidden meanings of the flints and oblong eyes.

On the surface, the sacrifice and the horrid violation are of the woman by the Little People. Her sacrifice begins with her disappearance, or rather kidnapping, by the Little People and continues through an ugly orgy of horror and ends in flame, leaving only her

---

17 Tellingly, over the course of the tale, Dr Black shrivels, as if the jewel that he hoards in his hovel abode drains his life-force.

18 In "The Red Hand," Phillips, searching for a commonplace solution to a murder with a primitive flint knife, says to Dyson, "I warn you I have done with mystery. We are to deal with facts now" (*White People* 5). But this is not how it all works out.

brooch, as her body and soul are consumed. However, the real sacrifice is the young woman by English gentlemen to the forces of darkness and "embodied deviance" (the Little People) for their viewing pleasure. The perpetrators of the sacrifice seem to be the Little People, but at that natural bowl at night Dyson and Vaughan are observers, like objective scientists gathering data on their field study, detached from their subject.

After Dyson figures out the clues, like an amateur sleuth getting the what, when, and where, they enjoy "six days of absolute inaction" (*Shining Pyramid* 34), forgetting about Annie Trevor. At the end of this sojourn in comfort, they finally go out at night to the site of a "circular depression, which might well have been a Roman amphitheatre, [with] ugly crags of limestone… [like] a broken wall" (33). They hide on the rim amongst the limestone rocks "grim and hideous…[like] an idol of the South Seas" (33). They sprawl on the ground and wait in the dark. At last they hear a low sound and then see a moving to and fro in the bowl. A mass of restless forms begins to appear, and they seem to speak to each other with a "hissing like snakes" (36). The two men watch as the hideous forms swell around a central object. They hear hissing "more venomous" and see "abominable limbs" (38) grope and grind—another twisted erotic image. Then they hear a faint moan but do not move. Suddenly, the things draw back and they glimpse "human arms" and then a large flame [the shining pyramid] erupts, and they hear screams in utter anguish and horror. Not once during this scene is Annie's name used; she has become a non-being, objectified, a sacrificial object. One of the real horrors in this story is the spinelessness of the heroes—they are voyeurs. Dyson is satisfied at the end of his unraveling of the mystery and reasons away his failure to intercede in the sacrifice of Annie.

The Little People are the imaginative re-creation of fairies in a form of terror. This is similar to Machen's work with Pan; he goes back to the original panic, the original forms. These are not the fairies of children's stories; here as elsewhere Machen uses atavisms to reverse time and inverse morality. Graves in *The Greek Myths* suggests that fairies can be thought of as displaced early tribes forced into the wilds and woods, where they continue to haunt the imagination. Leslie Fiedler suggests that gnomes or kobolds are "the surviving image in the mind of homo sapiens of the stunted proto-men that they destroyed, the first dispossessed people, whose memory survives to haunt our fairy tales and nightmares" (369). In the story itself, the Little People portrayed are identified with "prehistoric Turanian inhabitants" (45). The stories imagine the return of these beings, bearing savagery upon the innocent. They are part of the awful aliveness of the landscape for Machen.

In the story, two English men ruminate on an archaeological mystery in the wilds but do nothing to help a young woman in danger. What was of value to those two men? It was old silver plate, especially a silver bowl. But mostly the solving of a puzzle, like doing a crossword puzzle while smoking a pipe. To Dyson and Salisbury the small flints left in varying patterns are of value and worth pondering, as are the increasing number of oblong eyes on a wall, but not the disappearance of a young girl of a lower class. In a sense, Machen is mocking the search for false knowledge or a false search for knowledge, the unraveling of a superficial mystery. It is as if the protagonists focus on the lowest level of mystery, as in a detective story, and are unaware of or ignore the deeper mystery. They are voyeurs at the end, watching Annie Trevor's awful death from a hiding place. They are witnesses or perhaps accomplices to a sacrifice and seem to be so self-focused as to be blinded to the world.

The most carefully sketched character is the lurking wilderness with its feral nature and deep dread. Vaughan's house is "in the west with the ancient woods hanging all about it, and the wild, domed hills and the ragged land" (13). The landscape seems more alive than the male leads, especially "the ancient woods, and the stream drawn in and out between them; all gray and dim with morning mist beneath a gray sky in a hushed and haunted air" (23–24). There is a "desolate loneliness and strangeness of the land" (33) similar to the landscape in "The White People." Underneath everything, the story hints there are currents of great force at work, which Machen personifies as a grand conspiracy against humans.

In "The White People" the elaboration of this theme of sacrifice is completed. Here we hear the voice of the sacrificed one herself, through her journal or diary. Here we get to see an imaginary manuscript, which in the other of these stories is only hinted at or mentioned and not elaborated. She appears to be an only child, living in the countryside and ignored by her father. A nurse initiates her into the mysteries embedded in the wild landscapes surrounding her home and into ancient rituals that appear magical and terrifying. It seems to be nearly an alternative religion and the "nurse must have been a prophet" (*House of Souls* 161). The diary recounts the child's experiences with the nurse and on her own after the nurse has been let go. These latter adventures become increasingly strange and wonderful, all within a deepening feeling of existential loss and elegiac despair. The child finds a most secret place within the "secret wood which must not be described" (161) and performs a series of rituals and something is revealed to her. The diary ends with her writing of the nymphs both dark and bright and how she called them and a dark nymph appeared and "turned the pool of water into a pool of fire" (163). The "diary" is framed with a prologue and epilogue where Cotgrave listens to Ambrose ruminate on good and evil.

This is a tale from innocence and of innocence violated, as there is a hint of sexual abuse. In the frame tale, when Ambrose is about to lend his green book to Cotgrave, "He fondled the fading binding" (123) as if he were fondling the young girl, whom he knew. The girl's father is detached and in a sense not there at all, while a nurse plays the role of parent for a time for the young girl. We read of her experiences in fragments, and much is hidden of the wonders and strangeness that she experiences. She uses wonderful words, such as the Chian language, Aklo letters, the Mao games, or the Dols, Jeelo, and voolas, along with the Xu language and voorish things and shib-show. These all dance in the voice of the child narrator,[19]

19 The book is "full of secrets" and she has written "a great many other books of secrets...hidden in a safe place" (125), but not everything is written down,

giving a sense of the surreal to her experiences. But the central mystery is with the white people.

Keepers of the old pagan faith appear in the story. There is Lady Avelin, who may be a leader of an underground secret society of witches. She is being forced into marriage but rebels and uses occult means to kill her suitors one by one, nearly a retelling of the suicides caused by Helen Vaughan. And in this story she is also found out and is sacrificed by fire. Each of the four stories has a scene or two with fire as an emblem of death. Perhaps Machen intended this to be a cleansing of evil through fire or a specter of hell. Machen injects distorted erotic images of women into the telling. Lady Avelin cavorts with great serpents in the woods; they "twisted round her, round her body, and her arms and her neck, till she was covered with writhing serpents" (150). The serpents always blessed her with a glame stone (a magical totem), for her pleasures. But Lady Avelin also is emblematic of women who rebel against the rules ordering women into certain roles. Hence she is sacrificed for social control, although perhaps Machen had her sacrificed for being in league with the devil. That lesson for the young girl may result in what is apparently her "self-sacrifice" in a sacred grove near a Roman statue, where "she poisoned herself[20]—in time." But "in time" against what? Or was it a suicide? Is Ambrose to be trusted, or did he drive her to death through his abuse that was not caught by her non-observant father, who is distant, aloof, away from the events, and ignorant of what is happening to his own daughter? Valentine suggests it was the fear of becoming like Helen Vaughan or Helen's mother, Mary, that is, becoming the she-devil or spawning one.

The girl's travels through the wild landscapes are like dreamscapes. Jack Sullivan characterizes the story as having a "trance-like lyricism and spontaneity" where "beauty and horror ring out at precisely the same moment" (114). H. P. Lovecraft extolled the merits of the story, calling the narrative "a triumph of skillful

as if she is aware that someone may take her books, as in fact happens.

20 Shortly before the journal breaks off abruptly, the young girl, after her moment of rapture, writes "I wished that the years were gone by, and that I had not so long a time to wait before I was happy for ever and ever" (161).

selectiveness and restraint [that] accumulates enormous power as it flows on in a stream of innocent childish prattle" (424). Lovecraft admired the craft and praised the overall sense of a horrid sentience behind the words of the young girl.

The landscape she travels is foreboding and alive with danger. As she clambers among the megaliths, she describes them:

> . . . dreadful rocks. There were hundreds and hundreds of them. Some were like horrid-grinning men; I could see their faces as if they would jump at me out of the stone, and catch hold of me, and drag me with them back into the rock, so that I should always be there. And there were other rocks that were like animals, creeping, horrible animals, putting out their tongues, and others were like words that I could not say, and others like dead people lying on the grass. (128–29)

This is all under a sky, "heavy and gray and sad, like a wicked voorish dome in Deep Dendo" (128). Ordinary things come alive. Matter seems to be malleable.

The girl's language is akin to stream-of-consciousness writing, as pointed out by Joshi. It is a wondrous stream, but also there is something beyond or below the surface. There is an overall sadness and feeling of loss and vulnerability in the story. It tells of abandonment and the torture of separation and loss; and there seems to be something non-childhood about her experiences, as if she has been robbed of her innocence. There is a deep despair and a feeling of absence in the marvelous flow of words.

After the nurse is let go, the girl roams the wild countryside on her own with no friends or companions or chaperons. She is alone in the landscape of bewitchment. And the landscape is not in one form but in many forms, a shapeshifting world, a world with a broken epistemology. The little girl thinks of it this way: "all alone on the hill I wondered what was true" (156).

The frame tales of this artifact may be characterized as a "Luciferian philosophy," to use Murdoch's turn of phrase. It articulates a voyeuristic sordidness, expressed through the fingering of the green book as if it is flesh. The book is one of Ambrose's "choicer items" and is treated as a specimen, or rather a trophy. He lingers over the book and parts "with difficulty, it seemed from his treasure" (124), as he hands it to Cotgrave. This story is a treasure from the horror zone. The frame tale speaks of mysteriousness including both good and evil. In a sense they are both indefinable and can only be hinted at or spoken of in allusions, like the ancient Mysteries.

Murdoch jokes that only angels could define the good, so perhaps only devils define evil, and this seems to be the point of the frame tale.[21] It is as if the there is a deep, old urge to worship, to strive toward the sacred, as Murdoch argues; but in Machen's tales this urge does not reach for the good or for the sacred but delivers suffering and evil.

Landscapes of Wonder and Terror

As Machen writes, "if there is a landscape of sadness, there is certainly also a landscape of a horror of darkness and evil" ("The Children of the Pool," *Tales of Horror and the Supernatural* 320). St Armand argues that this is the natural corollary to a theory assuming that nature possesses a spirit as well as a self, that it is, in some measure, conscious and alive. Valentine sees Machen's landscapes as replete with "active, brooding evil" yet also a "sacred splendour" (24). There are atavistic haunts in these four stories. Over the wonder or terror of existence there is a mask or cloak or veil. The great weeping beauty of nature hides a terror, as in "The Damned" of Algernon Blackwood, where the hero flees in panic from the woods as he hears the despairing clamor at the gates of hell. There is a deep fear of the forest as it takes us back to the primitive, to the campfires and howling of the wild. But Machen also transforms the street of London into a forest of dark night.

In each story's landscapes, there are objects, relics, or statues from the past which personify evil or are fetishes reifying a fear. Megaliths appear in these stories like sentinels from the pagan

---

21 Ambrose says that sin "is an effort to gain the ecstasy and the knowledge that pertain alone to angels. And in making this effort man becomes a demon" (117). This is traced through the stories.

world, along with relics from Rome. The use of ancient images, ruins, or statues is common in Machen and is used to signal the return of the past, the revolt of the dead, an awful history.

In "The Shining Pyramid" there are contrasting objects. First there are the flints left by the Little People, but there is also the silver, symbolic of old England and the stability of the world. There are the limestone megaliths in the hills and a limestone pillar by Vaughan's garden wall that was "a place of meeting before the Celts set foot in Britain" (*Shining Pyramid* 46).

The landscape in "The White People" is overwhelming, "a strange, desolate land" (*House of Souls* 165). The green book itself—a journal of the evil years, so to speak—is the prime relic. There are megaliths in abundance. And there is the stone image, "of Roman workmanship…white and luminous" (166), where Ambrose found the young girl's body. He demolishes it to kill the pagan world or hide his own sin.

In "The Inmost Light" the landscape is the foreboding, dank atmosphere of London and its maze of streets. The dying Dr Black resides in an area where the houses seem to have been "sordid and hideous enough when new" but aged in "foulness with every year and seemed to lean and totter to their fall" (*House of Souls* 271). In this urban landscape of darkness, the key object is the jewel, the host of Mrs Black's soul. Its crushing snuffs out any hope for transcendence.

There is "the stone head of grotesque appearance" which was "of the Roman period" (*House of Souls* 186) in "The Great God Pan." The view of this head causes such a shock to the boy Trevor, in whom Helen had precipitated a vision of "the strange naked man," that it leads to a "weakness of intellect" (184), as if Helen has stolen away his knowledge. In the closing pages of "The Great God Pan," Clarke writes to Dr Raymond about the life of Helen Vaughan and recounts his recent stay at Caermaen with its "mouldering Roman walls" (239). Near the grounds of an old temple to the god of the deeps was the house where Helen had lived when younger. Off the old Roman road Helen had seduced her first victim, Rachel, who was introduced to the powers of night in the "maze of the forest" (239).

A Science of Evil

The sequence of stories is close to a critique of Victorian scientific research with human subjects.

There are observers and non-interventionists of natural events in "The Shining Pyramid." Observational reason here views the suffering of the innocent but does nothing. Is it simply fear or the failure of morality, or the mocking of scientific objectivity? There is experimentation on human subjects, without consent,[22] in "The Great God Pan" and "The Inmost Light." Finally we witness complete detachment and theorizing in "The White People," akin to a single-subject case study design. A child is heard but her voice is framed by the voyeuristic, perhaps abusive, voice of a man. In the end it is all about the sacrifice of women to appease the desires of men for knowledge and control. And the sacrifice calls up cosmic terror. In a way, the stories, solidly in the Gothic tradition, give voice to an underclass against a distorted and immoral ruling order, which uses whatever means to maintain its control. In the stories, men engineer the intrusion of horror by sacrificing women. It is as if women are scapegoats to appease the great unknown and allow the gathering of data and knowledge by men. The troubling center of these stories is precisely the act of violent sacrifice of women.

These stories may be seen as critiques of the cult of science as the highest form of human activity. Christine Ferguson writes of decadence as the logical conclusion of one of the most fundamental of all Victorian values, scientific positivism. Salomon argues that Machen, along with Lovecraft and Bierce, attacked the limited acceptable worldview of nineteenth- and twentieth-century scientific positivist empiricism, which rejected any horror or disorder or atavistic haunts from the past as having any place in a narrative structure. Salomon sees Machen as disrupting the accepted sense of truth as given to us by empiricism; he also hints that this disruption applies to conventional morality and ethics. The dominance

---

22 In a sense, these are cautionary tales about the lack of ethics in the conduct of research on human subjects; this attitude reached its epitome in Nazi Germany. After the war the Nuremburg Code finally elaborated a set of principles to guide such research, one of which was that researchers should be willing to subject themselves to any research. The principles, standards, and controls over research with human participants have evolved since then.

of positivistic science and logical positivism were distasteful for Machen. Ferguson argues that if science is too worshiped for its mathematical logic and the fruits of its experimental methodology, then the moral practice of its experiments is secondary and ethical considerations are unnecessary. Machen exposes this. The *reductio ad absurdum* is that in science all is allowed and that the resulting knowledge sanctifies all means for its achievement.

The Victorian anti-vivisectionist and feminist Frances Power Cobbe warned of the consequences of science penetrating into "regions where it has no proper place" (quoted by Ferguson 468), such as emotions and ethics. Cobbe argued that the over-veneration of science could lead to a disruption of common human morality. Cobbe's *Wife Torture in England* unveiled the Victorian-age beatings of women. Susan Hamilton writes how Cobbe let light into the horrid details of the violent acts against Victorian women's bodies. For her the Victorian age was a culture of violence against women. The central core of Machen's four stories is violence against women; it is as if the search for knowledge and the power structure sanctifies suffering and evil.

A Negative Vision

Machen's quartet of stories deconstruct established Victorian notions such as empiricism, rationality, social control, and sexuality. Although part of this is a Romantic reaction to reasoning and the praise of vision to really experience being, Machen's sundering of the veil reveals horror. The invisible world is not like the Romantic ideal, as Emerson wrote:

> If the Reason be stimulated to more earnest vision, outlines and surfaces become transparent, and are no longer seen; causes and spirits are seen through them. The best moments of life are these delicious awakenings of the higher powers and the reverential withdrawing of nature before its God. ("Nature," *Works* 558)

In these stories the god, so to speak, brings panic not wonder; it is a revealing of a negative vision. The dropping of a veil is revolting and hideous, the mysteries infected with blasphemy and despair. There is only fear and trembling, and the face of the god revealed is of a corpse or worse. The sight does not elicit feelings of the sublime but rather of dread and panic. Of course, this is the Gothic. There is no sublime, only an unnamable dread.

The sacrifices are the terror. In each of the four stories there is a sacrifice of a woman at the hands of men. Although the sacrifices take on different forms and the actions of the men, as agents or abettors of the sacrifices, are somewhat different, the essential theme is the killing of women. These sacrifices are set in a pornography of suffering and evil. The rituals are performed in alien landscapes misted in misery, haunted by atavistic relics, and distorted with repellent erotic images.

In "The White People" Ambrose says that real evil is akin to trying to take heaven by storm. Perhaps that is what the men in these stories are doing by sacrificing women—women who end up like Mrs Black, "a cinder, black and crumbling to the touch" (*House of Souls* 286); or Annie Trevor, "a heap of gray ashes" (*Shining Pyramid* 40); or the young woman's beloved statue in "The White People," "dust and fragments" (*House of Souls* 166); or Helen Vaughan "a horrible and unspeakable form" before her "death" (*House of Souls* 237).

Works Cited

Beer, William. *Women and Sacrifice: Male Narcissism and the Psychology of Religion*. Detroit: Wayne State University Press, 1992.

Bloom, Clive. *Gothic Histories: The Taste for Terror, 1764 to the Present*. London: Continuum, 2010.

Boardman, John. *The Great God Pan*. New York: Thames & Hudson, 1998.

Browning, Elizabeth Barrett. *The Complete Poetical Works of Mrs Browning*. Boston: Houghton Mifflin, 1900.

Burkert, Walter. *Greek Religion*. Tr. John Raffan. Cambridge, MA: Harvard University Press, 1985.

——. *Ancient Mystery Cults*. Cambridge, MA: Harvard University Press, 1987.

Dodds, E.R. *The Greeks and the Irrational*. Berkeley: University of California Press, 1951.

Emerson, Ralph Waldo. *Works*. London: George Routledge & Sons, 1883.

Fiedler, Leslie A. *Love and Death in the American Novel*. 1960. Champaign, IL: Dalkey Archive Press, 1997.

Ferguson, Christine. "Decadence as Scientific Fulfillment."*PMLA* 117 (2002): 465–78.

Frazer, Sir James George. *The New Golden Bough*. Ed. Theodor H. Gaster. New York: Criterion, 1959.

Graves, Robert. *The White Goddess*. London: Faber & Faber, 1961.

——. *The Greek Myths: I*. Baltimore: Penguin, 1968.

Halberstam, Judith. *Skin Shows: Gothic Horror and the Technology of Monsters*. Durham, NC: Duke University Press, 2000.

Hamilton, Susan. "'A Whole Series of Frightful Cases': Domestic Violence, the Periodical Press and Victorian Feminist Writing." *TOPIA* 13 (2005): 89–101.

Hubert, Henri, and Marcel Mauss. *Sacrifice: Its Nature and Function*. Chicago: University of Chicago Press, 1964.

Hurley, Kelly. "British Gothic Fiction: 1885–1930." In *The Cambridge Companion to Gothic Fiction*, ed. Jerrold E. Hogle. Cambridge: Cambridge University Press, 2002. 189–207.

Hyginus, Gaius Julius. *Astronomica, Part 2*. Tr. Mary Grant. Retrieved from http://www.theoi.com/Text/ HyginusAstronomica2.html

Irwin, W.R. "The Survival of Pan." *PMLA* 76 (1961): 159–67.

Joshi, S. T. *The Weird Tale*. 1990. Holicong, PA: Wildside Press. 2003.

Lovecraft, H. P. "Supernatural Horror in Literature." In *Dagon and Other Macabre Tales*. Ed. S. T. Joshi. Sauk City, WI: Arkham House, 1986.

Luck, Georg. *Arcana Mundi*. Baltimore: John Hopkins University Press, 1985.

Machen, Arthur. *The House of Souls*. New York: Alfred A. Knopf, 1922.

——. *Selected Letters*. Ed. Roger Dobson, Godfrey Brangham, and R.A. Gilbert. Wellingborough, UK: Aquarian Press, 1988.

———. *The Shining Pyramid*. New York: Alfred A. Knopf, 1925.

———. *Tales of Horror and the Supernatural*. New York: Pinnacle Books, 1983.

———. *The Three Impostors and Other Stories*. Ed. S. T. Joshi. Hayward, CA: Chaosium, 2001.

———. *The White People and Other Stories*. Ed. S. T. Joshi. Hayward, CA: Chaosium, 2003.

Marlowe, Christopher. *The Tragicall Historie of Doctor Faustus.* In *The Works of Christopher Marlowe.* Ed. C.F. Tucker Brooke. London: Oxford University Press, 1910. 139–94.

Meyer, Marvin, W. "Introduction." In *The Ancient Mysteries: A Sourcebook of Sacred Texts*, ed. Marvin W. Meyer. Philadelphia: University of Pennsylvania Press, 1999.

Murdoch, Iris. *The Sovereignty of Good.* London: Routledge Classics, 2001.

Pasi, Marco. "Arthur Machen's Panic Fears: Western Esotericism and the Irruption of Negative Epistemology." *Aries* 7 (2007): 63–83.

Russell, Jeffrey Burton. *Witchcraft in the Middle Ages*. Ithaca, NY: Cornell University Press, 1972.

Salomon, Roger B. *Mazes of the Serpent: An Anatomy of Horror Narrative*. Ithaca, NY: Cornell University Press, 2002.

Scarborough, Dorothy. *The Supernatural in Modern English Fiction*. New York: G.P. Putman's Sons, 1917.

St. Armand, Barton Levi. "The 'Mysteries' of Edgar Poe: The Quest for a Monomyth in Gothic Literature." In *The Tales of Poe*, ed. Harold Bloom. New York: Chelsea House, 1987. 25–54.

Starrett, Vincent. *Arthur Machen: A Novelist of Ecstasy and Sin*. Chicago: Walter M. Hill, 1918.

Sullivan, Jack. *Elegant Nightmares: The English Ghost Story from Le Fanu to Blackwood*. Athens: Ohio University Press, 1978.

Sweetser, Wesley D. *Arthur Machen*. New York: Twayne, 1964.

Valentine, Mark. *Arthur Machen*. Bridgend, Wales: Seren, 1995.

Valerius Flaccus. *Argonautia*, Tr. J. H. Mozley. Cambridge, MA: Loeb Classical Library, 1934.

JONATHAN THOMAS

The Copper God's Treat

> There's a snap in the grass behind your feet
>   and a tap upon your shoulder,
> And the thin wind crawls along your neck:
>   it's just the old gods getting older.
> Ian Anderson, "Beltane"

A friend at work lent Jared his cabin for a long weekend, on condition he wouldn't go kill himself there. Pretty insulting, whether meant facetiously or not, but Jared laughed it off. Why get huffy and jeopardize free digs? And to beg the broader question, were workplace cronies really convinced he was flailing on the edge? He wouldn't deny some moodiness of late, yes, for which he could cite ample justification. Suicide, though? That would be stupid after everything he'd gone through to stand scarred, abridged, but apparently cured.

The cabin marked the end of stony dirt road off a one-lane series of switchbacks scaling the heights outside Peterborough. Scant miles from small-town society as the crow flew, but a Saab hauling food and supplies had to labor the better part of an hour. For Jared, the sense of isolation was ideal.

What he knew damn well he needed was to "go walkabout," but expenses wouldn't spare him those weeks off the clock, his job wouldn't wait, and he was nowhere near fit yet for epic undertakings. Hence he had to make do with the balm of three days' wooded solitude to restore him after double crisis of disease and fiftieth birthday.

Amidst the moss and granite outcrops and grassy tufts in the clearing out front was a shallow, rock-lined firepit. Didn't smoke and flames traditionally purge the spirit, banish bad juju? Seems he'd absorbed that lesson from college reading or the History Channel or obscurer wellsprings, and it provided elegant rationale for a cookout. He darted about the woodsy fringes of the yard collecting birch and rowan twigs for kindling, and nobody would miss a few split logs from the cord against the house.

Besides, he had to gorge himself on roast hot dogs tonight. It had slipped his mind that the cabin was a world away from the electric grid. No fridge on the premises, nothing that didn't run on batteries or scary propane.

Before shadows had lengthened into twilight, Jared warmed his hands proudly at a campfire that might not have shamed a cub scout. The aromatic smoke, with any luck, would also deter mosquitoes, since he'd forgotten to buy 6-12. The gnats hovered undiscouraged. He went in to uncork a bottle of burgundy and fill a tumbler from the kitchen cupboard. He also retrieved his package of hot dogs, bag of buns, and a bread knife.

To sit cross-legged and focus on crackling, antic combustion while his rattled brain relaxed felt therapeutically primal. He lapsed into scoffing at his new-minted status as "cancer survivor," as if that should be the measure of a man. Technically he was less of a man forever for want of a prostate gland. But he was coping okay with that, as he had with the diagnostic needles and probes, the surgical ward and its factory ambience, even those ten heinous days till the catheter came out. And his prognosis couldn't be better. That was the good news.

No, Jared's bad attitude, his short fuse, stemmed entirely from a billing department hellbent on overcharging him all his savings plus IRAs for twenty-four hours in the hospital, on top of what insurance had kicked in. Most galling, though, was the call from a hospital stooge, three days post-op, to enlist him in a Penile Rehabilitation Program, as if Jared wasn't in deep enough hock. The flack only backed off when Jared spelled out his brusque acceptance that God had slammed a door on his dick. As it was, he'd have to retain a *pro bono* lawyer to wrangle with "healthcare providers" who'd saved his skin and hence felt entitled to clean him out. How the hell could anyone recuperate under that load of stress?

And how to benefit from "weekend walkabout" unless he left his cares behind and properly observed this major milestone of fifty years on earth? Oh God, there was another can of worms to boot around. More than halfway to the boneyard, with or without cancer, and what did he have to show, what had he accomplished? Humanity's tritest birthday question, perhaps, but no less legit for that.

He slashed open the hot dogs and skewered one on knifepoint and thrust it toward the fire. It slid off the blade and plopped among the embers. Jared took a deep breath. All right, hold that temper. Let's not add heart attack to the menu of woes. At least he hadn't knocked over the increasingly precious glass of wine between his feet. He set undivided attention on raising a toast to himself, the "cancer survivor," the aging Walpurgisnacht baby. The sizzle and scent of meat sacrificed to carelessness made him salivate, but what of it?

Then he had to guffaw or else throw a tantrum and his drink as well. A gnat was paddling frantically across the expanse of wine. He clenched his teeth and briskly tipped and jerked his glass above the fire, to rid it of bug while saving most of the beverage. Studying vacant red surface against the flickering glow finally gave him cause to cheer. Success was success, no matter how puny the scale.

A reverberant voice of authority, to all intents from the void, accosted him. "I need you to move away from the fire!" Wonderful. Was roving forest ranger about to bust him for illegal outdoor burning?

Jared managed to scuttle beyond the fringe of warmth without spilling a drop. In the chilly dusk he squinted around for covert ranger and blinked in bewilderment as someone lunged straight through the smoke, fist over coughing mouth as he came to a swaying halt mere inches from squatting Jared.

"Bah. Not used to wood smoke anymore," the foolhardy stranger complained. "It's been ages."

"Are you all right? Do you want some of this?" Jared essayed no bolder move than to lift his glass toward hacking guest, not without more detailed mental appraisal. The man wasn't in Parks Department uniform or prison jumpsuit. His costume, for it definitely wasn't routine civvies, consisted of collarless red smock and loose gray leggings, of cloth like linen but heavily stitched like cattle hides, and fancy latticework sandals. The fabric was also evidently flame-retardant and resistant to smoke stains. He cleared his throat and sniffed, "Do I want any of that? To drink? No, it's fulfilled its purpose."

Sporting braidably long copper hair and droopy mustache, this fussy party-crasher could have passed for a re-enactor of "The Dying Gaul" or a member of the Allman Brothers, and despite his lean and hungry look was almost delicately handsome. He smiled with disarming gentility and reached forth a hand to help Jared up. It seemed unwise to refuse.

The stranger held on and treated Jared to a hearty handshake, just long enough to make him uncomfortable. "I happened to be in range, and to find you paying respects like that made me so happy I had to thank you in person. Such a rare show of devotion in this negligent era." He had a vaguely Brit or German accent, too protean to pin down.

"Pay my respects? What?" Funny how a minute ago Jared had been craving distance from earthly troubles, and now here he was haplessly at sea. In the best-case scenario he could picture, this was an elaborate hidden camera stunt rigged up by workplace pal.

"Hidden camera stunt? Ah, a practical joke." The stranger shook his head indulgently as Jared, reeling at this demonstration of apparent telepathy, wished for more of a barricade between himself and this spooky character than a glass of wine. "Jared, Jared. Didn't you light the sacred wood and offer roasting flesh and pour out the libation?"

Had he done all that? Uh, those were the only sticks around, the hot dog fell in accidentally, and he was trying to dump a gnat out of his drink. This list of corrections no sooner occurred to him than he suppressed it lest psychic "Dying Gaul" were still eavesdropping and easily offended.

"Well, the important thing, Jared, is that your actions honored me, and here I am. And who am I, you ask? If you were to conduct a poll of everyone who ever lived, a landslide majority would agree I'm a god."

Jared mechanically chugged at his wine without tasting it till his Adam's apple had bobbed three times.

"No? You don't believe me? Okay then, I'll prove it."

The tumbler flew from Jared's nerveless fingers as self-styled god clutched his wrist and skipped backward into the smoke, dragging Jared along. Jared ruefully clamped shut his eyes and mouth and heard glass smash against granite.

He staggered through the campfire and a heartbeat later was sitting on a bench, with a beaker of black ale to replace his tumbler of wine. Only a dreamer would take such a jump-cut transition for granted, and Jared provisionally chalked up his outlandish surroundings to hypnosis or smoke inhalation. In fact, the smell of smoke persisted but was impossible to localize in this echoing vastness of gilded beams, shadowy rafters, porthole windows, and endless trestle tables. It hearkened to a shore dinner hall from childhood beach vacation, and to the Adirondack lodge where youthful fiancée had chucked his ring into the squash purée.

The numberless multitude crowding around him would have qualified as bikers and pro wrestlers, except they were more muscular and wore outfits from the same tailor as the "god's" across from him, and also were much bigger, practically giants, though in panoramic terms they came no closer to making a dent in this space than fresh-mown grass came to blotting out the sky.

The upside, if dwelling on it didn't risk jinxing it? These brash, thirsty, quarrelsome, laughing bruisers were minding their own business, and he strove to uphold status quo by curbing eye contact and sharp movements. "You see my predicament," confided divine escort, arching rusty eyebrows toward the rowdy clientele at his elbow, "and why it's a pleasure talking with someone different like you, a mortal, who can lend a novel perspective."

"You brought me here purely to talk?" Jared hadn't yet ruled out that "here" was merely the interior of his skull. At the same time, his escort's glib manner, fiery advent, and overall color scheme did hoist a red flag, however silly Jared felt in heeding it. "That's all you want from me?"

Soft-spoken "god" drained his beaker, swiveled to lift and waggle it toward parts unknown, and wiped his mustache on absorbent sleeve, from which the taint of ale speedily faded. He narrowed pale blue eyes at Jared and simulated shock. "You're not mistaking me for the devil, are you? Most of us have had to put up with that since the Middle Ages, and it's exasperating. Besides, you don't believe in the devil."

Or in gods, Jared noted, and instantly censored his impudent self. "You're right, I don't. Sorry." Whatever the hell you are.

Unsampled ale was warming in his clammy grip. He swigged and weathered wrenching out-of-body experience. He'd never tasted anything at once as sweet and bitter, or as rich and tannic, literally hard to swallow. At the blurred periphery of vision, he suspected guzzling benchmates were jeering at his milquetoast constitution. Or maybe they were braying at his comrade, smooching brazenly with athletic, ravishing blonde in long blue gown who'd swooped in to replenish his ale. Better, he decided, that he never find out which. An instant later, the barmaid disappeared, the neighbors settled down, and fickle god resumed, his interlude promptly forgotten, "There, in a nutshell, is why I love this tête-à-tête of ours. You're afraid I want something from you, when it's always been the other way around, from the Ice Age forward. Worship, they called it. Bah."

He slid his beaker from hand to hand across the silvery veneer. "When the Europeans defected in bulk to the Church, we mostly heaved a sigh of relief and groaned at every pagan revival, be it in ancient Rome or recent Iceland."

He fixed Jared with a searching eye. "You used to work for the post office. You understand how it is. The crap never ends. You start to catch up, and then you're hit with more, always more." His shoulders slumped dejectedly. "No, if you'll pardon my bluntness, you couldn't understand the scope of our frustration. For millennia, to be accountable for every solstice, every equinox, every eclipse, every rainy season, nearly everything that we had nothing to do with. By and large we ignored the supplications, let 'em go to voicemail, as you say nowadays. The prayers piled up regardless. Nothing slowed them down."

Jared sipped more warily at his high-impact brew. He had no idea what was in store for him, but could guarantee he'd be on that bench a long while if he had to finish his drink. Meanwhile, grousing deity left off pushing beaker back and forth and emptied it at one slurping go. He repeated the waggling gesture, stole another sloppy kiss from the beautiful evanescent blonde amidst raucous approbation, and attended to Jared again. Jared regarded these displays of heavy drinking and heavy petting as tactless and insensitive in light of his recently ablated capacities, but what to say in present company that wouldn't lead to more scorn heaped upon him?

"And the torrents of shameless petty shit. You would be appalled, my corporeal friend. The incessant whining for love or money. Avarice devoid of originality. Disgruntled selfishness on a tremendous scale. Plus the centuries of spiteful, vindictive defixiones."

"I'm sorry. The what?"

"Curse plaques. I'm so glad the word is strange to you. Inscribed on lead usually, and dropped into sacred wells. Great for water quality. 'Please smite the landlord for making me pay up,'" he mockingly intoned. "'Please cripple the whore who laughed at my special needs.'"

Jared waffled over whether he ought to apologize for any sordid forebears. No, not an option. Futile trying to put a word in for now.

"Begging for miraculous cures. That was the pits. Subjecting us to nasty, gruesome figurines to show us where it hurt. Goose-egg eyes, crooked limbs, goiter, harelips, tumors everyplace." Third beaker he obsessively rotated, to imitate a squeaky wheel. It became irritating immediately.

"Even after Christianity raided the game, prayers to saints for healing and money and revenge, the same old same old, were routinely misrouted to our ears. Sometimes we were so fed up we made damn sure the sniveling pipsqueaks got the opposite of what they demanded, and you know what they did then? They'd take an icon of their venerated saint and pulverize it against the wall. Veneration indeed. We never tolerated that sort of disrespect."

He tossed off ale number three and peered skeptically at Jared's scarcely depleted first. "Go on, drink up! It's on my tab, you realize. I can spend eternity on something, but you can't."

Jared fidgeted to the edge of the bench and leaned forward. He may have been ensconced in some heroic fantasy, but his body's post-surgical limitations remained the same. Copper-headed god obligingly cocked an ear his way, as if well aware Jared wasn't keen on attracting macho audience. "I'd like to visit the bathroom."

"Not here you wouldn't. Trust me." Wry deity peered into Jared's liquor as if reading tea leaves. "I prefer the other place myself. More robust brews, roomier seating. Rougher customers, though. Not that I'd disparage our proprietress in a million years. I haven't in twice that time. You can feel the womanly touch here. More refined." He bent near and whispered, "She might be listening. Take my word, when you see the bouncers coming, it's too late." Then aloud, "Doesn't mean we shouldn't adjourn to a quieter venue where the drinks are more to your liking. No, don't get up."

Valiant self-control saved Jared from the faux pas of exposing how startled he was. Otherwise the piss in progress would have zigzagged out of quaint eggshell urinal and onto stamped-tin walls. In terms of one small blessing, the flanking urinals were unoccupied, though a duffer in dowdy tweed was scrutinizing him via the mirror above the sink where he was washing up, as if Jared had somehow behaved conspicuously. Had this second jarring "jump cut" wrung unseemly squawk from him, or unseemlier flatulence, before mind and body had rejoined? The duffer shot a baleful glance at him while stumping through a doorway propped wide open with a cannonball.

From a cubby for two with a beeline vantage of the restroom, the copper god waved Jared over. Well, if lofty deity didn't care if Jared's hands were clean, then neither did he. Or was this deity especially lofty? A prankish aura tinged those jolting shifts of scene, and hints of run-ins with bouncers were symptomatic of a troublemaker. To take him at his word that he wasn't Satan didn't mean he was on the up-and-up. Or that Jared wasn't really squatting temporarily insane beside a campfire outside Peterborough.

At least the present delusion boasted old-school appeal. Jared trod on creaking floorboards decked with sawdust, and noted darkly varnished walnut paneling, and dusty heads of bear and elk and boar mounted at a height secure from further human harm, and a pall of cigarette and sweeter pipe smoke, and a hairless, hulking, aproned barkeep who might have doubled as a butcher. Nothing showed through oriel window with leaded panes beyond lazy tapping branches and rural darkness. Topers cut from the same cloth as their colleague in the bathroom, or in equally threadbare serge and twill, prattled clannishly at the hinged end of mammoth Victorian bar, acknowledging neither Jared nor their barman nor the god among them. Their discussion was too cloistered for Jared to identify its language or even isolate any syllables.

The copper god now wore a cable sweater enlivened by rows of archers aiming at moose. He'd applied no makeover, however, to Jared's ill-matched beige fleece pullover and baggy green khakis. He remarked, as Jared squeezed into the pew across from his, "I thought you'd find this wayside den engaging."

A pair of pint glasses was sweating condensation on the narrow, spindly table, and they appeared to contain that same black ale Jared had so gratefully left behind. More trenchant humor from divine drinking partner, whose sixteen ounces were down to eight already? "You're in luck," the god announced, indicating their drafts with a flourish. "I have an in with the publican. Special reserve." He raised half-empty glass toward Jared with the chummy air of inflicting a high-five. "A toast." Jared half-heartedly brought his glass into clinking range. "To May Day and everything about it." And happy birthday to me, Jared mused gloomily. Would have been nice if omniscient god had mentioned that.

Jared saw no way around a trial swallow. He naïvely tried willing his taste buds to lie low, but yikes! "Special reserve" could have spewed from the same tap as that supernatural beer, except watered down for mortal palates. This lite version might have grown on him, were it not so onerous by association. In its favor, he could probably nurse it along without passing out, thereby staving off divine pressure to binge.

For now, though, self-absorbed god was off in the fog of memory lane. "You know, my personal connections with this locale run incredibly deep." He paused to tip remnant foam and droplets from the glass into his mouth. "Used to be a sacred grove where we're sitting now. Consecrated to me among others. Men of more than one race conjured me in various guises down the centuries. I had quite the following. You'd never guess, but the faithful flocked to this forlorn spot by the thousands. You should have seen the fear and awe when I showed up, which happened as often as not on May Day."

Wistful deity made a sign of *pax vobiscum* with uplifted arm to request a refill from the bartender. His frown into the gulf of history lapsed deeper into melancholy as two more pints, with nervous alacrity, plunked upon the table. "Oh, who am I kidding? Those sacrifices to me. Ugh. Nothing worse, here or elsewhere. A stink beyond your vilest nightmares. Scorching fur and viscera, rancid blood. Giant wicker men crammed with miscreants and cattle and put to the torch. Groves like the one on this site, with dozens of men and horses hanged on boughs, gutted and rotting until they dropped piecemeal like blighted fruit."

He grimaced as if his nostrils could inhale the past. "Uppsala, that had to be the nastiest. Every solstice, seventy-two victims at each go, nine days in a row, till nobody could duck into the arbor without getting soaked in blood and ghastlier fluids. And crow shit, I might add. Or does my nostalgia exaggerate?" He grinned cattily to ensure the irony registered. Jared would never have guessed that a god had so much to complain about.

"I stayed well away from there and all holy ground on most major holidays because of the stench and misery. We all did, so these grisly spectacles achieved the opposite of their purpose. They were god repellants, no less, the best ever devised, and your ancestors were too hidebound to figure that out. When the missionaries charged in purging and vandalizing and exorcising, nobody cheered louder than us, I can tell you." He pushed fresh pint across sticky oaken

94

surface to plink against Jared's first glass, which rested on the table, enclosed in his damp fingers. "Prosit."

Jared humored him with a token gulp. Foolish to provoke a deity who mightn't need much further working up before he started lobbing thunderbolts. The outsized barkeep shied timidly from meeting Jared's sidelong glance.

"Ah, delighted you're more receptive to these refreshments."

"Yes, thank you!" Jared chimed.

"You're welcome. See? This is nice. Some simple back-and-forth civility. Our dealings with the priests and supplicants were basically so impersonal. They never really knew or cared who fielded their petitions. Wotan, Zeus, Osiris, Baal, Thor, Enlil, Apollo, what was the difference from beggarly human viewpoint? And none of those, by the by, has ever been my name. You may have noticed I didn't come right out and introduce myself. That was deliberate. Experience has taught it's best to remain anonymous. No risk of seeding false expectations."

Jared's every gulp of "special reserve" helped dissolve its association with his celestial counterpart. He began warming to it, and loosening up, in spite of himself. "Okay, I understand your disgust, and I sympathize, and I'd never impose on your good graces. But if you'll pardon my asking, since you're so fed up with people, why did you respond to me and my cheap hot dog and a little spilled wine?" More politic, he decided, to skip the drowning gnat.

The copper god chose painstaking words. "Well now, to be pestered or fawned over, that's a nuisance, yes. Being worshiped is a burden, but who thrives on negligence? Everyone's entitled to their share of acknowledgment, aren't they?"

Jared nodded complaisantly, while repressing a suspicion that divine host was navigating the shoals of some duplicity.

"Let's say, for the sake of discussion, that my kind are gods second, and something more nuanced first. 'Gods.' That's a human label, just as our names for each other bear no relation to your names for us. Prior to *Homo sapiens*, we never called ourselves gods, but it's been so long we can't remember what we were before."

Pensive deity chugged, dourly restrained himself, smacked his glass back down with a fraction unconsumed. "We are what we are. Your species tells us we're gods. We've never genuinely understood the term any better than you do, or any better than you understand yourselves, for that matter. Turn it around, shall we? You're a man. Quick, what does that mean?"

Jared's wits fumbled pathetically at the unforeseen ball in his court. His mouth gaped open in advance of coherent reply.

"Not exactly child's play, to sum yourself up on the spur of the moment. Might come easier to you if you weren't lagging as far behind." Divine index finger nudged Jared's intact second pint almost indiscernibly closer, a gesture that carried much farther than the bare millimeter involved.

Jared took the hint and choked down an arduous slug of his first ale.

"That's more like it!" Nameless god clapped approving hand on Jared's flinching shoulder. The impact made him shudder head to toe.

Jared reckoned he was in his rights to plead, "I'm not in top form. I've been unwell, you see."

"Yes, yes, but you're better now," his host countered matter-of-factly, and with a broad streak of paternalism. Excuses, dammit, were always transparent to a god. That was one thing that made one a god, wasn't it?

"Honestly, I'm not fishing for sympathy. And I'm not moping around sorry for myself." Uh-oh, were those the mild initial wobbles of headspin? Impossible! He'd only had, what was it, half an ale here and a couple of sips from the heavenly beaker? He forged intrepidly toward clearing the air. "I don't have to explain 'going walkabout,' do I? You must have learned about that sometime in the last fifty thousand years. A walkabout, that's what I was doing, to the best of my paltry ability, when you homed in on me. Putting some distance between me and the bullshit. Promoting a little peace of mind. Healthier mind for a healthier body, as the cliché more or less goes. And if I'd had the resources to attempt it correctly, our paths would never have crossed."

"They wouldn't? You can't be too sure."

What the hell did that mean? Jared had no chance to ponder because the copper god was off on another tangent. "The humble scope of your effort isn't important. You still deserve a lot of credit for looking to your spiritual welfare after a life-threatening crisis. Not a high priority in your generation. You're not quite yet the man you were though, are you?" Compassion shone plain through diaphanous blue eyes, but Jared squirmed at the notion of supernal X-ray vision penetrating his underwear, lingering on absorbent pad. And on more chronic soft-tissue shortcomings to which he'd resigned himself.

"That's all right," he hastily asserted. "My identity isn't stuck in my pants."

"No, I'd never accuse you of machismo. And I'm satisfied you're not the grasping type, either." Immortal hand, with skin smooth as marble, patted Jared's consolingly, tarried there. "That's why I'm fully prepared to fix everything for you. As good as new. Just say the word."

Holy shit, was this a come-on? Jared's headspin accelerated a notch. Don't panic! Potentially disastrous to panic. He slowly withdrew his sweaty hand and wrapped it around his second pint, ridiculous though he must have looked with a glass in each mitt. Two-fisted drinker, indeed.

"No? As you wish." Godly expression continued placid and benign.

The tardy possibility occurred to Jared that "fixing everything" might extend to colossal hospital debt. But no, hell no, what was he playing with here? Maybe no *quid pro quo* was at stake, maybe he was jumping to wild conclusions, but that was preferable to the least likelihood of enlisting as divine boy-toy.

"In any case, Jared, on a purely academic note, how did you suppose our pleasant symposium was going to end?" Did Jared detect a cunning undertone, an indirect reminder that mortal misgivings were never secret in godly company?

He pursed his lips and hedged, "I've given up predicting what's around the corner. Any corner. I leave that to wiser heads such as yours."

"A reasonable life lesson after what you've been through." Copper god drained his glass but withheld the gesture for more.

Jared, meanwhile, seized upon a flash of insight. This drinking partner hadn't volunteered a name because he didn't have one. His unbridled smooching and imbibing, his "jump cuts" into the unknown, even his offer to "fix everything," all added up too handily as projections of Jared's insecurities, his yearnings to escape, his impractical wishes. And how about that remark implying he and deity would have met wherever Jared had been? Nonsense, or else dead giveaway, that alleged god and these environs were outright hallucinations. And that being the case, why not swill illusory alcohol, since his headspin, logically, wasn't for real, and neither would be his hangover? Manners decreed, however, that he attend to his imaginary friend.

"I do feel I owe you something, Jared. You've been so kind to hear me out and treat me with respect. There must be a way to repay you. 'A gift seeks a return,' to quote your nobler ancestry."

Jared guzzled past the verge of masochism. "Thanks, this beer is plenty," he gasped. "Nothing like it." Surprisingly, the beer was truly fine, once he'd set aside that foolish dread of repercussions.

"Glad you've acquired a taste for it, but let's not be naïve. You've got a god at your disposal, remember?" The towering barkeep had shambled over, perhaps because he'd seen the empty glass and dared not miss a cue. Arching russet eyebrows sent him scudding away. "This walkabout of yours, Jared. You can't allot a single weekend to it and expect much benefit. We're talking about the restoration of your *joie de vivre*, your sense of place in the universe, your self-worth, your very sanity."

Interesting, mused Jared, to be lectured by a delusion about sanity. He put a reckless dent in his first drink and ogled the next while asking, "Where would you have me go? The Australian outback is completely foreign to me. I've no affinity with it. I don't see it as helpful. Plus it's too hot and dangerous. The same goes for the Southwest and those vision quests. Nothing worse than the hubris of an Anglo like me going Native American." Another pull at his glass did it. One down.

"Where does it say you have to find yourself under a rock in the desert?" A spark ignited in pellucid blue eyes. Sly or inspired? "Dolmens are part of your cultural heritage, aren't they? Alias chamber tombs, cromlechs, portal graves, Hünengraber, dösar, or quoits? If you're hoping to find yourself under a rock, that might be your best bet. Waking up in one is reputedly auspicious, especially on May Day. Or that's the hype immemorial. An impeccably relevant place, ethnically speaking, for your renewal or rebirth, from which you can pursue therapeutic wanderlust in a temperate climate, with idyllic countryside and villages purveying food and shelter at your beck and call. And home? No more than a day's fleet journey away."

Jared marveled at the persuasiveness of this extraordinary sales pitch, but he foremost gave his benefactor the nod because no harm could come of humoring a figment, could it? He proffered a salute to anonymous god with uplifted glass, which he tossed back so zealously that liquor clogged his sinuses.

Elated deity clasped Jared's free hand heartily in both of his and proclaimed, "Congratulations! Your wish is good as granted. I postpone it only to advise you strongly to retire to the bathroom again. 'Travel in comfort' is a motto of yours, is it not?" He had Jared there, as none but a god or his subconscious incarnate could.

The table scraped harshly as he pushed it away and reeled toward the urinal. Yes, this pit stop was a grim necessity, he realized as his lurching stride kept jostling a tightly swollen water balloon behind his belt. The knot of codgers nattering at the bar steadfastly refused to see or hear him, despite the snickering pleasure that might have afforded them. Capricious god let him piss in peace, but after flushing, Jared reckoned, all bets were off. Between bathroom door and table, he suspected every logy blink, every faltering step would segue him into *terra incognita*. Or into another befuddling mirage, more like.

His unearthly guide, however, was steeped in somber reflection, studying empty glass from sundry angles, apparently as subject to beery mood swing as anyone. Did Jared have to clear his throat to establish he was back? Ahem. Yes, he did. Pretty selective omniscience, wasn't it? "Are you fashioned in our image, or we in yours?"

99

deity brooded. "As hackneyed as the riddle of the chicken and the egg. If I could only exhume those memories to solve it." Reviving smile, half-hidden under ruddy mustache, seemed more guarded now. "Well, let's get you sorted out."

As if that sentence cast a sedative spell, leaden fatigue descended on Jared, but why fight something that wasn't actually happening? He did crave one last mouthful of sumptuous "special reserve," unreal or not, and dragged it toward his parting lips. "One for the road," he slurred.

He sucked some in and savored it, sloshing it from cheek to cheek, and after he'd consigned it to his gullet, instinctively spat out foreign particle stranded among his molars. He squinted at the speck on oaken tabletop. A gnat? That boded more significance than his guttering faculties could process.

"In your parlance, don't sweat the small stuff." Tricky gleam in clear blue iris seemed at odds with mellow veneer. Inscrutable divinity blandly backhanded spent pints to smash upon the floor, and nodded in approval when sodden mortal reflexes didn't even twitch. "Yes, you go ahead and catch your forty winks. I'll handle the arrangements."

As his chin sank inexorably to the table, Jared invested his last grains of cogency to puzzle, If I'm dreaming already, is it really possible to fall asleep? Two fading snippets pierced the cotton in his ears. A profoundly sonorous hiccup preceded an ominous "Oops."

Jared was sitting up straight when his eyes reopened on dazzling blue sky. Pungent sea breeze fanned his face, and low morning sun deposed chill from his back. He felt fine, no headache, no queasy stomach, no distended bladder, except his ass was sore, as from too long a sojourn on a hard surface. That pew in the pub would be the obvious culprit.

He awoke at this special moment because someone was poking the soles of his loafers and shouting up at him. Best not to make too much of that yet. First let him get his bearings. Beneath cloudless sky was ocean of a more limpid blue, and leisurely wavelets broke sibilant on a beach shaggy with grasses above the tideline. As breaches of promise went, he could live with this, so far anyhow.

All around nicer than materializing in a dark, moldy underground crypt.

He squinched down at the party responsible for the fuss. Roughly ten feet below, a grizzled pensioner with bulbous nose and plaid soft cap and frayed gabardine jacket was literally hopping mad, stretching on tiptoes and launching himself tremblily inches into prodding range with his cane. His aim was remarkably good. He was grousing in what sounded like Welsh with a French accent, and after panting for breath, French with a Welsh accent. Where the hell was this?

The geezer was doubtless incensed because Jared was perched like a flagpole sitter on a narrow, battered monolith, cavalierly profaning a cherished ancient monument, at whose base was black entrance to long subterrene passage, with a ground-level roof of slabs like squarish turtles on the march. Tipsy deity must have meant to transport him inside.

Or was Jared still, as sanity would have it, spaced out beside the cooling embers of moribund campfire? He clamped his eyes shut and insisted that he was, that he'd open them in the middle of woodsy front yard. Nope. Hadn't budged an inch, which was just as well, considering his precarious station. Perhaps the codger's invective was too distracting for Jared to blink himself back to normality, and whether he were physically atop a menhir or not, he'd be foolhardy shutting his eyes again and letting a lucky prod topple him by surprise.

For lack of a better plan, Jared returned geriatric glower and began to exclaim, "Get a ladder!" The ornery cuss might not understand, but Jared's French was vestigial and his Welsh nonexistent. Eventually, he had to hope, his tormenter would perceive he was a Yank and fetch a bilingual friend.

Jared lapsed into bellowing autopilot while debating whether silver-tongued god really had misrouted him. That parting "oops" was a shade too coy, too staged. Of a piece with much else in his double-edged, smart-alecky deportment. Better late than never, Jared guessed why a god would prefer going nameless if he were archetypal joker, lord of tricksters Loki, whose powers to bamboozle would be compromised if mortal rubes were on to him. How manifest in 20-20 hindsight, as well it should have been even had he not squandered youthful hours on Loki's supervillain exploits in *Mighty Thor* comics. Yet here he huddled like an anchorite, the butt of a divine joke, no inkling where he was or how to make waspish native desist. Jared crossed his feet to elevate them out of dependable reach.

The counterintuitive hell of it was, he did feel optimistic, rejuvenated, ready for epic undertaking. Those hot dogs at the cabin must have spoiled hours ago, which would have bothered him yesterday, but on this glorious morning, so what? Hot dogs and medical bills and his job had become unreal specks in the astronomic distance. Maybe he'd never go home. Could he swing that somehow?

Anticipation and foreboding mixed restlessly in his stomach. Any serious god of mischief couldn't be through with him already, and Jared deep down banked on more chaos forthcoming to spice up his next fifty years. And if this was still a dream, he plainly wasn't in charge of waking up. But awake or not, the freedom to live as if he were dreaming might prove his best birthday gift ever. "Get a ladder!" he yelled, a bit hoarsely, for the umpteenth time.

Choir (of the Damned)

Charles Lovecraft

"Come, sing in unison. The madness peaks
 In voices from the pit. O ululate
 Despair of souls, excised, disconsolate,
 And give your blood and flesh to Him who seeks.
 The ancient thirst of that mad *seeker* wreaks
 The bedlam of the damned. It is a hate
 Which whelms, a hate indifferent and late,
 While from the goblet's tilt the droplets eke.

"Drink the mad chalice up, all ye who sing,
 Ye vile mad choristers. Slurp fluid red—
 And *make* the dead. On them replace the head,
 And place them right around, red, rolling things.
 The madness sings…and now the seeker comes!
 A shadow falls on singers now made dumb!"

The Black Abbess

Wade German

I died ten thousand years ago…then woke
In catacombs beneath the priory,
And raised my sisters sleeping near to me
By whispered necromancies that I spoke;
And now the chapel fills with censer smoke
As I resume my ancient ministry—
And in black rites of outer mystery
The names of patron demons I invoke.

Shadows obey me; lich and mummy show
Allegiance to my long-forgotten sect.
Like moths ensorcelled by the moon's green gloom,
My spectral envoys flit among the tombs
To whisper gospel, and I resurrect
The dreams of gods sepulchered long ago.

In…and Out

You'll read just about anything inside. Book's a book. Same as pussy. Pussy's pussy.

Breaks you outta the cell for a few is good.

Pearce pushed the book cart by every afternoon.

Always told him to skip the facts, didn't want some history of famous and free. Inside was the fact and I wanted out.

"Old, scary shit."

He'd smile.

"Liked monster movies as a kid. Stuff like them."

Slid one through the bars. *13 Monsters at Midnight*. Horror stories. Read it. Couldn't make out what the hell a few of them were about. Weirdass shit. King in Yellow? Crap. Tindalos? Bullshit about bullshit I didn't understand. Wanted a werewolf. Maybe some vampire with fangs buried deep in some number's neck.

Soft white skin. Big jugs. She sighs when the fangs slide in.

In. The hard fact.

Hadn't been in a long time.

5 to 7 is long.

Long time without.

Long time with punks and motherfuckers. Bad and monsters. Stayed away from the White Power assholes. Blacks and Latinos too. All hate. Hate's bad. Leads to shanks wanting to see your true colors. 'Less you're a Martian it's blood red, but these motherfuckers couldn't see that.

Did my time. Quiet when I could.

Time without carpets under your feet. No coffeepot. No Thai delivery with The Game on the Big Screen.

Slide the book back to Peace.

"Less weirdshit, more monsters."

"Try this."

Tales from the Tomb of Terror. More weird, but I liked a few. Couple a lot. Finished the thing that night.

"This one was pretty good, weird alien monsters and things in tombs. Any more like it?"

"Not on the cart. But I think I've seen more by that editor. I'll look."

"Thanks."

He came up with three old paperbacks. *Devils & Demons*, *Shadows and Screams*, and *Hauntings and Horrors*. I liked a lot of the tales. Asked if there were books by the authors. Said he'd look.

Found a bunch. Two or three at a time he'd slide them through the bars.

And he kept them coming.

Wasn't long I thought Dracula sucked and Frankenstein was a big dummy. Wanted real evil. Things with business on their mind that was never human.

Trapped I wanted *out there*.

Let me out on a Tuesday.

Read every old paperback I could, needed a beer and a woman.

Bus took me where I needed to be.

City of Angels.

Vanished into a joint called the Ten Dimes with raggedy. Got a grip on a smoke and drank two beers.

Waited for night and women to come.

Slid next door to Black Jack's for a greasy cheesesteak, double fries. Licked my fingers clean.

Neon turns on the creatures of the night. Dementia trembles. Strange overtakes people. What's inside twists and while trotting past ruin forgets about dishes in the sink and that there was ever a sun.

My kind of crowd.

Stirred up, drums and dirty guitars come out of club doors. Hopeful goes in.

They been told never trust your eyes, but everybody looks in keyholes. Deadbeats. Hostages. Daddies, slippery repertoires sharpening anecdotal, and punks. Maybes hopin' the jingle in their pocket is enough to make it to 2 AM. No one's looking to change the world, ain't no bitchass-politicians scrubbed and pressed in million-dollar-lies walkin' the avenue, but a better seat at the bar, bet your ass. They all want. That's what I fixed on.

One with two legs that would spread for my stick of dynamite and a big set of jugs is what my solitaire wanted for a cure.

Let my eyes do the walkin'.

Flash of red said MULHOLLAND. Not unique by the look of it, but I let it insist.

In.

Grabbed a stool with a view. Heat on, shark bites and masquerades, celebrating with separate realities cocktails. Hothouse of silicone twins and daughters and child's play. Half-ass hustlers who didn't grasp the fundamentals. Boozers. A Big Daddy Thug wannabe talkin' an-shit, yo. Laughed, never heard of a vampire-gangsta before. Posse of two, LOUD counterfeit everything, double brainless, thought they were the hottest trim in L.A.—weren't. All night dancers burning to ash. Midnight shift ready to deal into a few hours of good time. Scannin' the court for one at the top of her game.

Radar lock.

Maxx—million-dollar-no-bullshit. Goth chic by the look of her, hungry, but she wasn't a swinging door. Expensive sleeves, and big jugs. Plump hips too, I like my cushions soft. She was eyein' my joint tacs and my crotch. I was skiing her slopes. Eyed that ass too.

She brought her show over to my stool. Talk about the circus coming to town—looked at its midway, yeah, tunnel of love. Bought her a beer.

We sowed a few words then she bought me one, had the bartender put a Maker's Mark next to it. Offered to take me outside to smoke a joint.

Did.

Then I let her take me home.

Long time since I had any pussy. Showed her how much I missed it.

Kissed it. Registered for the deed on it.

Washed out the shit in my soul with it.

No candles no candy. Skipped the "I'm—from—you?—I love puppies—hate liars—great movie" over dinner. Drink and cut to the chase. She unfolded her sweet and blossomed.

Morrison sang about eatin' more chicken than any man. Wrong about that, Mr Mojo Risin'! I'm the hoochie coochie man. Showed her I am.

Twice.

Beer. At it again.

Had half a cold pizza in the fridge, brought it to me with a beer. The perfume of sex and sweat dried on us. Satisfaction.

She put on a T-shirt, didn't bother with panties. Drank a beer. No bullshit.

Didn't jabber away.

When she finished her beer she asked if I wanted another.

"Sure. Thanks."

She ran off to grab it. Made a point of showing me her ass when she picked up my empty.

When you ain't in 5½ and you hide in books not to think about it, it's like cash and honey and the penthouse of the Grand Hotel on Easy Street beach in Hawaii. Forget you ever lived off nickel-and-diming and want.

She came back in and handed me the beer. Not a word as she bent over and took me in her mouth.

My hungry MORE was begging finish me off.

Lay there wanting this to last forever.

End of my first day out. Fed, a soft spot to sleep, and the pussy was better than I remembered.

Nodded off.

Woke up. Smell of eggs and fresh coffee killed groggy. If she wanted me to say I love you, would have.

Ate. It reminded my taste buds they were boats.

Talked some.

Looked around while we talked.

Goth chic, Goth apartment. Black and dark purples, touch of

red here and there. Two stuffed bats on the mantel, painting—large and it looked pricey—of a witch doing a spell over a cauldron above the mantle. Kind of classy, nothing Halloweenie. Lot of books, lot of DVDs. High-end stereo, components. 42-inch 1080p. She had shit, looked great—better than great, and fucked like a junkie with a howling jones.

Wanted more of this. Sly kicking ass as Rambo, game and beers, takeout. More of her sweet ass. Maybe shakin' to some tunes.

Skipped the bullshit. Told her so.

She told me I'd get it.

She saw me eyeing her place. Asked if I thought she was weird.

"No."

I like monsters and movies, her ass too.

Laughed.

Talked.

Grew up in a middle-class San Diego subdivision. Came to L.A. the day she turned eighteen. Tried acting. Waitress, barmaid, even a brief stint stripping. "Two years, just another Angelino applying for top-of-the-world. Took a while in hell to *see*." String of days in the life of…She told me of her journey from magic to witchcraft and the occult to vampires—"Got sucked into that scene for a while"—to Satan and beyond—"Grew up, became whole—*Trying to*…I discovered me."

She was interesting. I listened.

Sketch of my life is boring, but I ticked it off . . .

Finally got around to my bit.

Thief.

Safes. Security systems.

Partner screwed up. I got caught in a play with no exit.

Told me she needed a thief.

Told me she was a practicing witch, not Satanic—not for years, not the Halloween variety, her own blend, and could see things. Pointed at her crystal ball.

Didn't laugh.

I know righteous when it hits me and she was giving it to me.

Had been watching me.

"In that?" It was the size of a bowling ball.

"Yes."

Skipped how. "Why?"

"Everyone needs something. I need you."

Still truth.

Out it came.

Was part of a coven until she moved in different directions. Cauldron didn't have room for compromise, got stormy. Bad blood when she split. Then she really screwed up, bumped into an old coven member, had drinks—"I was feeling…*lonely*"—slept with him. His wife, now not her best friend and still the High Priestess of the coven, didn't like it. Decided to make her pay.

"I was out of town and she had someone break into my apartment and they took my two most prized possessions. I need you to get them back.

"I know where they are. It should be very easy for someone with your skills."

Waited to hear about the pay side.

"You get this."

My eyes skipped mapmaking, but didn't fail to be detonated by the flourishes of the currency she flashed.

"And I've got funds in the bank to go along with it."

Lit a smoke and waited for the boot to drop. "And just what is it you want me to get?"

"My athame—a ceremonial knife—and a book, grimoire."

"Witch's cookbook. You ain't planning on eating me up are you?" Grinned.

"Did and plan to again." Smile was hotter than last night's sex.

"You might be able to talk me into it."

Shower. Sex—my insatiable locked on thigh and nipple. Thai delivery, beer, the Lakers at home in a full-court feud with Boston on the 42-inch 1080p. Sex, translating muscle-squirm-inhabit from frenzy to satisfied.

Nourished till I busted.

Slept like a baby.

Western omelet and fresh coffee.

Out shopping for clothes and accessories for me. Hit Barnes &
Noble, four DVDs—I'd missed Sly's last couple, two books—thick,
The Best Horror of the Year, and a CD box set of old Chess Blues. All
for me with a smile and a "You'll *pay* for those." Put three grand
on her plastic didn't flinch.

Sex—greedy smothered in the grind, every shade of high, cleav-
age—yeah—room ringin'—hips—yeah—

"YESsssssssssssS!"

Roasted chicken and fresh veggies, pasta and shrimp, steaks . . .

And sex—my lips and eyes incarcerated in full go-go . . .

And planning the job.

Names. Numbers. Details and descriptions. She had a photograph of her blade. Drew the marking on the cover of the book.
No bullshit.

Set cash on the table for my tools.

Didn't ask when.

Did the prep work.

The food was great. She was attentive, never bugged or bothered me. Sex was sensual or wild like she could read my felt. Every
tango I made sure her wings, velocity a flesh-eating thing, melted.

"It's for five days."

"Use your plastic. Buy shoes, a blouse. Eat in the same place, a
good one, every night. Charge it.

"Be seen. Leave fingerprints."

Lousy poker face, didn't say don't sleep with anyone, but it was
there on the table.

"While I'm in New York?"

Nodded my yeah.

Predator's grin. Shifted position, didn't pull any punches, blend
of bright from her core set fire to my fantasize.

"They'll be someplace safe when you get back."

Hugged me. Never been that appreciated. Never.

Straight into the bedroom. I embraced her slow sweetness that
night. Thought this is why people go to church, to get this kind of
grace in their marrow.

Read . . .

Watched some movies . . .

Saturday evening we went for a walk in the park. Hand in hand just like a couple . . .

. . . Placed a charm around my neck. "Wear this and do not look in any mirrors while you're inside. It will protect you."

"Okay."

"Trust me about this."

Did.

She kissed me and I watched her heels…and the door close.

Sat in the kitchen. Smoked a smoke. Drank a beer.

Let my schooling reexamine every detail.

Rich and powerful her ex's left info everywhere. Saturday night, they were holding court over a long-planned social function. Across town. Staff off and gone by eight. Simple security system. 6+ hour window for a job I could flow through in an hour tops.

Waited for Saturday.

Walked to Starbucks a few times for coffee. Bought milk and chips and dip…napped…exercised…Looked out the window.

Missed her.

Panties or no, I was going to show her how much soon as she walked through the door.

Sat on the edge of the bed. Thought about sweet. Thought about bright, about earrings and mascara and her laugh . . .

Sat on the sofa. Hit the clicker, sports recap, and hit the clicker . . .

Walked, let traffic inward to work on the echoes of waiting . . .

Looked out the window. East—

Saturday. Everything ready. Waited on the clock.

Rolling.

10 PM. Their function working up to high gear.

By the numbers.

In. Clean.

I was inanimate, just another object in the room.

Second floor. Maxx's things sat on a shelf in a closet. I put them in a bag.

What's that thing little kids say? "Easy peazy." Out. Breeze.

No trace.

Stashed her property in a safe place I'd procured and went home. ESPN and a beer. Waited for Sunday's redeye.

ESPN…Thai… pizza… beer…looked through her books and DVDs…read, really liked a couple of the new writers I discovered, made note of them…caught up on a few movies I'd missed . . .

Walked around the apartment . . .

Went to the park. Sat on the bench we'd sat on . . .

Looked in her crystal ball a few times. Brought in a kitchen chair and sat there. Stared. Couldn't see a thing except my reflection and this thing must have cost a bundle.

Not many other things in her dining room. Wooden box large as a coffin, top was made up like an altar. Pair of silver candlesticks—expensive ones, 12 inches tall, $1,000 give or take. Black feathers, a lot of black feathers, lying on the black altar cloth with embroidered witchy symbols. The feathers looked arranged to me.

Comes to any spirituality-thing deal me out. I'm a here-and-now guy. You stop breathing it's nothing but gone. Pussy's Heaven, street's Hell. Apocalypse is a car crash, gun or shank, or cancer. No moving on, no coming back.

Okay, she had her thing. I've got mine. I can live with that. Figured I'd kick it around with her and see if she could.

She came home. Showed me the panties she'd bought for me in New York.

I showed her what 5½ days without after 5½ without meant.

I made the coffee and breakfast the next morning.

Left for an hour to pick up her package.

Handed it to her.

My reward left me breathless.

"I'm going to be a little busy for a few weeks. Let's see if we can find you some type of diversion."

We went shopping.

"Would you like an Xbox?"

"Nah. Not into shooting things."

"Maybe a laptop?"

"Thanks, but I don't see what I'd do with it."

Hit a sale on DVDs. "Dig in." That's what she said. She liked horror movies and documentaries on history and science, me, action. I like my scares in books. Loaded up on bang-bang-shoot-'em-up and badasses on fire.

I enjoyed my freedom and Maxx.

She spent time in her book. A lot of it.

Oldest most beat-up and falling-apart thing I ever saw, but she loved it. More than once I heard her say, "Resurrected." It sure was and I was raking in the points for it.

Cashed them in every night.

One night she whispered, "... shifting currents and converging planets." The rest fell off into some deep inner. Thought, *Yeah, she's right.* Time for me to look around, scope another job.

That began to take up some of my time.

The book took up hers.

Month on Easy Street.

Blacks in the joint say livin' large. I was. Out of the joint and doin' a stretch of SWEET. Had my feet up—Put me down for a life jolt.

She made enchiladas.

Never had better.

"You're turning me into a new man." Patted the new inch I'd added to my waist.

"I wanted to discuss developing."

First time whoa hit me.

She smiled. "It's not like that.

"I've always been a seeker. I've sought power and gold, enlightenment. As a teenager I began to search for ways to enrich my spirit. Theology, psychology. Crowley and the occult. Egypt and the stars. I've looked under a lot of rocks." Smiled.

"There is a planetary convergence coming and I need to perform a private ceremony to further my...*goals.*"

"Okay. I know you're into that. From what I've seen and heard, I can live with it."

"I need an assistant for this rite." Her eyes added the will you please?

"Me?" Didn't laugh.

"Not my thing. Don't you need to be a believer to add *energy*, or whatever you call it, to these…things?"

"Not for this one. You lie upon my altar and I use you as the ceremonial offering."

Smiled. "Wave your blade over me and chant?" Did chuckle.

She smiled. "Yes."

Truth.

"Okay."

"You will?"

"Yeah. Anything for you, baby."

She was on my lap and in my arms.

Sugar time. With extra sugar.

Panties didn't stay on long.

Her *thing* was in two weeks. We talked about it here and there. General details. Showed me her blade. No bullshit.

"Okay, yeah. Anything for you, baby. Sure." Didn't chuckle. Hell or high water wanted to keep my lady happy.

New moon. Always thought, maybe from books and movies, these things only happened when the moon was full. Didn't ask about why hers wasn't. This was her thing. Do it. Be a good sport and rack up some major brownie points.

Maxx had me take a bath. Some herbs and oils in it. Had this white linen robe for me to put on. Looked like some Muslim-thing.

Drank something she whipped up.

She had me lay on the altar.

Kept my mouth shut. Tried not to grin.

Started to feel a little groggy.

She looked in her book.

Maxx was chanting quietly. Half of it sounded liked growling.

Went on for a while.

Didn't get raised in church, but you know religious-lingo when you hear if even if it's in a language you can't speak.

She meant it.

Fine with me as long as you don't jam it down my throat.

Her chanting became a lulling singsong thing. That and her brew were putting me in a place with no map, no detail—

Something scratching in me—

Veins a boat of error—

Hazy—valley—dead noise forming the shape of a bruise—bad folding, surfing the doorstep and pages of me—

Solid-myself *less*—

Her blade was high above my chest. Saw the look in her eyes. Seen it before—Motherfucker pushin' all the ill he can muster into his shank. Dulled headed-to-shut-down *ain't* when you're lookin' at tits-up—

Brain latched on to FUCK!

Seeking old devils, like it was back then.

I had hope, man, I could see light, and right outta nowhere she wanted me dry.

I'd had enough Charles Bukowski territory, LA hard-bite speed-loader, trials with tough guys, self-destructive surges of loneliness slurring its secrets, and living that would starve you to death, and sure-as-shit, dead was not on any menu I wanted to read.

Fuck that.

Wasn't putting me on the plate.

Wanted me to steal something for her.

Did.

Was a witch, some weird-thing she was into.

Okay.

Had a holy knife. Wanted me to be the blood sacrifice. Had used her body to keep me under her thumb.

Lied.

Doped me up and her knife was ready to sink in deep.

Lied.

Fuck.

FUCK!

Barking strange words—

Crazy lyin'ass bitch wanted to put me back in the box. Zero me.

Scared serious.

Cut her before she could cut me.

Looked at her body. Noticed her book. She'd written a word

on one page. She believed her book was that *Necronomicon*-thing. Like in Lovecraft.

I read a few things by him. Liked his rats story a lot. Not the others. Didn't buy into his tentacle-bullshit. Squid is for eating, don't scare me.

She had.

You want things that pull you out of this lyin'ass jungle of gray citizens squeezing the clock; sometimes you get 'em.

Her blade got the blood it wanted. She died.

Waste of good pussy.

Then again I had her stuff and maybe a couple of rich buyers.

(various tracks by Al Kooper, Paul Butterfield,
Buddy Guy, and Muddy Waters)

Wind Shift

by Ann K. Schwader

In autumn, the leaves grow heavy with omens
cryptic & golden, poisoned & red
as stepmother's apples. Edged with light
already tilting overhead,

already weighted toward the grave,
they flutter like the tongues of masks
about to drop. What lies beneath
may wait in silence & unasked

another year. Or not. Such shades
as these distract our dreaming minds
from darkness & the earth stripped clear
of consequence. Yet still behind

these burning visions, twilight slips
inexorably. Broken seals
which once secured our blindness leave
the twisted bones of things revealed.

MARYANNE K. SNYDER AND W. H. PUGMIRE

Your Seventh Eikon

We rode beneath the vast mauve sky and its scintillating sun, she on her stallion, me on my mule. The dry wind rustled her clothing and headdress, but the latter had been securely fastened and would not fall. I opened my mouth and drank in the dry wind and particles of dust as I continued my song in honor of dark Khroyd'hon and its illicit valley, to which we journeyed. When at last we came upon a pond, we stopped to allow our beasts to drink; and when, while exploring the territory, I came upon a forsaken altar, I pulled a pinch of oakmoss from my pouch and set it alight in honor of the deity that was my especial doom. Seeing me prance about the altar and wail inarticulate psalms, Euryale laughed and tapped her brass hands together in time to my frolic. I stopped my gambol in the meadow grass when she knelt near to me, and I lifted my face to the bright sun and shut my eyes as Euryale sliced one of her metal talons into my forehead and replenished the insignia that had been etched into my dusky flesh.

"Open your eyes, my dwarf, and read the shadows within mine own," my Lady commanded; and so I exposed my purple pupils and peered into her emerald orbs, where I beheld the coils of blackness that moved as ghosts of serpent ink behind the surface of her organs; and when I read the secrets of their forms, I smiled and winked. "From your mask of mirth I assume that all is well, and so let us continue on our way; for the sky will soon turn to blood and diamonds, and we must reach foreboding Khroyd'hon before that instant."

I returned to my mule and continued our expedition, across the meadow-grass and over hillocks of dust, until we came to the haunted forest before which our nervous beasts hesitated. I sang with soothing tones as I hopped off my mule and led her into the dim realm of dark mute trees on which fungoid faces watched our progress. Finally we stopped, at the place where the forest momentarily ended, and we gazed down the sloping terrain, into Khroyd'hon, as above us the mauve sky darkened into a scarlet sea within which golden stars glinted as they circled the ginger moon. I walked beside my weary beast, down the inclined earth, and sang to the woman who followed close behind on her stallion. Above us the sky congealed and darkened as if composed of ingredients of antique gore in which its scab, the moon, hung like an emblem of decease. I leaned against my mule's muzzle and sighed as she bathed me with her breath. Perhaps she sensed her fate—animals are far wiser than we can comprehend.

I stared, as we descended, at the twin-peaked mountain from which the valley took its name—at the crimson stone that glistened like new-shed blood, at the impossibly high twin peaks, lean and curved like the wings on a slumbering daemon's back. The trees were now few and far between, and the soil on which we trod was chill and rigid. We followed where that soil led, to the squat neglected temple that was our destination. Its hoary stone was enshrouded with the dust of ages, and one dark vine clung to its wall in such a fashion as to resemble a fissure extending in a zigzag line from the roof of the edifice to the lush grass from out of which the temple ascended. Looking away from it, I espied the area of blue stone that was Circle of Sacrifice, and to that I led my beloved beast. We stepped onto the smooth blue stone and I knelt beside my mule, which lowered to her knees and pressed her snout to my eyes one final time. Gazing at the orange moon, I made to it the Sign of Forfeit, and I shuddered at the beam that shot from that bloated sphere onto my mule; and I wept as my beast bayed in torment until it dissipated before me as dust. Wiping woe from my murky eyes, I watched as my Lady dismounted her stallion and stood before me.

The magnificent she, silhouetted against the red sky and its golden stars. She stood tall and potent, attired in a robe that concealed most of her celadon skin. Her chiseled countenance was very proud and persuasive, and one could have gazed for an eternity into her diamond eyes. Clapping her brass hands, she pointed to the temple and hissed my name; and so I lifted to my feet, removed myself from the Circle of Sacrifice, and crept into the sanctuary. I stopped first at the pool of bones, wherein creatures had drowned themselves in honor of the Goddess; and it was in its water that I beheld my clear impression, the small thick frame of dusky flesh, the misshapen head and its grotesque face. I had been reviled as a leprous thing because of my ugliness, and had fled the people among whom I was raised so as to live a solitary life, a difficult existence. But then, one gloomy afternoon, my Lady discovered me, and soothed me, and coaxed me to follow her. And when I slept between her thighs I was enchanted with perfumed memory of things that I had forgotten or knew of in dream only.

I moved along, into the temple, where stones of fire set in places of the wall provided queer illumination; and it was in that extraordinary light that I beheld the six stone figures, the sight of which I had seen in deepest delusion. And I saw that each was of my height and form and possessed faces similar to my own. And on each wide forehead I beheld the insignia of the Goddess, cut deep into the surface of stone as mine was etched into my flesh. And as I peered at their rigid faces I felt a sense of belonging, almost a euphoria of joy. And so I took my place within their tribe and watched as Euryale lifted her hands of brass so as to remove the covering from her serpent hair. And I wept one final tear in memory of my beloved beast, who had been my only friend in life, as I transformed as she had. Yet unlike her, I did not disintegrate into a cloud of mortal dust to be tossed into the wind, but rather my limbs hardened as smooth mineral, kissed by the potent alchemy that spilled into my eyes as I beheld my Lady's serpent-hair. And although my eyes are things of stone, yet can they see her still, standing in all her glory; and I am happy to be her Seventh Eikon, to dwell here with my kindred for all ages.

The Demon Sea

Wade German

 Its shoreline borders on the edge of Time
Where demon-throated winds eternally moan
Across red sands and jutting, giant bones
Of alien sea-things, wreathed by weeds and slime.
Out in the gulf, huge shadows flit below
The raving waves in ever-shifting tides
Ensorcelled by the seven moons, which glide
Like ghosts above the sea's vermilion glow.

And in the churning chaos of the waves,
Vast hulks of vessels built by unknown race
Seem ruined castles and necropoli,
Where bloated devils like black octopi
Breed eldritch, evil dreams among the graves
Of mariners once lured here through deep space.

RICHARD THOMAS

Flowers for Jessica

The doctors had no answer for me, something wrong with her heart—that's all that I heard, all they could hint at with their stone faces and cold hands, constantly checking their watches, places they needed to be. Except, now that Jessica was gone, there was nowhere I needed to be and nowhere I wanted to go. She liked the woods, embraced nature with every fiber of her constantly distracted mind. She wandered off every chance she got—communing and dancing, her silhouette spinning in many a field of wildflowers. It gave me great pleasure to share that joy with her.

When I found her body in the deep grasses—weeds and vines bent over from the edge of the forest—she looked peaceful, asleep, hands resting on her chest. We'd been hiding from each other, playing a little game. The reward was supposed to be her soft kisses, my hands traversing her ivory skin, a stolen moment away from the city, away from the smoke and noise and drudgery of work and broken dreams. It only took a short drive north, away from our home and the echoes of lost children, the bloody rags that lined our garbage cans, the dusty crib that lay barren and quiet. I didn't bring it up anymore, didn't dare ask where we were, what the plan was, or how to move forward.

Too many nights I'd find her at the kitchen table, empty glass of wine, empty bottle, her eyes a million miles away, her hands torn and bleeding, wads of paper in her mouth as she chewed, broken glass littering the table. It was a room filled with anger, a thick layer of frustration, sadness, and an undying urge to hurt someone, to strike out in vengeance for the random pain that surrounded us. I'd carry her upstairs, a bundle of sticks, and place her on our bed.

123

When she'd reach for me, catatonic, dead behind the eyes, I'd push her away. It wasn't her. Her body called to me, begged me to fill her with life, but her eyes, her diminished mind, was anywhere but here.

Fractured. That's the word that comes to mind. I can see myself in my car, drifting down the highway. I can see her at the table, a ghost. I can picture the forest, her lying in the damp green blanket of grass, and I can see what I did next in excruciating detail.

It started as a way to honor her, to hold on to her shape, her shadow, the outline of her body flattening the greenery, the death of the grasses, the weeds withering and turning brown, flower buds that had borne witness to her heartbreak, shriveled and lying on the ground. I simply lay down in her outline, lay there in the woods, the grass, and tried to imagine what she had been thinking, tried to embrace her pain and longing. Insects buzzed at the periphery of my body heat, the sun above cooking the forest, the fields, a shimmer washing over me. My body glistened with sweat, the droplets running off of my bare skin and into the earth below me. Soon my tears joined the trickle of sweat, running down the sides of my face, as I bellowed and wailed, alone in the world. Things were just beginning.

Days later, unable to focus on life in the real world, unable to be anywhere else, I returned to the forest to find the dark outline of my body, overlapping the space where she expired, filled with tiny flowers, buds of yellow and pink and lavender, pushing up from the shadows. Wildflowers. I didn't dare lie down on them, these slivers of sweetness and light. I had no water with me, no creek nearby—nothing but blue sky and a shiver in my bones.

When I returned the next day, I stopped at the edge of the clearing, sucking in air, frozen. The flowers had grown, weaving in amongst themselves, her shape appearing in the layers of green. I held in my hands an old milk jug filled with water, heavy and slick in my sweating fingers. I approached her with apprehension, wind pushing through the leaves of the forest, small creatures tangled in the undergrowth, cracking and rustling, the shrill cry of some lost and frightened bird. I opened the jug and poured it over her, over the flowers, and vines, and grasses. I traced the outline, down her

124

head, over her shoulders, to her arms and legs and back to the top again. I created a small puddle where her brain would surely grow, another in her chest, where a heart might come to life. And then I walked away. Unsteady, I tripped over my feet, glancing back over my shoulder. My desire was uncertain.

I didn't come back the next day. Busy at work, I thought. Things I needed to do. These were the lies that I told myself, when she came to me in my dreams—in the dark. I ached for her, my hands trembling constantly, a dull throbbing at my temples. And yet, I'd lost my mind. Nowhere else to go, my vision filled with flashes of wildflowers and creeping vines, and I found myself back in the forest.

I stood at the edge of the clearing, her body expanding and contracting, her chest filling with air. She was still a shell, one glorious red rose in the center of her heart, a gathering of white buds at her head. When I summoned the courage to approach and kneel next to her, the wind picked up, whispering to me, things I needed to do. I shook my head. The trees bent under the gusts of wind, the long grasses of the field waving back and forth.

"More," it whispered. I lay next to Jessica, and the rustle of flowers and leaves as her head turned toward me—it caused my pounding heart to shudder and stop. I listened to her wishes, to the wind and the heady perfume of the wildflowers. I was weak. I stood as the sun set and unzipped my jeans and drenched the flowers and grass. There was a withering crawl of vines, the minerals and vitamins of my urine washing over her translucent skin. Nausea rolled over me and I turned and walked away. What was I doing?

Again I stayed away, fearful of what might come next. But she haunted my dreams, begged me to return, to finish the job, to bring her all the way back. I hesitated at the door to our home, several times. I'd retreat into the house and pour myself a tumbler of amber, over and over, until her voice faded into the walls. It was no use. I could not stay away.

Her final request was beyond me, and the thought of such action repulsed me. I told her it was impossible, I couldn't make lust out of wishes. Her skin was no longer translucent—it was a pale earthtone, the creeping vines still visible under her skin, the blooming rose sighing in her chest. Two violet blossoms stared back at me from her hardening skull—tracking my every move. I could see her naked form now as I stood above her, her body writhing in the grass and shadows, begging me to complete this act, to plant my seed among the other buds and seedlings that trembled at my feet. Two pink buds stood out in her chest, her right hand drifting down into the mossy growth between her legs, the wind picking up again, a hot breath at my ears, my neck, a desert of heat emerging from nowhere. I found myself aroused. As the sun disappeared into the horizon and the darkness pulled us in, I ran my hand up and down my slick flesh, a stammering in my chest, my breath caught and lost. Bountiful, she gasped and trembled, my prayers for forgiveness disappearing into the woods.

It took me a week to come back, and a part of me thought that maybe I could stay away forever. That maybe I didn't need to see this to completion, my insanity confirmed, my selfish needs and desire to see Jessica again, manifested in some horror of acts committed out of desperation. But I returned, eventually. Was there ever really any doubt?

She was lying at the edge of the forest, naked in the sunlight that pushed to the rim of the woods, her fragile silhouette disappearing in the sunbeams, reappearing in the shade. She didn't say anything when I came upon her. She didn't ask why it had taken me so long to return. She didn't question the tears that ran down my face. She opened her arms and beckoned me to her, and I knelt down, and then lay down, her arms wrapping around me, then her legs—pulling me in, pulling me under, until we were whole once again.

The Suitors

Michael Fantina

These sable midnight cliffs rise dark and sheer,
High straggling loons now circle overhead,
The scudding clouds all dark as pencil lead,
This winter's eve is chilly dark and drear.
The werewolf's wail it echoes sharp and clear,
Deep in half sunken caverns wake the dead,
Who float up from their damp and salty bed,
And to the unsuspecting will appear.

The tide's now pulled, dark and sidereal,
Against these soaring cliffs along these coasts,
While from the sea a spirit, half ethereal,
Will rise, a girl, the loveliest of ghosts,
Whom all the other spirits will pursue,
And, mad with longing, eagerly will woo.

In the Silent House

by Phillip A. Ellis

Where time's abeyant, space, in turn, is coiled
upon itself; where life is slave to schemes
of chaos, there the massive suns have boiled
away to wisps of scattered, frozen steams,
seemingly veils of darkness: know then, dreamers,
know as you know your bodies, born from curled
and convoluted foetuses, we deem,
in the silent house, the gods are witless churls.

We may take blades against them, take up foils
or sabres, take up books with verse, as reams
of satire, rank invective, written on coils
of skin or paper, take up bleeding fleams
to let their ichor, take up anger's memes
and motifs, all like flags let fly unfurled
and windbrave, knowing well, where marshlight gleams
in the silent house, the gods are witless churls.

Yet their dreams die, although the dreamers toil
in vain: the dreams are rotten, broken themes
both burdensome and squalid, rank as oil
that's soured, stained and bloody, half agleam
with hatred, rancour; their dreams die, spiremes
decayed, corrupted, far from gold impearled
sans tarnish, but marred by rust although it seems,
in the silent house, the gods are witless churls.

Reader, if in the fields of academe
or Sheols of toil, if homebound, heartcracked, earls
or philosophes, or fools, where silence screams
in the silent house the gods are witless churls.

GALLERY
JASON ZERRILLO

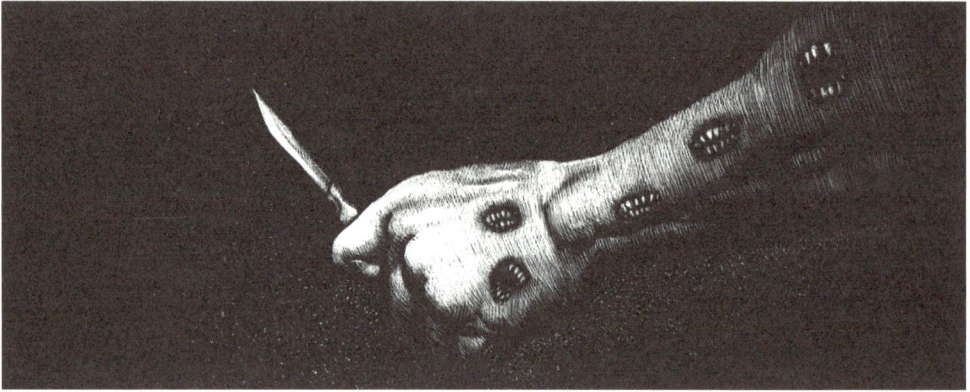

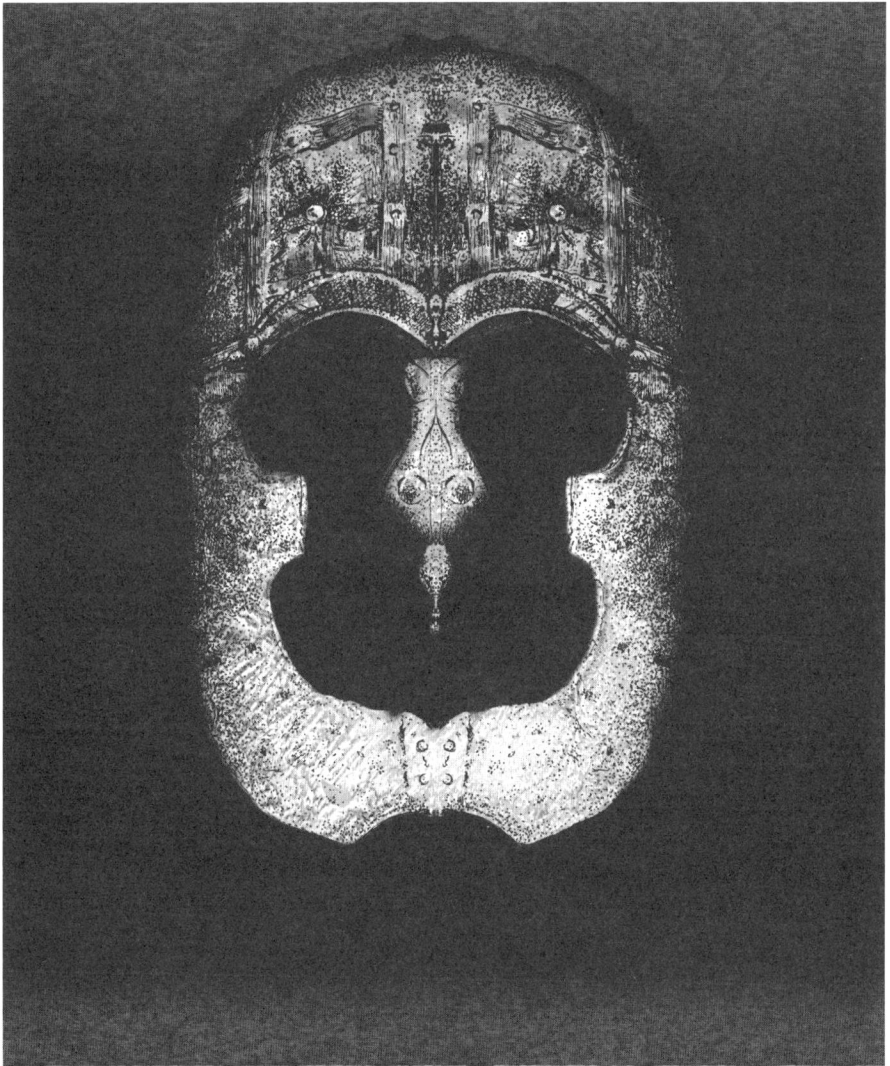

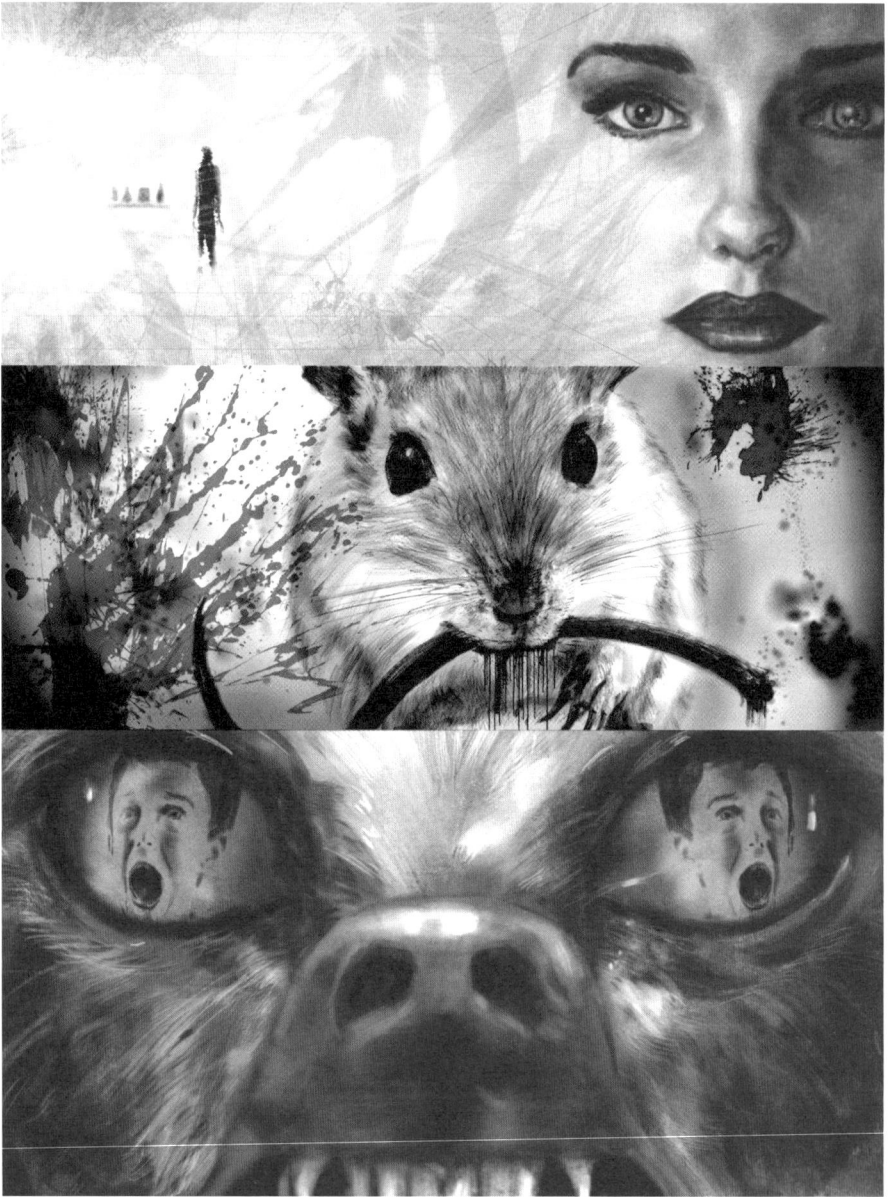

Jason Zerrillo lives and works in upstate
New York doing freelance art and illustration.
A World Fantasy Award nominee, he's worked
for publishers such as Ash-Tree Press, Fantasist
Enterprises, and Centipede Press. He particularly
loves the collaborative nature of illustration, such as
orking with the authors and publishers to synthesize
the best piece of work possible, informed by the
creativity and intelligence of all involved.

ROBERT H. WAUGH

In Her Eye

The only trace of the event that Barbara can find today, now that she is ready to go home, is a fragment of pale bone through which a mesquite spears its bitter branch; each green leaf casts a sparse shadow onto the gnawed bone. The bone will not be folded into mud to fossilize, it will not be found. Nothing will be left when winter comes. Roger Kensington had showed her much more bone and flesh at the beginning of the summer. Coyotes and vultures, flies, ants, bacteria, in their various cleanly fashions, have gorged. She had not meant to cater the feast, but she does not begrudge them; they never eat too much, none of them. The most marginal beast knows better than to eat too much; but it eats enough.

She still wonders what she had actually been doing when the earth shook. Roger was quite clear about the time. For her it was ten minutes after two o'clock in the afternoon of the second Friday in March. But since she only learned of the event three days later when Roger called on Sunday night, she finds it difficult to recall where she was, what she was holding, what she was looking at, what was in the air, what was the set of her mind. Most probably she was sitting at her desk, dissatisfied with the numbers Mr Olsen had provided on the screen, her cold fingers poking at the empty in-out tray, or staring across the Charles at the pyramids and mortuary domes of MIT. But she could as well have been on break, reaching for her bottle of water from the refrigerator or in the bathroom, squatting and waiting. Though she had been sick to her stomach that morning, she had seen no reason why she shouldn't go to the office, and the walk had invigorated her. Her work is perfunctory; forms come in, bearing the heading of the plaintiff, are manipulated, and depart transformed. When she came home in the afternoon, walking with her usual economy past the station on Huntington Street, past the church, stopping in the grocery store and the yarn shop, she found the end of the day as satisfactory as she had found the morning. She ate and worked and went to bed. This is satisfaction, this is enough.

So she wonders what she could have been thinking at that instant. And was it prayer?

She doesn't believe it was prayer. She was finished with prayer since the day she came back from the Vineyard and told Joshua that she couldn't see him anymore, that it was dangerous. Because prayer, she knew, could do nothing.

"Listen to yourself," his voice had said calling from Newton that night. "You're not a child anymore, you really aren't. You can't expect that something that big can be saved when it comes rolling in at high tide. And you can't just cut someone off like this, out of the blue."

But Joshua didn't understand how little she wanted. She hadn't expected anything more than a gesture from God. Not even when she was a child did she expect more than the smallest brightening of the tip of the candle on either side of the altar, and when she was older she expected no more than the usual acts of kindness in a day, just the sight of one person giving one penny to a beggar.

So now both she and God had to pay for the dismissal they had both suffered in those weeks last summer when the right whale had come ashore east of Gay's Head and heaved its helpless lungs beneath the weight of its tossed-up flesh. The experts from Woods Hole along with volunteers from up and down the island gathered on the beach but could not repeat the successes to which they had become accustomed in earlier incidents. Incidents. Its size, forty-four feet long and eighteen shaking tons, was too daunting to handle gently. The polite meadows upwind stank from its decomposition for days before the authorities determined that the only way to remove it was to call in butchers to haul off the slabs of blubber and thick cords of bone; the beach still stank for weeks.

And no one knew why. Perhaps whales follow a migratory track that existed across this beach millennia before the land silted and lifted; perhaps their sonars are distressed and disrupted by the increasing cacophony we make as we re-enter the sea. Every season a new theory comes into fashion to explain the gross waste on the beaches. That was the way of it again. This whale stank and died, and no one knew why.

The waste was more than she could bear. And the fact that it was the carcass of a right whale made the waste all the worse, the more desperate. It was right for the butchers who multiplied on the land, right for the lamps that shone on the enterprise of human use until now, as she had heard with Joshua on the whale-watch boat off Hyannis the summer before the beaching; the right whales of the North Atlantic are reduced to a community of barely three hundred. The seas and the songs are drying up, and few of the whales can hear a thing that the others are saying as they roll along scattered, murmuring to themselves the trivia of their private isolations, homeless in the dead seas.

After standing on the beach where a few hacked bones still lay in the dunes, after finding her way to Newton through the bustle of Boston, after eating the appetizer of the meal Joshua had prepared for her return and she couldn't eat a bite more, she couldn't help herself from suddenly saying that she had to create her own retreat, though she shrank from uttering the word solidarity. But it was a solidarity of flesh without fuss. Because so little was left.

That meal was a year ago. So she was in no way prepared for the significance of Roger Kensington's story, a story meant for her alone, when her phone rang that Sunday night. And her phone never rang.

"But I don't know you at all," she protested, after he allowed that a call from West Texas was nothing she ought to expect.

"Ms Matthews," he said with that *Ms.* of the South, she could catch the difference in the slight lilt, "I can't begin to tell you how I know your name. I don't know what connection you have to what's happened out here. But you listen and you judge. If you think I'm crazy you hang up, change your number, tell the police about me, whatever makes you feel safe. But me and my wife's seen something that you can be sure concerns you. I mailed this letter today, you'll get it real soon. But I'll say this now. I've seen your whale."

Then he said, "Must be your whale. In West Texas. In my front yard."

After the call she sat for an hour next to the phone trying to remember what she had been thinking on Friday at ten minutes past two. It was not a prayer. What had come out of her heart? Hurled itself out of her heart without her knowing? Help? Increase my heart? Feed me?

Roger Kensington had told her something else. She wouldn't believe him, he said, if he didn't tell her. "After you got home Friday, you opened the second drawer of the desk in your bedroom, lifted out some pieces of glass on a handkerchief, and cut the inside of your arm. Not much. Then you put the pieces back." She wouldn't have believed him, no.

She'd bought the figurine two years ago in the booth in front of the whale watch office. A clear-glass whale, no bigger than her palm. Joshua offered to buy it but she shook her head, it was her purchase, her whale; then he smiled and passed the tips of his fingers lightly across her belly, and she rippled. He'd never done that before. A year later, back in her apartment with the smell of the butchered whale still thick in her hair she had taken the figurine down from the bookcase and smashed it circumspectly in her folded handkerchief. Then she sat down to the absence of prayer.

But her year-long retreat had at least the character of prayer in its single-mindedness and the meager means it sought for itself. There was only so much she could deal with: the papers at the office, the grocery store, the yarn and the knitting, the Center off Commonwealth, paying the bills, pulling on the quilt, the necessity for sleep. Labor's more itself without pretense. Joshua had learned that it made no sense to phone or to visit; she taught him that. When he sat beside her the last time in September next to the river she had not said a word and not missed a stitch as he blamed her for the end of the world. That ended long before she was born.

146

When her mother phoned she said that she was doing well; she was. She was intimately in touch with the very center of what life there was as she became more spare in her space, more in control of what it meant to be in solidarity with the flesh of the displaced world, more mute in the hands of her needles as they gave away the little warmth that she could find to Rebecca or Kathy or Falla, sitting exhausted at the Center. They told her the worst was their families were scattered; they were scattered too, in their heads. They were cold. But what they looked at, she looked at: the street was the street, the rain was the rain, the stink of their flesh was the stink of flesh. Her mother in Ohio had no way to know this, the street or the rain or the flesh or the stripped-off oceans around us, and she had no way to tell her.

"Mother, I'm fine. No, I don't see Joshua anymore. Yes, he was very nice." He was. He was quizzical, light. His blond hair slopping across his freckled face made the world much better than it was. His barbecued chicken, rolled in the pungent rosemary that he grew in his window-box at the side of the bed that faced the morning sun, filled the empty parts of her body that obeyed the tongue. But the nice world protects you too much. The spice overlays the carrion.

Joshua had insisted that they go on the whale-watch, but he hadn't understood how shaken she was when that smooth skin of the ocean had lifted itself gently from the swell of the waves as though that darker wave were a dark organ the ocean displayed as it turned itself inside out and said *Love me*. In the wide forehead of the whale letting the water pour off it the ocean had said *You can love me*. It said *I don't care what the wound is*. And the whale was too big for any such words to sound perverse. As that powerful smooth back of the beast slid below the surface and the guide began chattering the statistics again, the statistics that you knew would kill the beast with well-meaning, Barbara had burst into tears and run for the door of the toilet where she could throw up her shame with as little fuss as possible.

Joshua thought she was seasick, but she wasn't. It was the shock of the animal's enormous, bodily generosity in the midst of its desolation that had shamed her. The beached whale the following summer had shown her that such generosity meant nothing, nothing at all.

How to respond to Roger Kensington's summons perplexed her; she was living on the edge of her means as it was. But Jane, when she told her that she had to fly to Texas—and she could tell the truth, that much of it, to Jane who was totally incurious—pointed out that someone who lived the spare life she did and always paid her bills must have a very good rating with the credit union. They were happy to lend her more than she needed, and left her bemused at this easy trust in a world that was getting by on less. And she had never taken as much vacation as she might have, especially this last year. She called Roger and asked him to pick her up at the Lubbock airport.

But all those days as she planned her trip she kept seeing in front of her eyes his account of the event that she had received in the mail two days after the call. As the plane began to lift off from the runway at Logan and bank over the Atlantic, her stomach and breasts could feel the event like a slow turn in the air.

"I've lived man and boy in Slayton for forty-five years. My wife says we just passed our silver anniversary, and she must be right, she always knows what she's saying. I work in town, we farm a bit too. It's bleak as anything all year round, but you get a living. My wife Lurlene saw this herself, like me.

"We were sitting on the porch at 12:10, heard the day's weather on the radio, just had lunch when we saw it rushing up, rising up from the ground fifty feet away across the drive, real near the other side of the flowers. It didn't come out of the ground, and it didn't just flash appear, didn't come out just head first either, then the rest. It was like it come surging up from that heat line you sometimes see out here hanging ten feet from the ground, like it was leaping from the waves; maybe it thought it was. So the thing, this huge thing, flung itself into that hot noon sun and took a slow turn in the air like it was going to circle for the rest of its life like some hawk. And then it fell smack on that flat desert floor, and from fifty feet away where we were sitting the porch shook beneath us. That was

148

it. Must have died like that. But Miss Matthews, I know it's your whale. Not that there's anything anyone can do about it."

When she walked into the Lubbock terminal he lifted his hat to her at once; he had no doubt who she was, and as she looked at the gray bare slope of the scrub across the tarmac she knew that she stuck out among all the other people landing in this small airport totally off the end of the world. He was not her picture of him. He was large, pot-bellied, weathered, soft, and his coppery face was washed-out above his buttoned-up shirt. She flushed to think how she looked to him, slight, pale, fair-haired, sullen, and airless.

"What do you do, Mr Kensington?" she asked in his truck.

"I work for an appliance store in the middle of Slayton. I repair airconditioners. That's a good job here. I used to go out hunting sometimes." He gestured vaguely to the country he was driving through that to her eyes bled off lifeless as the seas off the Vineyard.

"Where's your tribe?"

"And some things I just don't talk about much at all."

"I'm sorry." She had felt so clever for a flash, had to show off, had to show him that she knew something too. Because he knew things about her.

"No need to apologize. It's just, people get this notion, you're a Native American"—he spoke the phrase as though it would taste queer in his mouth all his life—"you're into something that's going to save the world, or's going to do nothing, that's shoved off. My wife's real easy about the Indian thing. My tribe, well, we get to-gether. Now I'll tell you this. What I saw, what she saw, what you're going to see, I didn't see it because I'm what I am, and I didn't see it because I was drunk either. Don't touch the stuff."

She didn't see the shape from miles away; that was a fantasy. One moment they were driving along the main road, the next Roger had turned off up a hard dirt track that circled a small rise, pulling onto his land where dusty hollyhocks were blooming next to the house, flowers she had never expected that took her breath away with their sweet nodding to the wind under the wall of the suburban house; dusty blackfoot daisies and zinnias edged the walk, and the doors of the garage opened as Roger drove in. None of it was Texas. So when she turned to look through the garage window the mass of the whale struck her as no more out of place than the garage and the house and the flowers, no more out of place than the man sitting next to her who repaired air-conditioners with his dark rough fingers, and no more out of place than Lurlene in her polyester apron getting up from the rocker on the porch to welcome her. So they had to talk and Lurlene had to go off to the kitchen for the iced tea before she could turn to the whale.

"You like sugar?"

It was not as big as the whale beached on the Vineyard. It was diminished; she hadn't taken into account that a week had passed since it fell to earth and shook the Kensingtons' porch as they rocked in the noontime heat. Roger didn't call in the butchers; he only called her. But the scavengers had heard the news, the coyotes and vultures and the hound down the road that belonged to the Kensingtons' neighbors. Every night it was becoming less and less. The tail was gone. The vestigial legs, long as her forearm, longer than she thought possible, showed teeth marks. The long ridge of the fin above the tail was shredded. The broken ribs jutted out of the mottled flesh that draped the remaining mass as though it were an old brown suit that the whale was about to contribute to Goodwill.

In this dry distant air the stench she had smelled at Gay's Head disappeared.

"It's a female," she said at last, after a long walking up and down, bending down, at last placing her hand on the stiff flesh.

"Yes. Hard now to see."

"Why's she lying like this?"

"When she came up like that wet, breaching you know, she was looking to fall back into whatever ocean she'd come out of. She came up turning, the tail came up and tossed out, the water spraying off her, and she lay there flat in the air for the damn longest time like she'd just come out of the belly of the sky—it was blue that day, the way it is here for day after day this time of year—and then she fell just that way, flat."

"Shook the ground in your backyard."

150

"Yeah."

"What comes eating?"

"Coyotes, vultures, ants. They all smell it. Nothing lasts very long out here. But they didn't get everything, her eye is still here. That's the surprise. The birds won't touch that eye for nothing."

Barbara looked into the clouded blue surface of the eye and thought she saw something move, a reflection.

"Anyway, we wouldn't let anything near it."

As she lay in bed that night next to the fireplace they'd lit for her against the March chill that started to seep through the walls, she tried again to make sense of it. Was it effective prayer, was it her prayer? Was it just a gasp, her breastbone grunting *The seas die*? Was it about the right whale whose carcass she could not forget rotting on the Vineyard, or about the one whose generosity she could not endure the summer before that? If the body out on the Kensingtons' front yard had been a right whale she wouldn't have been able to bear the possibility that she had somehow drawn her out of the depleted oceans. But she wasn't a right whale; and after he had examined some articles and a book or two carefully in the local library Kensington had discovered that no kind of whale like her swam on earth today. Not today.

West Texas wasn't always a desert. The inland sea once rolled here where she was trying to sleep, where she'd never get to sleep. She rolled over in bed, tucking up her knees, hugging herself tight, it was so cold. At the dawn of the world in that great hot humid world where the waters flooded and the first great flesh stood up in the leafy sun, the sun had poured through it all and the first whales had returned to the first home of us all. That soon dried up. Effective prayer. The attention of us all now in the world, listening to the hum of our air-conditioners, scattered through the sweaty streets, looking out our windows across rivers, it's our attention that hankers back for the first flesh. It's the weight of our pity that brought the flesh forward, to this sun, to this place of the emptied seabeds, breaching time. The weight of our pity, the force of our exhaustion, the plunge of our working hands.

Standing beside the mouth of the whale in the late afternoon light, she had felt an awful tenderness rush through her, bending down to stroke the black, fine threads that lined her lips, long, silky, tough, soft, pressing.

"But how did you know it was me, in Boston?" They were sitting at the table after supper; she felt unbalanced, forced. The setting sun lit up the wall of the family portraits that Lurlene had explained to her in detail. That's family, pictures going back to the turn of the century.

"I saw you in her eye."

She made a gesture as though pushing something off her face.

"When I first saw you, I could look at nothing else, I was just so dumbstruck. Lurlene too. You sat at a metal desk not quite your size, not made for you, maybe not made for anybody. When your face turned the eye turned with you, so that it was always looking just straight at your face. And then we saw the nameplate, Barbara Matthews. There you were, sitting in her eye."

"When we looked the next day," Lurlene added, "well, the eye was starting to film over, but you were there, silvery, sitting on a bench like on the side of a river, knitting and behind you there was a big skyscraper. Well, even out here in Slayton, Texas, we know what the Prudential looks like, and that that was Boston where Barbara Matthews lived."

"That first night after the whale fell out of her leap from the sky we saw you in your brass bed, sleeping by the light of the streetlamp outside."

"And that's how you knew me at the airport."

"Wherever you were, walking, waiting for the subway—"

"The T."

"—it didn't matter, you were still in her eye, no matter how cloudy it was getting. You're still there."

Lurlene got up and asked her to come out to the back porch where they couldn't see the body. "It's a good time to hear the whippoorwills. Roger, you stay put."

"Yeah, you ladies go talk."

Out in the warbling darkness, after they'd stood there for a time listening, looking out, Lurlene whispered, "You've got to forgive us, honey. We didn't know what we had here, we still don't. All we could do was watch. And we did watch, wherever you were, at the office, at your home. All the time. We saw you in the bathroom. We saw you throw up. Saw you crying. You've just got to forgive us, because that's why you had to come here, what we couldn't tell you on the phone. That we were perfect strangers who knew stuff about you that nobody knows."

How long does it take that massive body lying on the ground under the stars while the coyotes are gathering again, gathering hungry out there, how long does it take to die? How long do the thoughts take to pass through the brain in that dying? How long do the thoughts last that hold her? Lying in bed on her back, her hands at her side, she felt the tears press against the tissue of her throat again, her sore breast starting to hiccup, because it didn't matter. She would never pray again, she didn't need to; she couldn't get out of the sight of the dead eye.

Two weeks later, staring at the bone in the mesquite, she was still in her eye.

H.W. JANSON

Henry Fuseli's *The Nightmare*

Henry Fuseli—or Johann Heinrich Füssli, his original Swiss name—played a paradoxical role in the art of the late eighteenth century and the early years of the nineteenth. His fame was international, and his works, known practically everywhere through engravings, left their mark on artists as diverse as William Blake and Eugène Delacroix. He had, in fact, a most important catalytic function in the decades of "Sturm und Drang" and early Romanticism. Yet he never achieved popular success as a painter, and his most ambitious ventures, the vast cycles of the Shakespeare Gallery and the Milton Gallery, were resounding failures. Only once did Fuseli enjoy the wide acclaim he craved: in 1782, when he exhibited a picture entitled *The Nightmare* at the Royal Academy in London. And his modern fame, after a century of almost total neglect, also rests very largely on this one subject, which earned him a reputation among twentieth-century critics as a precursor of Surrealism.

The Nightmare, however, is not at all typical of Fuseli's work. John Knowles, in his *Life of Fuseli*, published in 1831, gives a list of the sixty-nine pictures exhibited by the artist at the Royal Academy between 1774 and 1825, and almost every one of them is based on a literary source—Homer, Sophocles, Dante, Milton, Shakespeare, Spenser, and many others—while no such source is indicated for *The Nightmare*. This record quite agrees with Fuseli's views on art as laid down in his numerous letters, Royal Academy lectures, and aphorisms. Art, he believed, must have a noble subject, and he found such subjects in the storehouse of the world's literature; when he pleads for freedom of invention, he means freedom to choose literary themes not previously illustrated, rather than the exploitation of subjective fancy. Among his aphorisms, it is true, we find one that says, "One of the most unexplored regions of art are [*sic*] dreams, and what may be called the personification of sentiment," but the dreams he had in mind were the dreams, visions, and apparitions of literature, such as the ghost in *Hamlet* or the dream of Richard III, not private nightmares. How, then, did he come to paint *The Nightmare*? Oddly enough, scholars so far have done very little to help us understand the genesis of the picture, or the extraordinary response it found among the public. The best-known version, now in the Goethemuseum at Frankfurt, has been reproduced countless times, but with a minimum of analytical comment. One might almost say of Fuseli's *Nightmare* what Mark Twain said of the weather—everybody is talking about it but nobody does anything about it.

There is, needless to say, no dearth of nightmares in literature (even Homer mentions them). Yet Fuseli seems to have been the first to attempt a visual representation of the subject. The basic difference between his conception and the traditional ways of depicting dreams is well illustrated by a comparison with Giulio Romano's *Dream of Hecuba*, a well-known Renaissance work that Fuseli saw during his Italian sojourn of 1770–78. It follows a traditional formula established in Western art ever since the ancient Greeks: Hecuba has the conventional pose of the dreamer—reclining but with the head supported by one arm instead of resting on the pillow, to signify sleep as distinct from death. Above her we see the content of her dream, a dark, cloud-borne winged genius with a flaming torch, prophetic of the destruction of Troy. Hecuba does not react in any way to his frightening presence; the two levels of reality are kept strictly separate. In *The Nightmare*, on the contrary, the dreamer is obviously in agony. She seems, indeed, near death. And the demon squatting on her chest, and the spectral, grinning horse, are the agents of her torture. Here the two levels of reality interact; the artist's main concern is the traumatic experience of a bad dream, not its content, whether symbolic, prophetic, or otherwise. With enormous effectiveness, Fuseli has succeeded in visualizing something that had never, so far as we know, been visualized before.

This is particularly evident when we turn from the Frankfurt painting to the earliest known version of *The Nightmare* (and presumably the original one), a large drawing in the British Museum dated March 1781. It is described by Knowles, who owned it at the time he published his *Life of Fuseli*, and it is the first version known to him. The demon here is far larger and more frightening than in the Frankfurt canvas; the horse, surprisingly, is absent; and the young woman is stretched out, almost like a corpse, parallel to the picture plane. She is in fact modeled on a corpse—the corpse in the center of the *Noah* panel on the East Doors of the Florentine Baptistery, by Lorenzo Ghiberti. For that Early Renaissance master, this is an unusually expressive figure, inspired not by classical sources but by certain Gothic representations of the Dead Christ. Fuseli could have taken it from the engraving here reproduced, one of a set issued in 1774 and illustrating the East Doors in detail; but I prefer to think that he studied the Noah panel directly and made a drawing of this figure when he was in Florence in 1777, since his tortured dreamer stresses all the expressive aspects of Ghiberti's corpse, which are somewhat softened in the engraving. Ghiberti's fame was just then rising once more, after centuries of neglect, and Fuseli had a special reason to study the East Doors: had not his idol, Michelangelo, pronounced them worthy to be the Gates of Paradise? The Noah panel, moreover, must have held particular interest for him; a few years before, he had illustrated an epic poem on the life of Noah by his mentor, the Zürich professor Johann Jakob Bodmer. (It was Bodmer who introduced Fuseli to Shakespeare and Milton; he had translated *Paradise Lost* into German and had written his Noah epic as a sort of sequel to Milton's poem.) Be that as it may, Fuseli knew the East Doors well, for in one of his Royal Academy lectures many years later he gave a lengthy and accurate description of certain details of the work. He even transmitted the Ghiberti corpse to his friend William Blake, who used it for the figure of Dante in his engraving of the Paolo and Francesca scene in the *Inferno*. Dante, after telling the story of the two lovers, wrote that "I fell to the ground like a dead body"; Blake could hardly have chosen a more suitable prototype. John Knowles remarks that the *Nightmare* drawing of 1781 lacks the horse's head. This, he says, was added in the painting of 1782. The picture, according to Knowles, was sold for twenty guineas. An engraving of it by Burke was so popular, he tells us, that the publisher made a profit of more than 500 pounds even though the prints sold for a few pennies apiece. Although the painting disappeared from public view—it turned up a few years ago and is now in the Detroit Institute of Arts—the engraving traveled far and wide. A few months after its publication on January 30, 1783, it was available at the Leipzig Fair, where it was admired by Goethe's patron, the young duke Carl August ("I have not seen anything for a long time," he wrote, "that gives me as much pleasure"). This, then, is *Nightmare II*, as against *Nightmare I*, the drawing of 1781. According to Knowles, Fuseli did several more Nightmares after the big success of 1782, each different from the others. The Frankfurt canvas, or *Nightmare III*, must be one of these; it was probably painted toward 1790, since there is an engraving after it dated 1791. Although it is the most melodramatic of the group, it has become famous only in modern times. The composition that made Fuseli known all over Europe was *Nightmare II*.

Except for the addition of the horse and the somewhat less rigid attitude of the maiden, *Nightmare II* closely resembles *Nightmare I*. The animal pokes its head through the drapery at the foot of the bed, and its questioning expression is directed at the incubus-demon. Its function is still a subsidiary and far from frightening one; it even wears a collar, as well it might, for it represents the demon's means of transportation. We gather this from the four-line verse below the engraving, which reads:

> —on his Night-Mare, thro' the evening fog,
> Flits the squab fiend, o'er fen, and lake, and bog,
> Seeks some love-wilder'd maid by steep opprest,
> Alights, and grinning, sits upon her breast.

Is this quotation the literary source of the picture? Or did Fuseli

The Nightmare, *ca. 1781*   *Freies Deutsches Hochstift, Goethemuseum*

compose it himself? Here again Knowles comes to our aid; he cites
a description of the picture in verse by Erasmus Darwin (a physician and poet, the grandfather of Charles), and its first four lines
agree with the words on the engraving. This description—which
is a great deal longer than Knowles acknowledges—appears in
part II of Darwin's *The Botanic Garden,* subtitled "The Loves of
the Plants," a long discourse in verse, part allegorical, part scientific, that enjoyed great popular favor. The first edition, however,
was not published until 1789, six years after the engraving. There
was, then, an intimate association between Darwin and Fuseli;
they shared the same publisher, Joseph Johnson, who must have
brought them together soon after Fuseli's return from Italy. Thus
Darwin (who had been at work on *The Botanic Garden* since 1777)
probably saw *Nightmare II* before the canvas was finished and

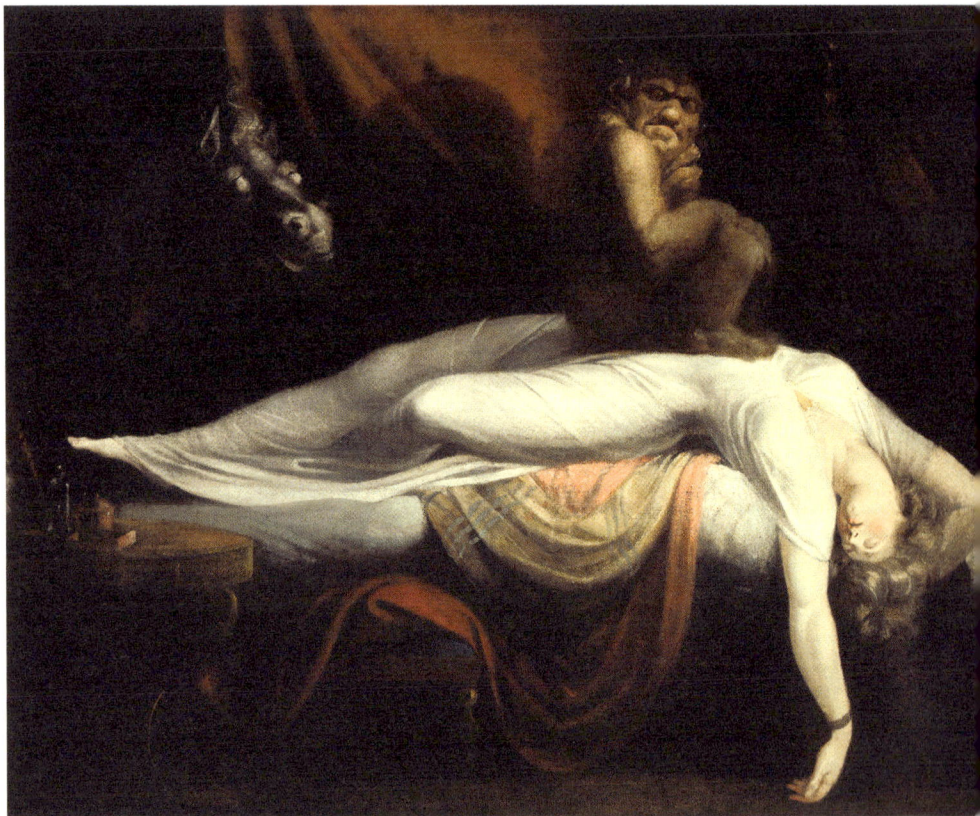

The Nightmare, 1781   Oil on canvas   101.6 cm × 127 cm (40 in × 50 in)   Detroit Institute of Arts

decided to incorporate a description of it in his poem. It may indeed have been he who was responsible for the addition of the horse, a somewhat distracting element in the picture, that apparently was introduced because of the punning line, " — on his Night-Mare…flits the squab fiend . . ." Etymologically, the "mare" of "nightmare" is quite distinct from "mare" meaning a female horse, although in folklore the two were often compounded. In England, the nightmare (i.e., the night demon that sits on the sleeper's chest and thus causes the feeling of suffocation characteristic of the pathology of nightmares), was often thought of as female, a night-hag or night-witch, while in German-speaking areas such as Fuseli's hometown of Zürich, it was masculine ("Nachtmar" or "Alp"). In either case, the incubus would "ride" his victim, or at times even assume the shape of a horse. But the notion that the night-mare is the steed which carries the demon from one victim to the next seems to have no antecedent in the vast literature on nightmares; in all likelihood, it was invented specifically for *Nightmare II*.

But why did the picture have such fascination for Darwin? The reason becomes evident from his discussion of it, which follows a passage concerning the Pythian priestess, drunk with a poisonous decoction of laurel, who "speaks…with words unwill'd, and wisdom not her own." The nightmare, too, he says, illustrates a suspension of the power of the will. Fuseli's maiden experiences not the incubus but a train of frightful images set off by the demon's pressure on her chest:

> Then shrieks of captur'd towns, and widows' tears,
> Pale lovers stretch'd upon their blood-stain'd biers,
> The headlong precipice that thwarts her flight,
> The trackless desert, the cold starless night,
> And stern-eyed murderer with his knife behind,
> In dread succession agonize her mind.
> In vain she *wills* to run, fly, swim, walk, creep;
> The WILL presides not in the bower of SLEEP.

In a long footnote appended to the last line, Darwin restates the nature of sleep in scientific terms: the sensory organs remain alert but cannot perceive external objects so long as volition is suspended. "When there arises in sleep a painful desire to exert the voluntary motions, it is called the nightmare or incubus." And, he claims, a similar state of reverie, or suspension of the will, occurs when we contemplate a great work of art; hence an artist with sufficient powers of persuasion, such as Fuseli, can with impunity violate every standard of verisimilitude. Only if the image presented to our imagination is an unbearably horrid one will we endeavor to rouse ourselves from our reverie, as from a nightmare. Darwin here draws upon a tradition of physiological psychology ultimately based on Sir Isaac Newton, developed by Berkeley, Locke, Hume, and Gay, and popularized in the later eighteenth century by David Hartley's *Observations on Man*. Fuseli's *Nightmare* must have seemed to him an admirable illustration of this theory, and many other contemporary admirers of the picture may have had similar thoughts, since the "new psychology" had aroused considerable interest among the educated public.

If Darwin's intervention accounts for the difference between *Nightmare I* and *Nightmare II*, Fuseli alone appears to be responsible for the further development of the composition in *Nightmare III*. There the entire design has been rearranged within a vertical format; the horse now looms as the most conspicuously frightening creature; the incubus, smaller and less weighty, looks as if he might be squatting beside the sleeper, rather than on her; and the maiden is placed obliquely, her head toward the beholder. *Nightmare III* thus appears both more Baroque and more "Gothic" (in the eighteenth-century sense) than its predecessors. There is, at Chatsworth, a painting of c. 1630 by Jacques Blanchard that may have suggested the new position of the sleeper; it represents the death of Cleopatra, whose body appears in a similarly foreshortened view. The picture was already at Chatsworth in Fuseli's day, and there also was an engraving after it, so Fuseli very probably knew it, directly or indirectly. The new role of the horse is less easy to account for. Here apparently the artist recalled a picture he had painted in 1779 on his way back from Italy, while stopping at Zürich. It shows him in conversation with his revered friend Bodmer, while a huge bust of Homer looms between them. In *Nightmare III*, the bust's place has been taken by the horse—an evil spirit usurping the dominant role of a beneficent one. The fascinating spectral, luminescent quality of the horse would seem to reflect a much earlier source: the wild horses in a woodcut by Hans Baldung Grien of 1534. In his youth, Fuseli had made numerous drawings after German and Swiss sixteenth-century prints such as this. These studies, which are among the earliest examples of the "Gothic Revival," were inspired by a national pride, a patriotic interest in one's own local past, that was a characteristic feature of early Romanticism, fostered among others by Bodmer, who was professor of Swiss history at Zürich. Fuseli even then may have been attracted by Hans Baldung's preoccupation with witches and

162

demons, and the wild expressiveness, the strange luminous eyes of Baldung's horses, must have stuck in his memory.

One final question remains to be answered: what was the genesis of *Nightmare I*? Why did Fuseli conceive it at the time he did, soon after his return from Italy, and why does the motif have so isolated a position in his oeuvre? As Ernest Jones has amply documented in his psychoanalytic study of the subject, nightmares always have a strongly sexual connotation, sometimes quite openly expressed, at other times concealed behind a variety of disguises. In the voluminous literature on nightmares from the fifteenth to the eighteenth century (a field halfway between demonology and medicine), the incubus "riding" its victim is almost invariably of the opposite sex. John Bond, whose *Essay on the Incubus or Nightmare* of 1753 Fuseli might well have known, lists "fond pining lovers" among the chief victims of the affliction, and Burton, in his *Anatomy of Melancholy*, regards nightmares as a symptom of the melancholy of maids, nuns, and widows, adding that the cure is marriage. Against this background, we must now take a glance at Fuseli's own love life. While in Italy, he seems to have been something of a gay dog, without any serious emotional attachments. He liked to tell how he used to lie on his back day after day musing on the splendors of the Sistine Ceiling, and that "such a posture of repose was necessary for a body

fatigued like his with the pleasant gratifications of a luxurious city."
The passage suggests that perhaps he identified himself to some
extent with the prone male body he found in Ghiberti's *Noah* panel.
On his return trip to England in 1779, however, he fell violently
in love, apparently for the last time in his life (he was then thirty-
eight), with a young niece of his friend, the physiognomist Lavater.
His passion came to nothing, and soon after he reached London
he learned, to his great distress, that the girl had been married to a
respectable merchant, in accordance with the wishes of her family.
Fuseli was terribly upset through most of the year 1779, and probably for some time thereafter. Whether he wrote directly to the lady
of his dreams we do not know, but we have a series of extravagantly
passionate love poems, as well as letters to Lavater and others who
knew the girl and whom Fuseli somehow expected to plead his
cause. One of these letters is particularly revealing in our context:
"Is she in Zürich now? [Fuseli was writing to Lavater from London.] Last night I had her in bed with me — tossed my bedclothes
hugger-mugger — wound my hot and tightclasped hands about
her — fused her body and her soul together with my own — poured
into her my spirit, breath, and strength. Anyone who touches her
now commits adultery and incest! She is *mine*, and I am *hers*. And
have her I will — I will toil and sweat for her, and lie alone, until I

164

have won her." In another letter, he expressed the hope that the heart of his beloved would respond to his vibrations from afar, and continued, "Each earthly night since I left her, I have lain in her bed …" And all this despite the fact that while Fuseli was in Switzerland he had never dared to declare his love to the girl! Is it too bold a conjecture to think that the "love-wilder'd maid" of *Nightmare I* is a projection of his "dream-girl," with the incubus-demon taking the place of the artist himself? The drawing dates from early 1781, but its highly finished character indicates that it is not a first sketch but the result of previous studies that may well go back a year or more. We have no likeness of the girl in question, although Fuseli surely made drawings of her while in Switzerland. Perhaps he destroyed them in despair at the news of her marriage. Did he try to paint her in London on the basis of these sketches? After the Detroit Institute of Arts acquired the painting of *Nightmare II*, it was found that a second piece of canvas had been pasted on its back; when the restorer removed it, he found underneath an unfinished but fascinating portrait of a beautiful young woman. If the front of the picture is Fuseli's original *Nightmare II*, rather than a copy, then the portrait, too, must be by Fuseli, and its sensuously seductive quality suggests that it represents the artist's beloved. By the time he painted *Nightmare III*, Fuseli's personal involvement had abated to the point where he was able to push the incubus-demon aside and develop the melodramatic aspects of the composition, now centered in the mare's head.

As a postscript, it is worth noting that one of the owners of the engraving after *Nightmare II* was Sigmund Freud; a framed specimen of the print hung for years in his Vienna apartment. Did he sense the fascinating psychological aspects of Fuseli's picture? Ernest Jones, who began his work on nightmares as early as 1909, makes no reference to that engraving. Instead, the book that eventually resulted from his studies carries *Nightmare III* as a frontispiece. It is tempting to think, though, that perhaps Jones's interest in the subject was first aroused when, as a pupil of Freud, he saw the print of *Nightmare II* on the wall of his teacher's study.

JAPOŃSKI

JEDYNEK POTWORÓW

SERIA: INOSHIRO HONDA

OLACH GŁÓWNYCH:

TAMBLYN

MIZUNO

SAHARA

UKCJA: TOHO

STUART GALBRAITH IV

Frankenstein Brothers:
A Look at *War of the Gargantuas*

War of the Gargantuas (*Furankenshutain no kaijû: Sanda tai Gaira*, 1966) exists as a kind of monster movie Nirvana, a film that delivers on the promise of its ingenious title in an orgy of gargantua vs gargantua action, with kindly (if plug-ugly) Brown Gargantua battling his equally hairy and scaly half-brother, the dreaded Green Gargantua, as both play hide-and-seek with the Japanese Self Defense Forces whose electrically charged Maser Cannons skewer them with electric bolts like colossal cattle prods. The movie was long a late-night favorite whose hypnotic qualities transfixed insomniac TV viewers and worked a similar magic on children when it was shown on Saturday afternoon monster movie shows, before local airwaves were taken over by infomercials and direct-to-syndication exploitation.

The film is a bastard sequel to *Frankenstein Conquers the World* (*Furankenshutain tai chitei kaiju Baragon*, 1965). It was written with that film's leading characters—played in the film by Nick Adams, Kumi Mizuno, and Tadao Takashima—in mind, but for reasons lost in the mists of time, the characters' names were changed and Russ Tamblyn replaced Adams, while Kenji Sahara pinch-hit for Takashima. Nevertheless, it is quite obvious to anyone watching the films back-to-back that they are essentially playing the same characters, especially considering that the events in *Gargantuas* make little sense without Frankenstein's backstory.

Indeed, without this backstory *War of the Gargantuas* has hardly any story at all. When a giant green, er, gargantua (called Gaira

167

in the Japanese version) begins attacking ships at sea, then comes ashore to gobble up tourists at Haneda Airport, investigators turn their attention to Kyoto-based researcher Dr Paul Stewart (Russ Tamblyn). Working with assistant Akemi (Kumi Mizuno) and scientist Yuzo Mamiya (Kenji Sahara), the three had raised a seemingly gentle Ewok-like creature (called Sanda in the Japanese version) that had grown to tremendous size and, like the Frankenstein monster in the previous film, had lost its hand trying to escape. Akemi alludes to the creature's death on Mt Fuji, but none of this is shown or particularly explained, giving the film a dreamlike absence of causal relationships.

With both the press and the military convinced Gaira and Sanda are one and the same, Paul, Akemi, and Yuzo do a little investigating on their own, and the vast majority of the picture has the trio racing to find Sanda before the military does. Meanwhile, Gaira wreaks all manner of havoc, until the kinder, gentler Sanda tries to put a stop to his half-brother's dire deeds. But, like a supersized Cain and Abel, the two are destined to fight to the finish, and after trashing Tokyo they fall into the bay where a providential volcano boils them alive like lobsters.

War of the Gargantuas was a Japanese production whose stateside funding was, at best, minor. Though billed in its U.S. version as a Henry G. Saperstein Enterprises presentation co-produced by Saperstein and his frequent partner, television writer Reuben Bercovitch, the Japanese credits make no mention of either man, though Saperstein did apparently insist on the giant octopus vs Green Gargantua duel that opens the picture, as if to suggest the battle shot but ultimately scrapped between the Frankenstein Monster and a giant mollusk for the intended climax of *Frankenstein Conquers the World* had waged on for many months, and far out to sea. Early drafts of the script, dating back to autumn 1965, more explicitly connect the two pictures, and earlier drafts were variously titled *Frankenstein Brothers* (*Furankenshutain no kyodai*), *Frankenstein's Battle* (*Furankenshutain no toso*), and *Frankenstein's Duel* (*Furankenshutain no ketto*).

Here was a giant monster that actually ate people, spitting out their blood-soaked clothes like watermelon pits.

A further sign that the relationship between Saperstein/Benedict and Toho had eroded can be seen in Russ Tamblyn's embarrassing billing. While Nick Adams was billed second after Akira Takarada (then a big draw in Japan) in *Monster Zero* (*Kaiju dai senso*, 1965) and was top-billed over both Kumi Mizuno and Tadao Takashima in *Frankenstein Conquers the World*, Tamblyn is billed third on *Gargantuas* behind Kenji Sahara and Kumi Mizuno. (The onscreen credits cheat somewhat, positioning their names Tamblyn—Mizuno—Sahara, with the layout implying but not insisting they be read right-to-left. Posters, however, clearly bill Tamblyn third.) Saperstein likely brought to the film little more than Tamblyn's commitment to do the picture and possibly his salary. The only other American in the cast is "Special Guest Star" (so billed in the American credits only) Kipp Hamilton, a struggling glamour girl/actress whose career was going nowhere fast after small roles in *Never So Few* (1959) and *The Unforgiven* (1960). Though she once dated Frank Sinatra, by 1966 she was, according to Tamblyn, dating Saperstein, who got her the role she'd live to regret. As a lounge singer at a rooftop beer garden (a summertime perennial in Japan to this day), Hamilton sings the infamously awful "Feel in My Heart," better known by its signature line, "The Words Get Stuck in My Throat." In all fairness it is not entirely clear whether it is Hamilton actually singing on the soundtrack, and with those lyrics it is unlikely that even Ella Fitzgerald would have sounded anything other than ridiculous. Hamilton died in 1981.

169

Many Japanese who saw *War of the Gargantuas* as children re-member to their surprise being horrified by its relative gruesome-ness: here was a giant monster that actually ate people, spitting out their blood-soaked clothes like watermelon pits. (This tasteless shot does not appear in the Japanese version, which opts for a more poetic cutaway to a dropped bouquet of flowers instead.) Special Effects Director Eiji Tsuburaya preferred his monster shows bloodless, but times were changing and it is also likely that Saperstein, with the American market in mind, insisted on a more graphic approach. However, it is also worth noting that rival Daiei had debuted its *Gamera* (the flying prehistoric extraterrestrial turtle) series eight months prior to *Gargantuas'* release, and both *Giant Monster Gamera* (*Daikaiju Gamera*, released December 1965) and the immediate follow-up, *Gamera vs Barugon* (aka *War of the Monsters; Daikaijû kessen: Gamera tai Barugon*, April 1966) featured a level of bloodletting unseen at Toho in its *kaiju eiga*. Equally notable is that while *Gamera vs Barugon* was given a first-class A-budget, it quickly became apparent to Daiei's executives that that series' audience was primarily children, gore not withstanding.

Toho saw the writing on the wall and, somewhat surprisingly, marketed *War of the Gargantuas* at children. Such had not been the case with *Frankenstein Conquers the World*, which had been half of a double bill that included *Standby Collegiate* (*Umi no wakadaisho*, or "Young Guy of the Sea"), the fifth in a long-running film series about handsome, athletic college student Yuichi Tanuma (Yuzo Kayama) and his travels and romances. That series' appeal was mainly to teenagers, comparable to those in America watching Frankie and Annette at their varied beach parties. But Kenji Sahara's billing over Tamblyn in *Gargantuas* suggests that Toho recognized the rapidly shifting market for its *kaiju eiga*. Sahara had just finished his run on the Tsuburaya-produced television series *Ultra Q*, the forerunner to the more famous *Ultraman*. Moreover, in its initial release in Japan *War of the Gargantuas* was part of a package that included *Emperor of the Jungle* (*Jyanguru taite*), a 75-minute anime adapted from the same cartoon series later imported to America as *Kimba, the White Lion*. Also on the bill was another cartoon, *We*

Russ Tamblyn wisecracks his way through the performance with a look of total boredom.

Pay Our Kindnesses (*Tsuru no ongaishi*), an 18-minute short adapted from the Japanese folktale. Clearly, *War of the Gargantuas* was not intended for adults.

Unlike the Italians, who in the mid-1960s shot everything silent, looping their films in postproduction, Toho and the other big studios in Japan recorded as much dialogue as was possible live; listen carefully and you can hear the quiet whir of the camera in some shots. During production, Tamblyn spoke his lines in English while the rest of the cast spoke theirs in Japanese. Though the Japanese trailer features exactly that (with Tamblyn's lines helpfully subtitled), for the Japanese release his voice was dubbed by Goro Mutsumi, who made his film debut starring in Koji Wakamatsu's first film and who would later amusingly play yakuza-like aliens in both *Godzilla vs Mechagodzilla* (*Gojira tai Mekagojira*, 1974) and *Terror of Mechagodzilla* (*Mekagojira no gyakushu*, 1975). More recently Mutsumi played another memorable yakuza, one of domestic origin, in Juzo Itami's *Minbo; or the Gentle Art of Japanese Extortion* (*Minbo no onna*, 1992).

According to Tamblyn, Saperstein claimed to have lost the dialogue tracks containing Tamblyn's voice, forcing the actor to loop his entire performance, a good deal of it from memory as Tamblyn had altered much of the pidgin English dialogue directly translated from the Japanese script. Not surprisingly, this only made his bad performance seem even worse. Tamblyn claims never to have seen the finished picture until November 2004, just shy of his seventieth

"An Important Film of Our Age! — Filmed in Absolute Realism!"

birthday. With *Seven Brides for Seven Brothers* (1954), *Peyton Place* (1957, for which Tamblyn was nominated for an Oscar), *West Side Story* (1961), *The Wonderful World of the Brothers Grimm* (1962), and *The Haunting* (1963) a not-too-distant memory, working—third-billed, no less—in a Japanese monster movie must have been a depressing comedown for the former MGM contractee, who admits he took the part solely for the money and the free trip to Japan. By all accounts he rarely socialized with the cast and crew, quite a contrast from his predecessor, the gregarious, eager-to-please Nick Adams. He wisecracks his way through the performance with a look of total boredom, in a character not unlike the one he had played in *The Haunting*, but where there he had been funny and likeable, here he is only smarmy and somnambulistic. That the Japanese actors play their scenes in the Japanese manner, at a higher pitch than Hollywood actors, only further emphasizes the inadequacy of Tamblyn's performance. (Adams wisely compensated, perhaps overcompensated, in his Japanese films.)

War of the Gargantuas opened in Japan on July 31, 1966, with posters declaring "Crises Erupt from the Mountain and the Seas! The Tokyo Metropolis is a Battlefield of Death! The World-Famous Toho Studios Presents the Monster Film of the Century!" (The international trailer is equally hyperbolic, unwisely promising "An Important Film of Our Age! —Filmed in Absolute Realism!")

War of the Gargantuas was not released stateside until four years later, in the summer of 1970, and then only via spotty distribution

Various posters and case designs for War of the Gargantuas.

to drive-ins by the long-defunct Maron Films. Why the delay? Saperstein, who died in June 1998, a month after the American-made *Godzilla* (a project he had spearheaded for years) stumbled into theaters, never gave a straight answer, claiming it took that long for him and/or Toho to prepare an international release version. While there are some differences between the Japanese and U.S. versions—there is a smattering of additional effects shots, and much of Akira Ifukube's memorable if severely repetitive score was replaced with stock music, the same Capitol Records Hi-Q stock themes by William Loose that also turned up in *Night of the Living Dead*—it is balderdash to suggest this process was dragged out for as long as it was. More likely, by the summer of 1966 Saperstein's competitive partnership with Sam Arkoff at AIP had soured utterly, leaving Saperstein's UPA with neither the capital nor the theatrical distribution network to release his co-productions with Toho. (Several other deals Saperstein had made with Toho were similarly orphaned, including *Monster Zero*, which was double billed with *Gargantuas*, and a big-scale war movie for which Saperstein had bought the U.S. rights, *Retreat from Kiska*, which debuted on local U.S. television stations in 1973, some eight years after it was made.)

As a movie, *War of the Gargantuas* is only average. As a result of his lackluster performance, Tamblyn has none of the likeability of Nick Adams, nor does Takeshi Kimura's script (writing as Kaoru Mabuchi) make any effort to expand upon the cross-cultural

173

The design of the monsters and their relative agility comes as a surprise and gives the film its own look.

romance with Sueko/Akemi intriguingly introduced in *Franken-stein Conquers the World*. There are more special effects shots in this than perhaps any previous Toho monster movie, but the film is little more than a search-and-destroy mission, a hunt for a pathetic, if wild, wounded animal, and neither the Green Gargantua's viciousness nor the military's relentless attacks on it engender much sympathy. It is all vaguely depressing; after all, every effort by the leads to save Brown Gargantua fails completely, and the film ends pessimistically. Except for the early scenes, the movie is essentially one big military operation, devoid of story and characterization. "Actually, I find this one a little boring," admitted director Ishiro Honda to Guy Tucker in *Age of the Gods* (Daikaiju Publishing, 1996). "I'm glad it's popular, but that picture doesn't really have much heart."

Conversely, those with a fetish for military hardware will delight in all the high-techery, which includes the introduction of the Maser Cannon, an iconic bit of futuristic hardware that would turn up again and again in Toho monster movies, sometimes in new footage, but more often than not pilfered as stock footage.

The monster designs, by Ryo Narita and originally intended to be much closer to the design of the Frankenstein Monster of the previous film (with Gaira also looking a bit like the Creature from the Black Lagoon as well), are unique for the period, eschewing as they do the weighty rubber dinosaurish/buglike designs of the past in favor of something lightweight enough that actor-stuntmen

174

Flares are shot at one of the monsters, and the suit briefly catches on fire with the actor inside it.

Haruo Nakajima (as Gaira) and Hiroshi Sekita (as Sanda) are actually able to run through Eiji Tsuburaya's detailed miniatures. Their relative agility comes as a surprise and gives the film its own look, though the immobility of the rubber faces, perpetually scowling like a Paul Blaisdell monster, is a disappointment, and overall the costumes look rather like Vikings covered with divots. Nakajima and Sekita surely earned their pay, however. In one sequence what look like flares are shot at one of the monsters, and the suit briefly catches on fire with the actor inside it.

Despite its many flaws, *War of the Gargantuas* will probably always be remembered as a seminally 1960s Japanese monster movie. It is outrageous and more than a trifle silly, yet ultimately, oddly endearing.

Furankenshutain no kaiju — Sanda tai Gairah
("Frankenstein Monsters — Sanda vs. Gaira")

Producers, Tomoyuki Tanaka and Kenichiro Tsunoda; Associate Producers, Henry G. Saperstein and Reuben Bercovitch; Director, Ishiro Honda; Special Effects Director, Eiji Tsuburaya; Screenplay, Ishiro Honda and Kaoru Mabuchi [i.e., Takeshi Kimura]; English Dialogue, Reuben Bercovitch; Director of Photography, Hajime Koizumi; Art Director, Takeo Kita; Lighting, Toshio Takashima; Sound, Norio Tone; Music, Akira Ifukube; Chief Assistant Director, Koji Kajita; Production Manager, Shoichi Koga; Sound Effects, Hisashi Shimonaga. Toho Special Effects Group: Photography, Sadamasa Arikawa, Mototaka Tomioka; Production Manager, Yasuaki

175

Sakamoto; Art Director, Akira Wanatabe; Editor, Ryohei Fujii; Assistant to Tsuburaya, Teruyoshi Nakano; Optical Photography, Yoichi Manoda, Sadao Iizuka; Scene Manipulation, Fumio Nakadai.

Cast: Russ Tamblyn (Dr Paul Stewart), Kumi Mizuno (Akemi, his assistant), Kenji Sahara (Yuzo), Jun Tazaki (army commander), Kipp Hamilton (singer), Yoshifumi Tajima (policeman), Nobuo Nakamura (gray-haired biochemist), Hisaya Ito (Police Chief Izumida), Nadao Kirino, Kozo Nomura (military aides), Tadashi Okabe (reporter), Yutaka Oka (reporter in bow tie), Haruo Nakajima (Gaira), Hiroshi Sekita (Sanda), Ikio Sawamura (frightened fisherman), Ren Yamamoto (terrified sailor), Goro Mutsumi (voice characterization for Russ Tamblyn), Shoichi Hirose, Henry Okawa.

A Toho Co., Ltd. Production, in association with Benedict Pictures. A Toho Co., Ltd. Release. Eastman Color (processed by Tokyo Laboratory, Ltd.). Toho Scope. 93 minutes. Released July 31, 1966. U.S. Version: *War of the Gargantuas*. Released by Maron Films Ltd. English-dubbed. A United Productions of America Release. A Henry G. Saperstein Presentation. Executive Producers, Henry G. Saperstein and Reuben Bercovitch; Editor, Fredric Knudtson; Dialog Supervisor, Riley Jackson; Sound, Glen Glenn Sound Co.; Production Supervisor, S. Richard Krown; Song: "Feel in My Heart"; prints by Consolidated Film Industries. Double-billed with *Monster Zero* (q.v.). U.K. Title: *Duel of the Gargantuas*. 93 minutes. MPAA rating: G. Released July 29, 1970.

Notes: Tamblyn's voice is dubbed for the Japanese version. Toho did produce an English-dubbed version of this title. Its release, if any, is undetermined. A quasi-sequel to *Frankenstein Conquers the World* (*Furankenshutain tai chitei kaiju Baragon*, 1965), with Russ Tamblyn replacing Nick Adams. Significantly altered for release in America.

The Rhymeless Sonnet of Fear

Charles Lovecraft

What classic dreams avail the morbid-souled!
For them are ruined mausolea of
The night, and catacombs of Ptolemais.
For them, the eyes' eclipse that stares and stares
From phizes of surrounding formlessness.
Vaults of Yoh-Vombis bear maroonings in
Andromeda, while Serpens wriggles wild
Nearby and bares fanged teeth of sharpened star.

What classic dreams await the morbid-spelled.
Therein, the runes of Lovecraft, Smith, and Poe—
Who fully eldritch life bestow beyond
The pale—light up the hearth fires that beguile
With chill, regale lost wanderers in time—
And then make rote *the rhymeless sonnet of fear*.

BRADLEY H. SINOR

Excellence Demanded, Whiners Piss Off
The Last Interview of Karl Edward Wagner

You've just completed work on The Year's Best Horror
Stories: XXII. *What can you tell us about this volume?*
How does it differ from preceding ones?

XXII is the biggest volume to date, weighing in at thirty-one
stories and over 150,000 words. This is in part owing to the massive
proliferation of small press horror publications. It differs from
earlier volumes in the emergence of new writers, at least three of
whom weren't even born when the first volume appeared in 1970
from Sphere Books, the original publisher. As to its content, this
volume reflects the current trend toward the indefinable, toward
enigmatic horrors, toward the strange and disturbing. Horror is
moving beyond stalk-and-slash and into the mainstream. This is
not to say that there aren't a few take-no-prisoners horror stories
included, as well.

> *What sort of criteria do you use in selecting the stories that*
> *you want to include? How do you feel that your standards*
> *for selecting stories have evolved since you became editor of*
> *the series?*

I select the best stories of the year, regardless of category or
author. All types of horror are candidates: fantasy or non-fantasy,
traditional ghost story or splatterpunk, Lovecraftian or surreal,
subtle or gross, shivers or rotting zombies, enigma or in-your-face.
I play no favorites with authors. Big Name Pro has the same shot
as first story small press writer. I've run stories by Stephen King,

178

and I've run stories by writers who may have never written another story. I have maintained this attitude for fifteen years as editor: No taboos. No holds barred. No free rides. Excellence required. Whiners piss off.

> *How did you happen to be selected as editor for* The Year's Best Horror *series? I've heard some talk that you might be planning on stepping down in the next few years. Any truth to that report?*

Dave Drake and I were in New Orleans for DeepSouthCon fifteen years ago, strolling through the French Quarter in search of food with then-editor Gerald W. Page. Jerry said he had returned his contract for *The Year's Best Horror VIII* to DAW because he wanted to devote more time to his own writing. He wanted Dave to replace him. Dave said: "No way in Hell." I said: "I'll do it." Jerry said: "You were my next choice." Later, at SeaCon in Brighton, Don and Elsie Wollheim came up to my room and asked me to take over. Trying not to bite the side out of my glass, I said: "Sure!"

Stepping down as editor? No way. Never. Where do these rumors get started? I asked Elvis at the mall last night, and it was news to him. Probably started by disgruntled wannabes.

> *Okay, how about some basic biographical material?*

I was born in Knoxville, Tennessee, on December 12, 1945. I grew up there, survived high school and the 1950s, but never became part of the local culture. In 1967 I graduated from Kenyon College with an A.B. in history, but never became part of the Gambier, Ohio, culture. I then moved to Chapel Hill, North Carolina, to attend medical school at The University of North Carolina School of Medicine. I went for combined MD/PhD (neurobiology), but never became part of the culture, and dropped out for a few years to become a Haight-Ashbury hippie and to write. Not getting rich at that, I finished medical school and earned my MD in 1974, then began a brief career as a psychiatrist. Not long after, my books began to sell. Been writing full time ever since.

I suppose it's in the blood. My great-great-great-uncle was an opera composer named Richard. I learned to read from pre-code horror comics; gruesome fairy tales were my favorites. When I was five, I distressed my first-grade teacher by drawing horribly violent comic books with dialogue pretty much limited to "BOOO!" and "ARRGGHHAA!" Not much has changed in horror comics. I understand those grim fairy tales have since been censored. Twist kids' brains, they say. Can't think why.

When did you first start attempting to write and when did it really become serious for you? Where and when was your first sale?

My first stories were published in grammar school and high school newspapers. Lost now, I hope. As a high school sophomore, I wrote some of the worst Poe/Lovecraft pastiches ever attempted, but got good grades from my English teacher. I began writing *Bloodstone* at this time, in 1960, and copped an A for the prologue. At the time I was submitting various short stories to the existing markets, with success. In 1961 I completed the first Kane story, "The Treasure of Lynortis," which, while not bad for a sixteen-year-old punk, did not crash *F&SF*. This was completely rewritten as "Lynortis Reprise" years later. The original version was published in German and (in English) in the Italian magazine *Kadath*. If you find a copy, I'll hunt you down. Late at night. After ten years at this, I finally made my first sale, a Kane novel, to Powell Publications in 1969. I had written the novel during my senior year at Kenyon. It was bounced everywhere. Then, browsing the newsstand, I spotted a really tacky sword-and-sorcery novel from Powell, or something like that. Reasoning that any publisher who would publish something that putrid would publish me (this is amateur reasoning, by the way, and does not hold up in practice), I sent it to them, they bought it, the book came out in February, 1970. I got my copy whilst on pediatrics; my classmates asked if it were porno as I read it in the interns' lounge that night and…Well, it had been cut by about a third, and Kane had been changed into a black to match the cover of a black swordsman with a banana stuffed into his orange jock-strap, and the typos…In keeping with Powell's production values, they didn't change the description of Kane throughout: thus, Kane is a black or a red-haired blue-eyed fair-skinned type depending on the chapter. The reader may already have been confused by the unusual spelling of "spy" as "spry" or the spelling of "bireme" as "direme." Go figure.

But it was a first novel and a foot in the door. I took my next Kane book to Warner (then Paperback Library) as a published novelist looking for better pastures. Most important, I had saved a copy of my original manuscript, and all subsequent editions have been printed from that.

How do you feel that your medical education and training have affected your writing?

Never underestimate the value of a medical education. Good for background, good for realism, good for the discipline. I have written several stories (and am struggling through a novel) based on my background in medicine. I have to flail about reading splatterpunk stories in which the killer rips off a human face with one jerk. I have flayed human faces. I have dissected human corpses. I have participated in autopsies. To do a good job flaying a human face, you need good scalpels and a few hours—that's if the subject is dead. You might use a chainsaw, but the AMA doesn't approve.

After medical school I began a psychiatric residency at John Umstead hospital near Chapel Hill. This is the state mental hospital similar to that described in my story, "Into Whose Hands." During my residency, two things happened: my earlier books began to sell and I got Kirby McCauley as my agent. When I left my residency to write full time, I had two books under contract: one due on the day I left, the other the following month. I haven't looked back.

Kane is probably one of the best known fantasy/sword-and-sorcery heros/protagonists. How did you develop the character? Do you feel that your conception of him has evolved over the years?

Kane grew out of my childhood fascination for the villain. Kane is not a sword-and-sorcery hero; he is a Gothic hero/villain from the tradition of the Gothic novels of the eighteenth and early nineteenth centuries. Possibly his single greatest influence was the doomed hero/villain of Maturin's *Melmoth the Wanderer*, although there are very many other sources.

What I wanted to do was to create a mysterious amoral character, far more intelligent and far more physically powerful than his adversaries. Before Kane, villains were either twisted geniuses or hulking oafs. With Kane, I wanted a character who could master any situation intellectually, or rip off heads if push came to shove. Fu Manchu with muscles. Kane is closer to the Terminator than Conan, although neither comparison is really valid. I suppose the best description is to consider Kane a genetically engineered organic cyborg created via magic and alien science. But you'll find out more later.

My conception of Kane has not changed over some thirty-five years. I have always considered the series as horror (or Gothic) as opposed to sword-and-sorcery. When Powell published *Darkness Weaves*, I described the series as "Gothic fantasy" and Powell so labeled it in their edition. Later, when working with Gary Hoppenstand on his groundbreaking small press magazine *Midnight Sun*, I described the Kane stories as "dark fantasy." Gary liked that term, used it, and yes, I coined the term "dark fantasy."

You'll be seeing a lot more of him, from Eden to just down the block.

> *At what point do you feel that you made the jump from wanting to write sword-and-sorcery/fantasy to contemporary horror? Do you think that you would ever want to try your hand at sword-and-sorcery again?*

There never was a jump. My earliest published amateur stories were horror. I consider the Kane series to be horror rather than adventure, and *Darkness Weaves* was deliberately structured after the Gothic novel. The second Kane book, *Death Angel's Shadow*, appeared in 1973, the same month that *F&SF* published my vampire story "In the Pines." *Death Angel's Shadow* also includes a vampire story, as well as a werewolf story, *Legion from the Shadows*, which has a scene in which a girl's flayed skin is discovered sewn back together and stuffed with human eyeballs. The kickball scene in *Dark Crusade* resulted in my German publisher getting busted. Ever count all the survivors at the end of a Kane story? One hand is all you need. I'll be writing more 'costume' (if you will) fantasy, but don't look for cutesy elves.

> *When you sit down to write, how much of the story do you know in advance, a little or a lot?*

I usually have an entire story developed in my mind before I begin to write. Writing it down then becomes a matter of selection and control of language in order to achieve the desired effect. I suppose this is similar to a director looking at a script and deciding how to shoot it.

> *Do you have a quota of words or pages that you require of yourself?*

I have no quota of words to write each day. If I am bored or confused with what I'm writing, I can't expect my readers to do any better with it. Back burner city. Sometimes I go months without writing; on two occasions I have written 20,000 words of published prose within twenty-four hours. Not bad for a one-finger typist.

> *What do you consider to be the particular challenges for your short stories and in novels?*

Short stories demand a certain tightness in writing. Each word should count. Novels you can be loose with. One so-so chapter won't kill the book. Thus: short fiction requires intense concentration; novels are more relaxed. However, novels require greater organization, a long-term vision, and lots of white paper awaiting lots of words. Life's a bitch.

Karl Edward Wagner, c. mid-1970s. Photograph by Terry Murray.

How did you come to be writing Robert E. Howard
pastiches?

I was asked to write some Robert E. Howard pastiches by Glenn Lord via my agent, Kirby McCauley. None of us were happy with the sorry state of the then-current crop, and I was brought in as a hired gun to try to sort the matter out. *Legion from the Shadows* and *The Road of Kings* were both difficult to write. I wrote in my own style, remaining true to Howard's characters.

The second Bran Mak Morn novel, *Queen of the Night*, was held back for various reasons. It will be published in England later this year (1994) as a double volume.

What kind of approval system did the Howard estate/
Conan Properties have on the books? Were you ever inter-
ested in doing any more?

Glenn Lord knew what I could do, knew that I would stay true to Howard's creations, and gave me carte blanche. I was to have

184

written three Conan novels, but by then, Conan Properties had assumed control with Sprague de Camp at the helm. He killed my first version of *The Road of Kings*, which told of Conan's rise to king, on the basis that *he* meant to write that portion of the saga. Lost several months of work there. On the completely different novel of the same title, he made pages of quibbling and quarrelling objections. I was able to override them. After that, never again. Andy Offutt and Poul Anderson wrote the other two I'd been slated to do. Despite all this, Sprague and I have remained good friends. We're professionals, after all.

> *In the introductions to the three reprints of Howard's original versions of the Conan stories, you seemed to have been somewhat disdainful of pastiches in general. Do you regret doing this? How did L. Sprague de Camp, Glenn Lord, and the rest react to what you had to say? In the years since, have you changed your opinion or do you still feel that way about pastiches?*

I clearly and plainly stated my disdain for Howard pastiches in my introduction to the three authorized Conan collections, including advising readers that I, too, had written such pastiches, which they were welcome to read, just don't mistake them for the real thing. Glenn Lord agreed with me. Conan Properties killed the project, which would have completed the untampered-with Conan saga in three more volumes. Damn shame, that. My opinion remains the same as to pastiches. I gave the ones I wrote everything I had. I don't think Howard would have been ashamed. This morning on TV I saw a brainless Conan cartoon show, then an ad for Conan action figures. The pastiches were reverent. This…Bob, come on back. I'll help you blow these bastards to Hell.

> *I understand that you were supposed to write the screenplay for* Conan III *and had some rather interesting encounters with Dino De Laurentiis and company along the way. What happened to that project?*

I did indeed write the script for *Conan III*. Dino had a studio in

Wilmington, North Carolina, so it was easy to get together for conferences. Dino was great to work with, one of the last of the old-school producers. Stephen King recommended me to Dino, and things took off. Now, as a Writers Guild of America member, I get a $35,000 minimum for one script and two revisions, regardless whether the script is ever produced. Nice work, if you can get it.

The first version of *Conan III* was to have been shot in China with a $20,000,000 budget; Mako and Grace Jones (known to Dino as Macho and Girl-with-Stick) to continue their roles from *Conan the Destroyer*. "Give Girl-with-Stick big part," sez Dino. I was in L.A. for a final script conference with his daughter, the most excellent Raphaella, whilst David Lynch kept breaking in with problems on the final cut of *Dune*. He'd lost a can of film, but worse problems awaited. *Dune* was a megabomb, and Dino had to regroup.

The second script for *Conan III* was to be shot in Tunis on a much smaller budget. I was to downplay the special effects, and was told: "Girl-with-Stick. We kill her halfway through film." I wasn't certain how Grace Jones would react to this (she was a budget cut casualty), but I had her snuffed fighting a rearguard action against zombie priests as a whole mountain caved in. Uncle Richard would have been proud of that scene.

Dune really bombed. Raphaella's comment that she needed to make back $125 million on the film was a bad guess. The third version of *Conan III* was to be filmed in North Carolina, no special effects, and no Girl-with-Stick. I came up with a rousing adaptation of "Beyond the Black River," but by then *Dune* had put an end to Dino's major budget films and had killed *Conan III*.

> *What other film scriptwork have you been doing? How do you feel about the medium for writers?*

I did a treatment for *Delta Force* for Dino, but he didn't think the film would work. Another screenplay was *The Twist*, a film noir that Kirby McCauley was to produce, but that fizzled. Best near-miss was a teleplay of Howard's "The Horror from the Mound," which I did for Laurel for *Dark Side*. Kirby bought the script back from them to use as a Howard trilogy. I was to adapt "The Cairn on the

Headland" as well, and Stephen King was to adapt the Howard story of his choice. All to be shot on location. Sam Peckinpah was to direct. Kirby was discussing the project with Sam just days before Peckinpah died. So did the project.

Script work is no place for a real writer. You have to be a team player, which most writers aren't. You have to set aside your own creativity to accommodate the wishes of those who hire and fire. You have to put up with the madness of the Hollywood mindset. You have to roll with the punches, expect to get fucked over, and hope their checks will clear. Then you can laugh a lot.

> *Were there any films that you can look back on now and credit as an influence on your writing when you were growing up?*

Any number of films. Captain Nemo from *Twenty Thousand Leagues Under the Sea* and Caine Miro from Roger Corman's *Gunslinger* both merged into Kane. *Forbidden Planet* showed me the awesomeness of an unstoppable force. *Yojimbo* and *A Fistful of Dollars* brought home the fascination for the amoral wandering killer. And I have watched *The Wild Bunch* over a thousand times.

> *If they adapted your work to the screen, who would you like to see direct and star in it?*

That would, of course, depend on which work was adapted. Sam Peckinpah and Val Lewton would have worked, but…I was on location with Clive Barker along with Dennis Etchison and Charles L. Grant when Clive was directing *Hellraiser*. Clive had an idea for an anthology film in which each of the four of us would script and direct one of his own stories. I said I'd like to do "The River of Night's Dreaming" in black and white with handheld cameras. Maybe that's why the project never materialized.

When I saw William Smith in some 1970 biker films, I thought he would be a perfect Kane. Check out *The Ultimate Warrior*. He's a bit past it now, but I did get him the role of Conan's father in *Conan the Barbarian*. Rutger Hauer would be my choice now, although he's showing age. Check out *Flesh and Blood*. I think Rutger *is* Kane

Karl Edward Wagner, c. mid-1970s. Photograph by Terry Murray.

in that film.

Director? Again, depends upon what story is being adapted. A few names: Dario Argento, Walter Hill, Werner Herzog, Akira Kurosawa, Samuel Fuller, Louis Malle, John Millux, Roman Polanski, Oliver Stone. Dream on.

> *Do you see any particular themes running through your work?*

The primary theme is betrayal: characters betrayed by their lovers, their friends, their dreams, their past. Virtually all of my major protagonists are loners, alone against a hostile world. Some are destroyed; others, like Kane, manage to triumph.

> *What writers, both in and out of the genre, do you consider to have been influences on you?*

When you've been writing this long it's impossible to name all the writers who have influenced you. Here are some: Robert W. Chambers for his gift of placing a deliberate barrier to final comprehension; Walter de la Mare for rather the same; Charles Birkin and Thomas Burke for their command of controlled psychological sadism; Dashiell Hammett and Raymond Chandler for their precise control of the English language; Paul Busson and Leo Perutz for their ability to distort reality in the macabre; R.R. Ryan and Hanns Heinz Ewers for their elegant management of decadent cruelty; Edgar Wallace and Mickey Spillane for their tight writing and killer closing lines; Sax Rohmer and Lester Dent for headlong adventure; E.H. Visiak and David Lindsay for reaching beyond their readers' grasp.

Do you consider yourself to be a "Southern" writer?

No, I certainly do not consider myself to be a "Southern writer," although I have written about the South. The dust jacket copy to Doubleday's *First World Fantasy Awards* anthology calls me a British writer. Go figure. Well, I do use British settings a great deal and hang out in London a lot and have enough of a British accent so that American tourists come up to me in pubs to ask directions to the British Museum, but seriously ...

How did you happen to meet Manly Wade Wellman? How much of an influence on you and your work was he?

I first met Manly Wade Wellman in June of 1963. My brother had just graduated from the University of North Carolina, but had to turn in a late paper. He didn't want to make the long drive from Knoxville to Chapel Hill alone. I was mowing grass; Jim knew I was a Wellman fan and promised to introduce us; we piled into Dad's 1961 Thunderbird and took off.

Manly was discovered at the old Wilson Library on campus; we had a short conversation. I said I was writing fantasy stories; Manly wished me luck and said he was all through with fantasy now that Arkham House was bringing out *Who Fears the Devil?* Four years later I returned to Chapel Hill as a medical student and looked in on Manly. We became the best of friends, and so it remained until his death in 1986.

However, Manly was in no way any influence on my own writing. We had vastly dissimilar techniques and philosophies. Manly used to say that he would give me good solid advice and then I'd go out and do the opposite. Mostly true. When I gave him a copy of *Darkness Weaves*, he read it and scoffed: "The day will come when you will repudiate this." Considering the butchery of the text, I can't blame his attitude. Twenty-four years later, *Darkness Weaves* is still in print worldwide.

> *Can you tell me how you came to found the small press Carcosa? What current projects does Carcosa have in the works?*

During my hiatus from medical school, I decided to start my own small press, Carcosa, getting permission to revive the name from the four partners of the original Carcosa House, which published one book back in 1947 out in Los Angeles. With David Drake and my medical school roommate, Jim Groce, as backers, I arranged with Manly to bring out an expanded version of his collection *Worse Things Waiting*, originally accepted by a New York publisher who went bust at the close of the Depression, later accepted by Arkham House, but shelved after Wellman and August Derleth had a falling out.

Carcosa brought out four books, the last one in 1981. We have not done business since, and there are no plans for further books. Readers simply would not shell out the money for a deluxe limited edition; our stock rotted in storage, and we lost a bundle.

> *I realize that publishing goes in cycles and horror seems to be in a downturning cycle now. What do you think the sudden cancellation of the Pocket and Pinnacle horror lines and the reduction of Zebra to one a month portends for the immediate future of the genre?*

This is simply a matter of survival of the fittest. Maybe 90% of the horror novels of the past decade are pointless, derivative crap, churned out by hacks who will now go back to writing romances, or by amateurs who have seen a dozen splatter films, read a Stephen King novel, and now want to write the same. It was a feeding frenzy of schlock publishers going for the current fad with no concern for quality nor any knowledge of the genre. Tough luck now for the twit who hopes to sell his novel about vampire cockroaches. Tougher luck for writers who do have something new to say, but have been lumped together with the garbage and discarded as no longer commercially viable. The good writers will hang in there and survive.

> *There have been some complaints that some publishers are trying to force the horror genre into a very narrow definition. Do you think that this is true? And, if so, how do you feel about it?*

Are you defining crap artists like Zebra and Pinnacle as publishers? True, they bring out books, but these are not movers and shakers. What has damaged the horror genre is same-old-same-old. Same as splatter films. A group of victims get snuffed horribly but not before showing some T & A. Interchangeable shit. However, if readers demand nothing better and writers strive for nothing better, you can't blame a publisher for buying what's available and sells. Did Robert Aickman ever make the grocery store newsstands? I don't think so, gringo. Publishers publish what readers read. Raise your sights and share a vision.

> *I understand that you keep a commonplace book to record your dreams in, for possible story ideas. Can you point to any stories that have evolved out of ideas that you've gotten from dreams?*

Stories directly based on my dreams include "The River of Night's Dreaming," "Neither Brute Nor Human," "Endless Night," and "Cedar Lane." I am still puzzling over one such dream entry in my commonplace book which is simply "Nematodes."

> *What can you tell me about* Tell Me, Dark?

Tell Me, Dark was the greatest creative disaster of my life. I'm still trying to get over it.

Right. Artist Kent Williams approached me with a few pages showing this guy wandering about, seeing this girl, then getting blown away by her in his hotel room. Good paintings, but plotless. Can you write a story, sez Kent. Sure, sez Wagner, but we need to do something about having your man killed off on page 5. Sez Kent, I'll want some creative input in the story. Here Wagner should have finished his beer and walked.

It was to be an 80-page painted book, eight chapters. Kirby McCauley cut the deal at DC: 15 thou for me, rather more for Kent. Deluxe hardcover, mega promo. Clear sailing. Wrong. Outline accepted, worked on script and art begins. Two things happen.

Editor Karen Berger goes on extended maternity leave. Musical chairs editors accepts the script and pay off in full. Cool. Karen Berger, whose idea of writing is confined to dudes in tights and balloons with easy to read words, returns from leave and hates the script.

Meanwhile, back in Chapel Hill, Kent Williams has added his own creative input, turning a two-panel taxi ride into five pages of a taxi ride on a deserted M4 at rush hour, then has injected a similar long boring clot of pages involving a fat Mexican wrestler in a jockstrap and with a flour sack on his head cavorting in the sand while our woman clad in a bustier is buried up to her ass in the sand and our man wearing boxer shorts is sitting in a ladder-back chair taking all this in. Kent thought I could write it into the story. Arrogance and stupidity are not a pretty combination. The eight chapters became five chapters. Major scenes and crucial characters were tossed out. The climax, which should have been ten pages, came down to a few pages, in which I had to explain what was going on in the missing sections of the story. Not good.

Kent wouldn't change one brush stroke. Karen was clueless. Kent thought a concealed sawed-off shotgun could be carried about London even though it hadn't been sawed off. Karen thought my character, an American hit man, would be more sympathetic as a stockbroker who went broke during the recession and whose wife had left him. And so it went. There was no meeting of the minds, even assuming Kent and Karen had room temperature IQs.

I got fired on Saturday morning, by special FedEx Saturday morning delivery, just to make the break gracefully. This after wasting a year trying to resurrect my story from the shambles, all *after* I'd been paid in full. Does it get worse? Yes.

One of my closest friends, John Rieber, had been sucking up to the comic books crowds ever since I introduced him to the local colony. He really did want to be a writer. DC gave him the script to rewrite to fit Karen's muddled ideas and Kent's completed pages.

192

For three grand he sold out. Going rate used to be thirty pieces of silver. He and Kent magnanimously insisted that I receive partial credit (with Kent) for characters and situations on my butchered and plagiarized script.

Two years wasted. Two friendships lost. I refuse to look at the rape of my creation, but I'm told my hit man turned stockbroker wound up as a rock star. Hell, I'd seen it all in Hollywood, and I've been tossed out of better bars than DC.

> *So what do you like to do just to relax? What do you like to read?*

I like to pour a drink, cocoon on the couch, and play channel roulette with my cable box. If depressed, I turn my stereo way up and watch *The Wild Bunch* again, though not usually at once.

Best relaxing read: the grocery adverts in the newspaper. There's something about The Ramones, pump shotguns, and pictures of raw meat that soothes my tormented soul. Also I read dusty old tomes of eldritch horror that only Bob Hadji has ever heard of, then I reread *The Long Goodbye*.

> *To the best of my knowledge you've only done the one collaboration,* Killer, *with David Drake. How did that project come about?*

When Dave came back from Nam and returned to Duke Law School, he was still trying to make it as a writer. Some early sales to August Derleth (based on the date on letter and check, Dave almost certainly sold the last story that Derleth bought), but not much more, primarily because Dave was writing fantasy (a dead market just then) with solid historical backgrounds. Dave wrote a story, "Hunter's Moon," and submitted it to *Fantastic*, where Ted White ate it. Dave had only retained his rough draft of the story. Gary Hoppenstand had begun publishing the pioneering small press magazine, *Midnight Sun*. I had given him a number of my stories; Gary needed more free copy, and I thought Dave could use the exposure. Dave gave me the rough draft of "Hunter's Moon," which I rewrote as "Killer" and gave to Gary. This version has often been reprinted.

Karl Edward Wagner, c. mid-1970s. Photograph by Terry Murray.

Some years later Dave and I were sitting about, talking shop, and we suddenly decided that "Killer" could be expanded into a novel. We brainstormed a plot outline, Dave did the first draft and all the legwork on historical background, and I revised and wrote the final draft.

> *What do you think are your best written story and novel?*
> *What have been your most popular ones?*

I like all of my stories. Otherwise, no one else but the trash collector would have seen them. I don't submit anything I don't like. This is why I'm so prolific, right? If I had to choose, I'd say my best story is "The River of Night's Dreaming." My best novel is probably *Dark Crusade*. "Sticks" has easily been my most popular story. I've long ago lost track of reprints and translations. The story was dramatized for National Public Radio and bought for the *Dark Room* television show (which was canceled before the story was produced: William F. Nolan was to have scripted it). *Bloodstone* is probably my most popular novel.

What time of day is best for you to write in?

I used to write mostly late at night. The last few years I tend to work from late morning to mid-afternoon, assuming I'm not disturbed. I need a couple hours in the morning to clear my chest, and if I eat anything I get sleepy. So now I fast, argue with my muse, then relax in the evening.

What does your writing area look like? Is there anything that you like to keep around just for luck?

I have been writing out of the same study for over twenty-five years now. It is small, incredibly, *really incredibly*, cluttered. Last month I threw out utility bills from the early 1970s. My walls are covered with original art and photographs of Diana Rigg. I compose with a ballpoint on legal pads, type on the Royal manual portable I got in college, and play my stereo very loudly. I have a cheap Depression-era writing table, cluttered with such objects as an early '30s Packard hood ornament, beer steins, a bust of someone named Lydia, an Iron Cross, a '30s Coke tray, and lots of other neat stuff to fiddle with. For luck I keep a Colt Model 1911 A .45 in my desk drawer, cocked and locked.

I don't want to jinx anything, but can you talk about any of your current projects and upcoming publications?

I have a bunch of short stories forthcoming in various anthologies. I'll be collecting these and others for my third contemporary horror collection, *Exorcisms and Ecstasies*. *Queen of the Night* is headed for the UK. Much delayed *Satan's Gun* and *The Fourth Seal* are past due at Tor and Bantam. *At First Just Ghostly* awaits completion as a novel. *The Year's Best Horror Stories XXIII* will beckon at year's end. And I'm working on a novel version of *Tell Me, Dark*. Several Kane projects are slowly taking shape.

So what do you want to be when you grow up?

A lumberjack!

The Dark

Michael Fantina

On cold and autumn eves the shadows creep
Against these banks and hillock and the lane,
The branches of this oak tree stretch and strain
Toward hills and leas where patriarchs yet sleep.
The secrets of this glade are buried deep
Within these fallow fields of rye and cane
Where rest the troubled dead, the ancient slain,
As ghostly winds above them howl and sweep.

One lonely raven sits alone and caws
On branches of this old and tilting elm.
This place, obeying esoteric laws,
From some outré and little guessed dark realm,
Keeps all its secrets hidden like rare gold,
And only to the dark are they now told.

DARRELL SCHWEITZER

John W. Campbell's Lovecraftian Tale

Barry Malzberg remarks in his introduction to *A New Dawn*, the NESFA omnibus of John W. Campbell's "Don A. Stuart" stories—and he is almost certainly correct on this—that there will never be a biography of John W. Campbell, Jr. The reasons are that most of the people who knew him are now dead, and, furthermore, it is impossible to separate the man from his work. Other than his early career as a science fiction writer, and his much longer one as editor of *Astounding*, there is nothing particularly remarkable about Campbell. His extra-literary life contains little drama. His involvement in science fiction *was* his life.

That being so, the best, and virtually the only, source of information we have about Campbell's ideas, influences, and thoughts are his own writings, his editorials and occasional essays, and his letters. Like his older contemporary H. P. Lovecraft, he was a brilliant letter-writer, perhaps the greatest editorial letter-writer the science fiction field has ever seen. His specialty was starting arguments, without malice and in a sense of sportsmanship, which would stimulate new stories and new approaches from the recipients. Two volumes of his correspondence have been published to date.

The mention of H. P. Lovecraft is immediately relevant to the subject of this essay. What did John Campbell think about Lovecraft? He made himself clear enough in a letter to Robert Moore Williams dated August 14, 1952, explaining why the modern writer *shouldn't* lard on the adjectives:

> A good many years back, you started selling yarns that had a lot of "mood," and they went pretty well. They

were, in a way, rather like the Gothic horror story "The Fall of the House of Usher" sort of thing, built up with *Roget's Thesaurus*, and various sources of adjectives. Lovecraft did the same kind. I did some of 'em myself. As of the time and the slant of the field, they were right.

That was a dozen years ago, and the field's changed far and fast since then. We're older too, you and I, and we've got to change with the change. (*The John W. Campbell Letters* 1.66)

The remark "I did some of 'em myself" is interesting, and is the key to much of what follows here. Campbell is at least acknowledging that his work, at one point, was somewhat akin to Lovecraft's.

Elsewhere Campbell commented on the sort of story he wanted for his short-lived fantasy magazine, *Unknown*, explicitly rejecting the old-fashioned, Gothic approach of the traditional ghost story (and, by implication, of *Weird Tales*). He makes a specific, unfavorable reference to Lovecraft ("I do not want the sort of stuff Lovecraft doted on") in a letter to Jack Williamson from 1939 (quoted in Dziemianowicz 14).

What then is the Campbell-Lovecraft connection, if any, in the absence of direct epistolary evidence?

Campbell must have read both *At the Mountains of Madness* and "The Shadow out of Time" in *Astounding* in 1936. He probably read "The Colour out of Space" in *Amazing Stories* in 1927, though that is less certain. We can be certain that he *did* read the two *Astounding* stories if we keep in mind that in 1936, science fiction was a very small field indeed. Hugo Gernsback, who had founded the first all-science fiction magazine, *Amazing Stories*, in 1926 and with it the consciously aware genre itself, lost control almost immediately, due to inept editorial policies and business practices so bad that there really was a New York lawyer who specialized in collecting Gernsback debts. (We have this datum from Mike Ashley and Robert A.W. Lowndes's *The Gernsback Days*. Her name was Ione Weber.) Readers didn't want Gernsback's turgid science lessons disguised as fiction. They wanted stories. Authors preferred to be paid. So Gernsback was out. His *Wonder Stories* was dying in 1936, ending with the April issue, forced to sell out to a pulp chain and come back as the juvenile, formula-written *Thrilling Wonder Stories* later in the year. The original *Amazing Stories,* now edited by the aged T. O'Conor Sloane, was also very close to being on its last legs, so imaginatively barren and just plain dull that, for all Gernsback's shortcomings, it was clearly *Amazing Stories* that was third in a field of three. It too would sell out, in 1938.

Astounding Stories had seized the clear lead in science fiction in 1934, edited by the energetic F. Orlin Tremaine with an unbeatable combination of better (or at least more lively) writing, reliable payment, and a wider range of allowable imagination. Quite unlike the ultra-conservative Sloane, who didn't believe in space travel, Tremaine encouraged far-out speculations. The most extreme stories he tagged as "thought-variants," which proved very popular with his readers.

There was no question about it. Although *Amazing* and *Wonder* still limped along, and some science fiction was published in other pulps (notably *Blue Book, Argosy,* and *Weird Tales*), *Astounding Stories* was the place to be in science fiction in 1936. As is evident from interviews with writers of the period and memoirs and autobiographies, everything from Frederik Pohl's *The Way the Future Was* to Isaac Asimov's *In Memory Yet Green,* if you were a science fiction fan in 1936, that meant you read *Astounding.* You read every story, every month. You argued with other fans in the letters column, "Brass Tacks," making it a point to race your letter into the mails first, so it would be published as quickly as possible.

The professionals did pretty much the same. In this pressure-cooker environment, science fiction itself was like a heated, ongoing conversation at a closed party. Everybody had read the same things, discussed the same ideas, come down on one side or the other of the various controversies. This was a period in which the science fiction fan not only could, but was expected to, read everything published in the field. For John W. Campbell, as one of the top three writers in science fiction at the moment (the other two being E. E. "Doc" Smith and Stanley G. Weinbaum), *not* to have kept up with the only science fiction magazine that mattered, to which he was a regular contributor, would have been inconceivable. (Incidentally, Campbell has a science article in the June 1936 issue, which also features "The Shadow out of Time.")

So much for inference. We move on to hypothesis.

I suggest that John Campbell not only had Lovecraft in mind when he wrote his single most famous story, "Who Goes There?" (published in *Astounding*, August 1938), but that the story is a virtual critique of Lovecraft's *At the Mountains of Madness* (*Astounding*, February–April 1936). It seems to answer reader criticisms of Lovecraft, almost point-for-point.

Lovecraft's sudden appearance in *Astounding* was something of a fluke and, for Lovecraft, a miraculous bit of good luck. *At the Mountains of Madness* was written in early 1931 and was regarded by Lovecraft as a kind of magnum opus, certainly the most substantial thing he had written in years. It is his second longest fiction, surpassed only by *The Case of Charles Dexter Ward* (written in 1927), which he had repudiated and probably never expected to see published. The rejection of *At the Mountains of Madness* by *Weird Tales* was a devastating blow, which Lovecraft felt had pretty much finished his career as a fiction writer. The manuscript circulated among his friends thereafter and was eventually submitted to *Astounding* via the fan-turned-agent, Julius Schwartz, who has reported that Tremaine bought the story without reading it.

This makes a certain amount of sense. Tremaine, although already the unchallenged leader in the science fiction field, sought to consolidate his position by attracting all the important writers of the period into the pages of *Astounding*. He knew that Lovecraft was immensely popular in *Weird Tales* and revered by some of his friends who were regular *Astounding* contributors (such as Frank Belknap Long and Donald Wandrei), so when Schwartz said, "I have here a 35,000-word story by Lovecraft," Tremaine allegedly replied "Sold!"

At the Mountains of Madness is problematical in the Lovecraftian canon. It is undeniably an important work. Some Lovecraft readers admire it immensely. S. T. Joshi calls it "a triumph in every way" (*I Am Providence* 2.781). Others are not so sure.

That the short novel is densely written and slow, no one denies. It is the story, written in the form resembling a scientific report (although the narrator's intent is to reveal just enough to *discourage* further exploration), of an expedition to Antarctica, in which explorers from Miskatonic University discover the ruins of a vast, pre-human city half buried in the ice. They also uncover specimens of completely unknown life-forms, semi-vegetable, which resemble large, bat-winged cucumbers with a starfish-like head and a variety of tentacles. These creatures are clearly millions of years old. Their footprints have been found in stones from the era of the dinosaurs. Yet the "specimens" are surprisingly well preserved, and when disaster strikes a remote camp, where the complete "specimens" have disappeared, the more damaged ones are found ritually buried, and the camp has been smashed and all humans and dogs are either slain or missing, the explorers can only hypothesize madness, but any reader of *Astounding* knew perfectly well what had happened.

Here Lovecraft faced a problem inherent in any sort of genre writing. In the context of a science fiction magazine, *of course* we know that these ancient creatures have returned to life, but rational scientists in real life would be, at the very least, extremely reluctant to conclude that a million-year-old corpse just sat up on the dissection table; yet the *reader*, knowing that this is a science fiction story, becomes impatient. (Similarly, in a mystery story we *know*, merely from the fact that this is a mystery story, that the corpse must have been murdered, possibly well before a real detective could come to that conclusion. If you read a story in a ghost story anthology, you can be pretty certain that the thing bumping around in the attic *is* a ghost. An awareness of genre tends to defeat ambiguity.)

The narrator and a colleague take an airplane inland and discover the main city of the Old Ones, creatures that descended from the stars and colonized the Earth shortly after the planet cooled and before native life evolved. The Old Ones must be the most artistic species the universe has ever seen, because, over a period of several million years, they carved their entire history in fantastic detail into a series of reliefs which line the walls and corridors of their buildings. Furthermore, our heroes must be the most perceptive art critics and archeologists who ever lived, because in just a few hours, while making their way by flashlight through the ruins in an atmosphere of increasing dread, they are so able to interpret these carvings, which are not only the product of a hitherto unknown culture but of an unknown *species,* that the narrator can provide a vastly detailed history of the expansion and collapse of the Old Ones' civilization upon the Earth, complete with much about their government, biology, and culture. (For comparison, consider how much difficulty archeologists had making any sense at all out of Mayan or ancient Egyptian inscriptions.) This exposition goes on for many pages, until it almost seems that Lovecraft has abandoned writing a story altogether and is composing a pseudo-nonfiction treatise, rather like some of the works of Olaf Stapledon (a writer Lovecraft later read and admired, by the way).

At this point someone at *Astounding* must have become alarmed, because the short novel, as serialized, is heavily edited, his long paragraphs cut up into shorter ones in an attempt to give Lovecraft's prose a more conventional, jauntier pulp feel. (This outraged Lovecraft, who lapsed from his usual gentlemanly decorum in a letter to refer to "that goddamn'd dung of a hyaena Orlin Tremaine" [*O Fortunate Floridian* 335] and ultimately came to regard the story as unpublished. A fully restored text was not published until 1985.)

Toward the end of the story, things do pick up. The explorers learn that the ancient city was built with the aid of *shoggoths,* protoplasmic beings bred by the Old Ones and controlled through mental powers. However, over time the shoggoths got out of control, grew crafty, and revolted against their makers. They became the horror that even the Old Ones feared. There is a powerful moment when the explorers discover "degenerate" examples of the ubiquitous wall carvings, which seem to be mocking parodies of the Old Ones' work, which we realize must have been done more recently by semi-intelligent shoggoths.

Also discovered are the missing Old One "specimens," headless and covered with ooze, plus a couple sledges and the carefully wrapped bodies of a missing expedition member and a dog. It is clear what has happened. The perfectly preserved Old Ones awoke, finding one of their number being dissected by the humans. In the ensuing chaos, they killed the men and dogs that confronted then, then gathered together one specimen of each species for further study, plus assorted human artifacts, bundled them on sledges, and tried to make their way into the depths below the city, where (it is implied by the carvings) there is an opening to a vast sea beneath Earth, whence the last of the Old Ones have long since retreated. In an extraordinary passage, the narrator suddenly understands that these are not "monsters" at all: "Scientists to the last—what had they done that we would not have done in their place? God, what intelligence and persistence! What a facing of the incredible…! Radiates, vegetables, monstrosities, star-spawn—whatever they had been, they were men!" (*At the Mountains of Madness* 96).

Unfortunately, the surviving Old Ones then fell victim to still-lingering shoggoths, which implies, to the two humans who have discovered this, that the strange sounds and strange odors wafting up from the depths below do not bode well. In one of Lovecraft's most effective passages of sheer fright, the two are chased out of the ruins by a barely glimpsed shoggoth. The narrator, flying the airplane, does not see the final horror, but his colleague, looking back, glimpses *something* beyond the even vaster mountains beyond the city, and is never quite right in the head again…

This did not go over well with *Astounding*'s readership. While some letters in the "Brass Tacks" department praise Lovecraft, it is hard to find anything in the period which brought down such a deluge of complaint as *At the Mountains of Madness*. Readers found the story tedious. They objected to its total lack of dialogue. In the August 1936 issue, reader O.M. Davidson thought Lovecraft's work "too tedious, too monotonous to suit me," while admitting that the images of the Old Ones etc. would stay with him for a long time. Peter Ruzella, Jr, deemed Lovecraft "trash" and begged for no more. Andy Aprea called *At the Mountains of Madness* "drivel."

In the June issue Robert Thompson quipped, "I am glad to see the conclusion to 'At the Mountains of Madness' for reasons that would not be pleasant to Mr Lovecraft." Cleveland Soper, Jr, declared that he would "never forgive" the editor for having foisted such unscientific "bunk" on the readership. Davidson probably summed up the reservations of a lot of readers when he wrote, "If Lovecraft could only create real characters and action to go with his superb, but lifeless fantasy, he would put out some classics." And so on. The Lovecraft controversy sputtered through the rest of 1936.

Now it must be admitted that many of these readers do not seem to have been intellectual titans—indeed, many of them trash Lovecraft and clamor for the return of the Hawk Carse, the worst, most formulaic space opera from *Astounding*'s pre-Tremaine days—but they *were* the people forking out twenty cents a month for the magazines, so the editor had to listen to them.

One wonders: did John W. Campbell listen to them too? Did he read *At the Mountains of Madness* and decide to do it one better? Within the narrow confines of genre science fiction, an environment in which most of the writers know one another, read one another's work, and ideas are exchanged freely, it has long been the tradition to write subsequent stories in answer to an earlier one.

It would have been an interesting challenge, if John W. Campbell, arguably the best science fiction writer of the day and the man who would soon completely reshape the field around his own vision of it (the result being subsequently known as the Golden Age of SF), decided to improve on Lovecraft.

Did he? Consider:

Where Lovecraft's opening is the sort of "Had I but known . . ." sort of Gothic writing that Campbell warned his writers against:

> I am forced to speech because men of science have refused
> to follow my advice without knowing why. It is altogether
> against my will that I tell my reasons for opposing this con-
> templated invasion of the Antarctic—with its fossil-hunt and

wholesale boring and melting of the ancient ice-cap—and I
am the more reluctant because my warning may be in vain.
(*At the Mountains of Madness* 3)

Campbell's is a classic of vivid, you-are-there concreteness:

The place stank. A queer, mingled stench that only the
ice-buried cabins of an Antarctic camp know, compounded of reeking human sweat, and the heavy, fish-oil
stench of melted seal blubber. An overtone of liniment
combated the musty smell of sweat-and-snow-drenched
furs. The acrid odor of burnt cooking fat, and the animal, not-unpleasant smell of dogs, diluted by time, hung
in the air.
    Lingering odors of machine oil contrasted sharply
with the taint of harness dressing and leather. Yet,
somehow, through all the reek of human beings and
their associates—dogs, machines, and cooking—came
another taint. It was a queer, neck-ruffling thing, a
faintest suggestion of an odor alien among the smells
of industry and life. And it was a life-smell. But it came
from the thing that lay bound with cord and tarpaulin
on the table, dripping slowly, methodically onto the
heavy planks, dank and gaunt under the unshielded glare
of the electric light. (*A New Dawn* 335)

The situation in "Who Goes There?" is very similar to
Lovecraft's. An Antarctic expedition has discovered *something* in
the ice, which turns out to be an alien spaceship, millions of years
old. But the hull is made of an alloy of magnesium, which bursts
into flame when the explorers try to melt the ice with explosives.
After a tantalizing glimpse, everything is destroyed, except this one
specimen, which lies dripping on that table.
    It took Lovecraft several thousand words to get to this point.
Campbell has his "dead" alien in the second paragraph.
    He does write atmospherically, as he remarked in that 1952

letter to Robert Moore Williams. He does not engage very much in adjectivitis, although we do find a few passages like this: "It was lone and quiet out there in the Secondary Camp, where a wolf-wind howled down from the Pole. Wolf-wind howling in his sleep—winds droning and the evil, unspeakable face of that monster leering up as he'd seen it through clear, blue ice, with a bronze ice-axe buried in its skull" (340).

Campbell's creature has less in common with the Old Ones than it does with the shoggoths. Indeed, it might be seen as an improved shoggoth, a "jelly-like protoplasm" with the disquieting ability change its shape and to absorb and mimic any living thing, so that it can devour a dog—or a man—and then turn the victim's tissue into its own, the imitation being so good that it cannot even be detected under a microscope, but with an alien mind. Its ultimate purpose is to replace all life on Earth with itself. There is a strong implication that it did not build the spaceship it arrived in, but, like the Lovecraftian shoggoths mockingly mimicking the Old Ones, this creature has supplanted some technological species and then set forth into space in search of new prey.

Campbell's narrative style is seemingly as far removed from Lovecraft's as possible, for all that many of his aesthetic goals are quite similar. For the benefit of readers who complained about the lack of dialogue in Lovecraft, there is plenty of dialogue in Campbell. There is also physical action, beginning with the monster's almost-off-stage awakening, then several vivid battles with it.

Significantly, Campbell makes a distinct attempt to characterize the members of the expedition. Lovecraft's characters are complete ciphers, unimportant in his view in a story that is largely a static word-picture of vast, cosmic vistas. Campbell's characters are individuals, who argue, tell jokes, and respond differently to the mounting, increasingly paranoid crisis as the men realize that anyone among them could well be and probably *is* a monster from outer space. Two of them, in finest Lovecraftian fashion, go raving mad. The characterizations are not entirely successful, and the modern reader may still have trouble telling members of the large cast apart. A modern science fiction writer probably would have dealt with this problem by narrowing the viewpoint, so that everything is perceived through the eyes and mind of one person and the story is what these events meant to that person and how it changed him forever. This would have brought things into tighter focus, no doubt, but that is not the way pulp stories, which tended to be situation-oriented rather than character-oriented, were written in 1938, even by a writer as good as Campbell.

Again simplifying Lovecraft, Campbell leaves out the history of the aliens. We learn nothing more about the shape-changing monstrosity beyond the implication that it came from the distant stars, from a hotter world with a blue sun. There would, indeed, be no way for the human characters to have gained any more perspective, unless somebody had a long, telepathic rapport with the Thing, which would have slowed down the pace intolerably. Lovecraft, who was far more interested in sweeping visions of remote epochs, dealt more convincingly with the knowledge problem in his second *Astounding* story, "The Shadow out of Time." There, a man learns the history of a pre-human civilization by switching bodies with an alien and living in the remote past for several years, which is a more plausible method than just looking at wall-carvings for a few hours.

But Campbell's focus is more on the present, on what the men have to do *now*, to save themselves and the Earth. (They have no doubt that if this creature escapes from Antarctica, all life on Earth is finished.)

Campbell builds suspense in steady stages, through a combination of action and logic. Every time the men think they have destroyed the monster, someone comes up with a logical reason why they have not. On this level, the story generally holds together quite well, although there is a seeming lapse when one fellow, who has gone mad and made a nuisance of himself with constant prayers and hymn-singing, is found dead with a knife in his throat. Somebody snapped. This ironically proves that the murderer is human. But then it is discovered that the corpse is a monster, and previously we were told that the best way to tell a human from a monster would be to shoot him through the heart. The monster wouldn't die so easily. So why is the "madman" dead—or is he?

The monsters can be killed with a combination of a blowtorch, electricity, and acid. An effective method for detecting them is found. It looks as if the humans have won, but then, to their horror, they realize that one of their number, who had gone mad from fear and been isolated in a remote shack, has been left alone for a full week. They rush to the shack and discover that the thing within (yes, this was another monster, pretending to be an insane human) has been working unimpeded with available materials and developed an atomic power plant and an anti-gravity pack. In another half hour or so, it would have gone soaring off to South America and to world dominion.

In this way the emotional structure of Campbell's story continues to resemble Lovecraft's. After everything has been revealed, there is one last fright—though with the essential difference that with Campbell it is a threat narrowly averted and with Lovecraft it is an even larger threat, still very much present at the end of the story. (One naïve *Astounding* reader called for a sequel to *At the Mountains of Madness* in which the second Miskatonic expedition destroys the monsters and discovers the wonderful lost civilization. No, I do not think that is what Lovecraft had in mind...)

Has Campbell successfully "improved" upon *At the Mountains of Madness*? There is no question that "Who Goes There?" was an immediate success, far better received than the Lovecraft story by the readership, almost universally praised. It went on to become recognized as one of the great, early classics of genre science fiction. It has never been out of print since, and has been filmed twice. Its shape-changing monster, far more than Lovecraft's shoggoth, has spawned countless descendants in later stories, TV shows, and films.

There are undeniable flaws in the Campbell version, notably that the characterizations don't seem quite distinct enough for the reader to keep track of who's who, and that Campbell telegraphs his very effective punchline a few paragraphs earlier; but what he did, and did very effectively, was to take the material of *At the Mountains of Madness*, streamline it, and produce a more conventional story, with elements that would immediately seize and hold the reader's attention—the vividly concrete opening, the greater emphasis on human characterization and human interactions, and the physical action—while maintaining a great deal of atmosphere and suspense. He added the eerie, immensely dramatic notion that the monster could change shape and impersonate the man next to you, so that no one can trust anyone, and you could already be (though only one of the "madmen" might have come to such a conclusion) entirely surrounded by monsters, whose mock-humanity could, at any moment, literally melt away.

"Who Goes There?," like most Lovecraft stories, is primarily a story of cosmic fear. It has ideas in it, but its appeal is emotional. It is, indeed, one of the most effective blends of science fiction and horror ever written, a combination that, despite outsiders' ignorant notions that science fiction is all about monsters, is actually rather rare in the field.

"Who Goes There?" has a much stronger plot-engine than *At the Mountains of Madness*. Where Lovecraft's story is more of a subtly disquieting tableau almost until the end, Campbell's *moves*, and builds its own unique, paranoid intensity. It was very much more the kind of story that *Astounding*'s readers wanted. Of course, as I have mentioned, the readers of *Astounding* in the 1930s were not necessarily intellectual or aesthetic titans. That a story was popular in a pulp magazine in 1938 is of no consequence. Trash is often popular for a short time. Even Hawk Carse was popular in his day. What matters is that the Campbell story has shown real staying power. *At the Mountains of Madness* has since been appreciated, too, for its richness and complexity, but it took decades for it to gain recognition. "Who Goes There?" was an example of what is usually an oxymoron, an "instant classic." What proves its worth is that it stayed a classic, for decade after decade.

So the question is not, "Did Campbell do better than Lovecraft?"—even if that was what Campbell was trying to do. This is more like the case of H. Rider Haggard's *King Solomon's Mines* (1885). Haggard wrote his novel after his brother bet him that he couldn't produce a book better than Robert Louis Stevenson's

Treasure Island. It was a tall order. Did Haggard succeed? That is a matter of taste, but it is clear that Haggard also produced a classic, which has never been out of print after more than a century.

Keep in mind that science fiction, particularly in the science fiction field as it came to be dominated by Campbell in the 1940s and later, was a form of dialogue between editors and writers, and between writers and readers. How many subsequent stories were written as "answers" to such controversial classics as Tom Godwin's "The Cold Equations" or Robert A. Heinlein's *Starship Troopers*? What the subsequent writer was supposed to deliver was not an insult, in the sense of the famous remark of Beethoven's: "I liked your opera. I think I'll set it to music." Instead he would say, as one colleague to another, "Your version has undeniable validity, but have you considered this twist, or that angle?" and, rather like a shoggoth reproducing by fission, a second, often equally potent story would result. That was what Campbell, as editor, encouraged in his writers, to the extent of farming out ideas to more than one writer. Distinct ideational threads can be discerned in Campbellian science fiction. For example, the whole series of stories and novels about super-scientific, fake religions as tools of social engineering can be traced ultimately to an unpublished novelette by Campbell (who had to give up his writing career when he became editor of *Astounding*) called "All," which he showed to Robert A. Heinlein. The result was Heinlein's *Sixth Column* (later reprinted as *The Day After Tomorrow*), in response to which Fritz Leiber proposed that the only way to overcome super-scientific "miracles" of the oppressive church would be through super-scientific "witchcraft." He wrote *Gather, Darkness!*, which Campbell also published. And these were only the most famous two. There were others.

So what Campbell was doing, whether deliberately or not, and I think it was very deliberately, was *engaging in dialogue with Lovecraft*. He was saying that, yes, *At the Mountains of Madness* was impressive, but wouldn't it be a bit more dramatic if the monsters were up close and personal?

My guess is that if Lovecraft had lived a little longer, and still been around when Campbell actually became editor of *Astounding* in late 1937 (Lovecraft died in March), Campbell would have not only solicited material from Lovecraft but tried to *provoke* stories out of him. It would have been a sign of the greatness of both Campbell and Lovecraft that this was so.

Works Cited

Ashley, Mike, and Robert A.W. Lowndes. *The Gernsback Days.* Holicong, PA: Wildside Press, 2004.

Campbell, John W. Jr. *The John W. Campbell Letters.* Volume 1. Ed. Perry Chapdelaine, Sr., Tony Chapdelaine, and George Hay. Franklin, TN: AC Projects, 1985.

———. *A New Dawn: The Complete Don A. Stuart Stories.* Framingham, MA: NESFA Press, 2003.

Dziemianowicz, Stefan. *The Annotated Guide to* Unknown *and* Unknown Worlds. Mercer Island, WA: Starmont House, 1991.

Joshi, S. T. *I Am Providence: The Life and Times of H. P. Lovecraft.* New York: Hippocampus Press, 2010. 2 vols.

Lovecraft, H. P. *At the Mountains of Madness and Other Novels.* Sauk City, WI: Arkham House, 1985. Corrected fifth printing. (Note: This is the first publication of the complete text of the title story.)

———. *O Fortunate Floridian: H. P. Lovecraft's Letters to R. H. Barlow.* Ed. S. T. Joshi and David E. Schultz. Tampa, FL: University of Tampa Press, 2007.

DANEL OLSON

The Casket Letters: Reports on Recent Innovations in Dark Short, Long, and Graphic Fiction

As a professor who teaches the Gothic, the Horrifying, the Apocalyptic, and the Weird, I am always saddened to find that what makes for the most imaginative, stylish, sublime, curious, frightening, or unprecedented in new prose seldom makes for grand sales or even awards. H. P. Lovecraft opened the field beyond anyone's imagining, and yet was consistently unrewarded for it in his own time. Considering this sad reality, let me now suggest new works (a Weird six-pack: two stories, two novels, and two graphic fictions) that are outstanding and yet under-acclaimed, all in an effort to add to the staggering pile of morbid books featuring nightmare, disease, crime, corruption, and tentacles already on your bed-stand, and to reward those authors who are taking the harder road to create dark wonderment in us.

Disappointing has been the word for the twenty-three graphic novels of the last year which encounter (and are entangled by) Lovecraft's concepts, plots, and prose. Sometimes the graphic novels have been more about sexual attraction and eventual trysts among those who are on the chase of Old Ones, all of which is conspicuously absent in Lovecraft's oeuvre (though of course women themselves can be mentioned, if rarely, in HPL. Cf. "The Dunwich Horror," where mating with something awful does occur, if off page, and of course remember the possession by Asenath Waite in "The Thing on the Doorstep"). This attention on sex may sell the graphic novel to readers who have never read Lovecraft, but seems the keenest failure to anyone else, really downright absurd.

Admittedly when teaching Lovecraft, I share how he has entered pop culture in ways that none could have foreseen—I bow to his presence among computer games and even, recently, women's parfum (one of my students enjoys splashing a bit of "Chthulu" to enchant those sitting nearby, and let me tell you such stinkum doesn't come cheap). However, a graphic novelist representing Lovecraft's fiction and lasting creations to the world of Weirdness, or an update of them, takes the lowest path if there is almost no fidelity to the original stories. It's a pity that for many younger readers, some of the least authentic graphic novels will be their introduction to this American titan. Though I admire without reserve *V for Vendetta*, *Batman: The Killing Joke*, and *Watchmen* (all of which Alan Moore would have rightly deserved a Stoker win for), and though I teach his interviews on sequential art, I am dismayed at Alan Moore and Antony Johnston's *Neonomicon* (Rantoul, Il: Avatar Press, 2011, illustrated by Jacen Burrows, hdbk, $27.99). Leggy blonde detectives in tight silk charcoal blouses and blacker pistols with handsome FBI creature-stalker-men with smart phones were never part of the HPL package, and the "updating" within this impoverished homage, with its dull creamy readability, all seems an insult to Lovecraft's genius of horrifying madness, his difficulty, his layered levels of meaning—even if it is done by arguably one of the greatest living comics imagiers as Alan Moore. The attempt to make Lovecraft easy and approachable and mod, for people who are apparently evasive of reading, is ignoble. Moore himself, in the Bram Stoker Award acceptance speech he prepared, hinted at such doubts, "I spent a long time in fretful deliberation over *Neonomicon* and six months after finishing the work was still uncertain as to whether it was good or even publishable…" Well he's right: the anachronism and dissonance *is* hard to take. Too much stretching seems ill-advised, off-putting, and actually boring. We start to wonder, *Where is Lovecraft in all of this, Alan?* However, out of the pile of graphic novels that ponder past geniuses, two are worthy and even respectful of the novels that nourish them, though lamentably neither was nominated for a Stoker. Dan Lockwood arranges *The Lovecraft Anthology, Vol. I* (London: SelfMadeHero, 2011, ppk,

$21.95) with energetic graphic artists D'Israeli, Shane Ivan Oakley, I.N.J. Culbard, Mark Stafford, Leigh Gallagher, David Hartman, and Alice Duke. The lines spoken in the bubbles actually come out of Lovecraft stories including "The Call of Chthulhu," "The Haunter of the Dark," "The Dunwich Horror," "The Colour Out of Space," "The Shadow Over Innsmouth," "The Rats in the Walls," and "Dagon." What's striking about the richly colored and expressive collection is the sense of our complicity in finishing the action within each gutter between the frames: the devouring, drowning, smashing, and burning that must go on, but mostly in our own minds. Some of the Old Ones get a two-page spread, as should be. There is a genuine overturning of thought as we read and watch characters' ways of knowing disintegrate, facing the fact of our species' insignificance. As fine a mind as China Miéville has admired this title, praising its "non fawning homage to Lovecraft's extraordinary oeuvre—vivid, variegated and, where appropriate, vile." I look forward to *The Lovecraft Anthology, Vol. II* from SelfMadeHero in late 2012. Perhaps we will see new work from the same writing adapters in this notable franchise, including Ian Edginton, Rob Davis, David Hine, Leah Moor, John Reppion, and Dan Lockwood. For anyone who has ever taught *Frankenstein* several times, a serious measure of doubt rises in the creature's pledge to kill himself at novel's end. In a book noted for showing death when it happens, rather than letting it happen off page, any unshown death strikes us as unusual, even suspect. The American cartoonist Richard Sala evokes much that is unsettling and terrible from his French contemporary Joann Sfar (of *Grand Vampire 1-4*, Paris: Guy Delacourt Productions, 2001-2003; also, *The Dungeon*; *The Rabbi's Cat*; *Klezmer*). The two could actually be read side by side to inform us on the lasting power of the modern myth of the Frankenstein creature and also the ancient yet undiminished folklore of the vampire. Sala, who has also produced for Fantagraphics such macabre, murderous, and weird mysteries as *Peculia*, *Mad Night*, and *The Chuckling Whatsit*, has become one of my favorite American sequential artists because of his subtle tributes and expansions to four of the most memorable twentieth century American cartoonists—Charles Addams, Edward Gorey, Gahan Wilson, and Basil Wolverton. And for anyone who has never quite gotten over the creeping, flying, and peeking within German-born Max Ernst's *A Week of Kindness*, that "surrealistic novel in collage," than Sala is for you. Forbidding and weird seem like weak adjectives for Sala's *The Hidden*, and I urge you to open it (Seattle: Fantagraphics, 2011, hdbk, $19.99). Mix in dark desert highways, menacing canyons and hidden valleys of the American southwest, a wooly scientist in a cave who vacillates as much as Shelley's Dr Victor Frankenstein and who ominously is named "Victor," a woman, Colleen, who's handy with a hatchet, enclaves for the one percent, discussions on the worth of raising the dead, and monstrous transformation, and you are beginning to get the picture. Except for several pages of staring into the lovers' eyes and over-ubiquitous head traumas (even of key characters) that should make their fighting back nearly impossible, on the whole the narrative arc seems faultless, and the last panel a shocker to make all tremble and gasp. Give a standing order to Fantagraphics for any noirishly weird fictions forthcoming from Sala.

In terms of short stories, two that stunned were from opposing corners. The first, from legendary fiction heavyweight Gene Wolfe (he of the unforgettable *The Book of the New Sun*, Lakewood, CO: Centipede Press, hdbk) is "Why I Was Hanged," from one of the richest and most Gothically booby-trapped collections of 2011 (*Ghosts By Gaslight: Stories of Steampunk and Supernatural Suspense*, ed. by Jack Dann & Nick Gevers, New York: Harper, ppk, $14.99). The narrator of this tale-within-a-tale is from Victorian England: Dickens' *The Pickwick Papers* was evoked for me as I read of one basically "faithful valet" with a love for one gorgeous "Miss Landon who is quite alive, but whose ghost nonetheless bends over his bed at night." Miss Landon has a request (the ghost of her, that is): Will he honor her offer? Will she offer her honor? And what price will he pay if she does? Regrets, our valet will have a few…If the plot is not entrancing enough, the story in its issues of class, subjects (undying desires of a man of lower class to be accepted, desperate women pleading for help, hunger for vengeance, fin de siècle predictions: "There is a doctor in Vienna who holds that there is a second mind below the one we inhabit")—as well as inimitable style, tone, atmosphere, dialogue—will enmesh you quite. Wolfe still is our great noble beast of blackest fiction.

Quite capable newcomers came at us with ghosts recently too, however, as with New York Professor Carlos Hernandez in "The Aphotic Ghost" (*Bewere The Night*, ed. Ekaterina Sedia, Gaithersburg, MD: Prime, 2011, ppk, $14.95). It's a complicated and emotive story involving inhospitable places (bottom of the sea and roof of the world), protagonist Enrique Montenegro's wife who has vanished (and apparently died), his son (an oceanographer who investigated a kind of immortal jellyfish at great depths) who was lost on a recent climbing expedition up Everest, and a desire to bring them both back. Often in Horror and in the Weird, the most truly wicked things start from greatest innocence. But I'm not sure readers will concede this story must lead to wickedness, though it is like the new Prometheus we have been warned of since 1818. Hernandez is an academic grimscribe of great interest and a new story of his will appear in *Exotic Gothic 5* (Hornsea, UK: PS Publishing, 2013) called "More Than Pigs and Rosaries Can Give," contending with unlawful hungers and breaking the biological rules in his people's homeland, Cuba.

Certainly one of the recent novels most sensitive to the terrors of life as to its promises and to feverish desire for me was *Osama* by Israeli-born Lavie Tidhar (Hornsea: PS Publishing, 2011, £19.99, hdbk). In a Chandleresque style unfolds a gripping story of a detective named Joe who seems to have slipped into an alternate world to earth, a prostitute who knows something of this slippage, and agents out to extract whatever knowledge the detective has. One of these earths has had no Al Qaeda terrorism, and their other Osama bin Laden is actually a protagonist of semi-popular literary spook thrillers by a novelist named Mike Longshot, where the fight is against conformity, and the readers cheer Osama on as they may have in *V for Vendetta*. Indeed, at World Fantasy-like conventions, fans collect his signed works and hope for an appearance. Otherwise, the novel has striking verisimilitude and realism, crowds mill through King's Cross station and London's chartered streets. The inviting strangeness of this novel is in asking why one world has rampant terrorism and a cycle of American-launched wars attached to it, and why the other world has no conception. We just got stuck in the wrong one, apparently. It is a nostalgic horror story: one where the harder Joe tries to restrain his emotion and keep from mentally dissolving, the more we get invested.

The last recent novel to upend things was Steve Rasnic Tem's *Deadfall Hotel* (Lakewood, CO: Centipede Press, 2011, $75). This novel's weirdness comes early and looms over us until the last page, not just for myself, but for my college students who were presented with a portion of it before its whole publication (premiering in *Exotic Gothic 3*, Ashcroft, B.C.: The Ash-Tree Press, 2009). Because of his reliably transfixing prose, Tem, who has also written over 400 stories of terror and horror, can be called legendary without risking hyperbole. Richard is a gentle daddy widower with a minor daughter. He needs a job and takes one at a joy-killer of a hotel of deep dark secrets run for ghoulish types. I'm not sure we simply observe Richard Carter, the Manager of the Deadfall: I fear we become him. Tem's steady trade is in fear, death, monstrosity, and the costs to aberration, but there is a gentleness throughout the narrative as well, a reminder of how things could have been, if this person had not been lost or this path had not been taken. John Kenn Mortensen illustrates the book magically, causing Tem to confess that he worried its sales were due solely to the illustrations. That of course is just modesty, though the story and story and the pictures do work well together to achieve an aesthetic response in us of intimacy, vulnerability, wonder, regret, sadness. They both have a synergy, making our identity extend to that of the characters.

Very few writers I recall have attempted describing seriously what would happen if you took the job of manager for a hotel whose clientele was strictly monsters needing R & R. The idea beckons and, in a refreshing twist, Tem doesn't play it for laughs. He shows us vampires considering helpless prey as a girl jogs by, reveals what madness and lust ghosts can engender, has demons fill the invisible, whispers how serial killers dismember, lets pounce a changeable cat that could eat you, and has bob some humanlike black blobs that rise in the pool and make drowning seem a prime endangerment. Most remarkable is that Tem never has any of these characters raise their voices to have us be overcome by the terror: fright secretes from their pores, rises out of their shuffle, radiates from their eyes, melancholy pools at their dim feet. If you were a widower and had to raise a young girl in this despondent place, how would you get on (remembering no one else wants to hire you)? And how would you face it when you start falling for one of your guests who reminds you in all the right ways of your dead wife? If ever there was to be a hotel with a non-fraternization policy, this off-the-map, forlorn lodging is the place. Will your child—your last connection to this living world—be killed by any of the lodgers in this near-ruin, or will she simply go insane? Or worse, will she become one of them? Last, can Richard trust any of the Proprietor's advice, one Mr Jacob Ascher, the only non-monster at the place, and yet a kind of creepy Mr Rodgers doppelgänger, a bachelor we could imagine skulking in long black claw-hammer coat. Really there's no exit from *Deadfall Hotel* … a manager must see to all his "guests." As in life, so in Horror: you've just got to do your job the best that you can.

JOHN PELAN

Forgotten Masters of the Weird Tale #2
Southern Discomfort:
The Weird Tales of Wyatt Blassingame

Last time around we discussed Mary Dale Buckner (Donald Dale) and Greye La Spina, and I made brief mention of some of Ms. Buckner's contemporaries in the weird menace pulps who successfully transcended the limitations of the formulaic nature of the genre to produce some truly excellent weird tales. The author I'd like to discuss averaged close to a million words a year during his peak period and was one of the few authors allowed by editor Rogers Terrill to depart from the stringent formula of rationalized endings and write out-and-out supernatural stories. He was also one of the few weird menace authors who remained active in the genre to the very end without losing his edge, successfully transitioned to more prosaic detective fiction, and, despite averaging nearly a million words a year of top-quality weird tales, remained unreprinted and unanthologized for over seventy years…

I refer to Wyatt Blassingame, brother of top New York agent Lurton Blassingame and a mainstay of *Dime Mystery Magazine*, *Terror Tales*, and *Horror Stories*. In my last column I mentioned Blassingame as being on a level equal to Hugh B. Cave and thus in the upper echelons of writers specializing in the weird menace tale, with only a handful of authors who could truly be said to be his peer. How can a talent of this magnitude disappear so completely from the consciousness of readers?

Let's take a look at a short yet very productive career. Wyatt Blassingame seems to be one of those people destined for the writing game. Despite a fine education, he found himself knocking about the country during the height of the Depression, working briefly as a journalist, and found himself broke in New York City in 1933 wondering what fate had in store for him. What fate, in the person of his older brother, literary agent Lurton Blassingame, had in store for him was a stack of pulp magazines of various genres and the advice to study them and see if he could write similar stories.

The younger Blassingame rose to the occasion in fine form, and over the next decade wrote more than 400 stories. Mystery, sports, romance, air war, western, just about everything except the "true confession." However, one genre held a special fascination, and Wyatt Blassingame quickly became one of the best, if not the best, authors of the new brand of horror fiction called "weird menace."

The weird menace formula was created by editor Rogers Terrill at Popular Publications, who had been tasked with reviving the sagging sales of *Dime Mystery Magazine*. Like most good ideas, the concept was a simple one: combine the rationalized supernatural thriller, much in vogue at the time, with the lurid excesses of the Grand Guignol Theatre of Paris and throw in enough titillation to compete with the *risqué* covers that Margaret Brundage was painting for Popular's sister magazine, *Weird Tales*.

The genre debuted in the October 1933 issue of *Dime Mystery*. As an indication of what a quick study Blassingame was, he had a novelette in the December issue and had the lead "novel" in the January 1934 issue. This new style of horror story was a rousing success and Popular brought out a second magazine in September 1934, *Terror Tales*, to accommodate the ever-growing readership. Under his own name and his nom de plume, William B. Rainey, Blassingame had no fewer than seventeen stories, mostly novelettes or novellas, published in the two magazines in 1934 alone.

So what set Wyatt Blassingame apart from his colleagues? The author himself stated that he relied on two very basic formulas: 1. The protagonist is fleeing from a menace. He tries every possible method of escape. Despite his efforts, the menace overtakes him and all seems lost. Somehow the hero manages to turn the tables.

2. The hero and heroine are trapped in a dark room at night. Every side represents some element of danger. The walls begin to close in. The hero has to find a way out. Add to the mix the mandate of editor Terrill that a seemingly supernatural menace should be revealed to be of human origin at the story's denouement, and this would seem a rather fragile framework on which to hang a tale. A short story, possibly; a novella? Almost certainly not …

However, that's exactly what Wyatt Blassingame did and, with the possible exceptions of Hugh B. Cave, John H. Knox, and Arthur J. Burks, did better than anyone else. He pushed the boundaries of formula to the point that he was able to transcend the limitations of the form and create some truly exceptional weird tales. This is not to say that every story published under his name or the William B. Rainey byline was a gem or masterpiece of originality. No, Wyatt Blassingame wrote his fair share of standard thrillers in the prescribed mode, set above and apart from his fellows only by an excellent sense of pacing and a wonderful sense of place, generally the American South. In fact, one may consider a goodly portion of Blassingame's fiction to belong firmly in the canon of the Southern Gothic.

This willingness to utilize other locales is a large part of what sets the four authors referenced above apart from their peers. Burks, a career military man, was very well-traveled as a result, and from the very start of his career Hugh B. Cave had a fascination with the island of Hispaniola in general and Haiti in particular, which would lead to his relocating there some years later. Like his contemporary Jack Williamson, John H. Knox lived in West Texas and New Mexico when the latter was still in its early years of statehood and what are now full-size cities or centers of commerce were small trading posts where one could easily fill volumes just by transcribing local legends and lore. Needless to say, most of their contemporaries wrote what they knew, which generally was New York City, a fascinating place to be sure, but hardly a milieu conducive to providing an exotic or mysterious atmosphere.

Blassingame's milieu of choice was the deep South, not the "New South," but the South of William Faulkner and Flannery

O'Connor, where small towns held hideous secrets and grand old families kept skeletons in the ancestral closet that were too unspeakable to discuss. This isn't to imply that he *always* set his stories in the South or that all his tales were masterpieces of supernatural horror; they weren't. What Blassingame did was to establish himself very early on as a master of the weird menace formula, and once this was accomplished, he began to start bending and then breaking the rules with very satisfying results.

Wyatt Blassingame debuted in the horror genre in the December 1933 issue of *Dime Mystery* with a predictable but competently written yarn entitled "The Horror in the Hold." While this is a minor piece, it was enough to convince editor Rogers Terrill that in Wyatt Blassingame he had another author who "got it" and could be counted on to produce the novelette- or novella-length lead feature that was always in demand and could be touted as a "complete novel."

With the publication of the novella "Death Underground" in January 1934, Blassingame came into his own as a writer who could be relied on to deliver a compelling lead feature. While "Death Underground" is still firmly in the tradition of the rationalized explanation for seemingly supernatural events that was a central element of the weird menace formula, it also serves to show Blassingame's deft grasp of the mystery story. In fact, were the graphic elements (death by fire ants) toned down just a bit, "Death Underground" would have been a perfect fit at any of a number of more mainstream mystery magazines.

1934 was a year of development, wherein he wrote a mix of stories, some firmly set in the weird menace formula, but others that were, if not overtly supernatural, ambiguous enough to the point that they would have fit in very nicely at *Weird Tales*. As the Blassingame name was solidly associated with lead features in *Dime Mystery* and the new companion magazine *Terror Tales*, the nom de plume of William B. Rainey was created to handle the occasional short filler story that was sometimes needed to round out an issue. As there was no discernible difference in style or theme, and "Rainey" only appeared in issues wherein Blassingame had a lead novelette or novella, it seems likely that astute readers would have figured out the deception in short order.

By the middle of 1934 we start to see the caliber of fiction that should have assured Wyatt Blassingame's reputation as a "master of the weird tale." In April, the remarkably brutal and effective *conte cruel* "The Tongueless Horror" appeared in *Dime Mystery*, followed the next two months by "Mummy Medicine" and "Death Blisters," both excellent tales, though these too adhered to the rationalized supernatural ending common to the form. However, by the end of the year Blassingame had found his comfort zone and his productivity soared.

Frequently given the cover feature (even over such contemporaries as Arthur J. Burks and Hugh B. Cave), Blassingame was now in a position to start experimenting, and the result was not only some of his best work, but some of the very best weird tales that the shudder pulps had to offer. With "Honeymoon in Hell" (*Dime Mystery*, September 1934) the mystery element has several components, and while a goodly portion have very prosaic explanations, there remain enough unanswered questions that the supernatural seems not only a possible explanation, but *the most likely one*. It is with "Honeymoon in Hell" and "Dead Man's Bride" (*Terror Tales*, September 1934) that Blassingame started bending the rules and leaving it up to the reader to decide if there could be a logical explanation for events or if they had just read a supernatural tale.

From this point on Blassingame alternated between stories that followed the editorial dictates of having a rational explanation for the apparently supernatural events and brilliant pieces such as "The Unholy Goddess," one of the finest tales of lycanthropy to come from the pulps.

The next three years were the "golden age" for the genre, with new magazines such as *Thrilling Mystery* and *Horror Stories* entering the field and the pioneers of the genre such as Cave, Burks, Knox, Zagat, Rogers, and, of course, Blassingame doing much of their best work. Of this group, only Blassingame and Burks seemed inclined to stray from the prescribed formula with any regularity. It makes for an interesting scenario of "what if?" to speculate how things might have turned out for the field had there been more deviation from formula allowed…As it was, several of the better writers seemed to get burned out by the repetitive nature of what they were writing and began to focus on other markets. Even worse, this burnout was felt by the readers, and by late 1937 flagging sales were the result.

The magazines responded predictably by encouraging ever more graphic violence and titillation to the point where various watchdog groups began to snuffle about the newsstands in an unpleasant fashion. Interestingly enough, Blassingame continued to write excellent stories right up to the time the genre died out (coinciding with the outbreak of World War II).

To indicate the level that Blassingame attained during 1935–37, I'll refer to my own notes for those years made when I was assembling the anthology *The Century's Best Horror*. First and foremost, to say that the competition during those years was fierce is quite an understatement. Not only was *Weird Tales* at one of its peak periods, but, on the other side of the pond, Charles Birkin was editing the "Creeps" series with a substantial amount of new material. As those who have purchased the book know, in 1935 my selection was Clark Ashton Smith's "The Dark Eidolon," an exquisite mix of beauty and brutality set in Smith's world of Zothique. The runners-up were (in no particular order): Arthur J. Burks, "Six Doors to Horror"; C. L. Moore, "Jirel Meets Magic" (disqualified by the appearance of "Shambleau"); Arlton Eadie, "The Carnival of Death"; Kirk Mashburn, "The Toad Idol"; and finally, Clark Ashton Smith with both "Vulthoom" and "The Treader of the Dust," and Wyatt Blassingame with "The Song of the Dead" and "The Invisible Horror" both meriting strong consideration.

1936 was also a close one with Thorp McCluskey's "The Crawling Horror" narrowly edging out Blassingame's "The Horror at His Heels," perhaps his finest supernatural tale, calling to mind *The Rime of the Ancient Mariner*, with the unseen but all-too-tangible fiend pursuing the protagonist to his doom. In 1937 Blassingame was again a strong contender with two excellent tales, "Flesh for the Swamp Men" and "Goddess of Crawling Horrors." Unfortunately, that was the year that Howard Wandrei's best story, "The Eerie Mr Murphy," was published.

For some reason, 1938 was not a strong year for Blassingame in the horror field, though he was very much a presence elsewhere. In 1939 he was back in fine form with "Lady of the Yellow Death" and "Golden Nymphs of Horror," with the former getting very serious consideration. Actually, in any other year it might have been my selection, but 1939 saw the publication of Rober Barbour Johnson's "Far Below," not only easily the best story of the year, but one that I'd put in the top five for the entire decade.

With World War II inexorably drawing the U.S. in, Blassingame was called up for military service, and at about the same time the weird menace genre died out. Despite some talented new authors like Mary Dale Buckner and Ralston Shields entering the field, too many of the mainstays such as Burks, Zagat, Rogers, and Schachner were moving on to other types of fiction and were sorely missed. Added to that was the specter of censorship and the all-too-real threat of the magazines being yanked off of New York newsstands. The weird menace genre died out, and rather than try his hand at the low-paying *Weird Tales*, Blassingame made one more sale in the horror genre to *Strange Stories* in 1941 ("Appointment with a Lady") and then turned his attention to detective stories (and wrote some very good ones for *Thrilling Mystery* and *Dime Mystery*), before leaving the pulps entirely for the far more lucrative trade of writing historical novels for juveniles.

All told, Wyatt Blassingame's career as a writer of weird fiction totaled only seven years. Rather brief when we look at authors such as Hugh B. Cave, Jack Williamson, and Manly Wade Wellman, all of whom were active for over fifty years. Still, the level of quality and volume that Blassingame produced is formidable, with more than seventy pieces, most of which were of at least novelette length. Also, the number of cover features accorded to him certainly bears out the idea that Rogers Terrill considered him one of his major talents and that the appearance of his name on a cover would increase sales.

How, then, does an author of this caliber become so completely forgotten that for over thirty-five years, not a single anthology or magazine reprinted a Blassingame story? Several factors come into play. Blassingame seemed to have a genuine fondness for his pulp days, unlike some of his contemporaries, who when asked about their work of that time react much the way a Miss America contestant does when queried about an earlier career in pornography. However, during his post–World War II career there is nothing to indicate that he tried to market any of his earlier work either singly or as a collection. So we can say with some degree of certainty that the author's lack of interest played a role.

While I doubt that Donald Wollheim would have reprinted any Blassingame tales in the *Avon Fantasy Reader* (for reasons I'll get to next), I have little doubt but that Robert A.W. Lowndes would have used some of this material in *Magazine of Horror* or *Startling Mystery*, *had he been approached*. I can say this with reasonable certainty based on the inclusion of other pieces from the weird menace pulps, notably by Arthur J. Burks and Hugh B. Cave. Were Burks and Cave better writers of weird fiction? In my opinion, the best of Blassingame stands with the best of either man, but in the case of Cave there is a substantially greater quantity and greater variety, and Burks has the cachet of being an Arkham House author.

Is the Arkham House credential really a factor? How about having been a *Weird Tales* alumnus? With the advantage of well over fifty years of hindsight, I would have to say yes. For many years fans and collectors took an interesting view of the weird menace pulps, judging them to be something outside the genre of imaginative literature and having little merit. As early as the 1930s, people collected pulps featuring "off-trail" stories. Many times I've been called in to appraise a collection of this vintage, and it isn't at all unusual to find that a collector of *Amazing* and *Wonder Stories* also collected *Weird Tales* and frequently had bound excerpts from *Argosy* and *All-Story*. However, copies of the weird menace pulps would be nowhere to be found. For years this prejudice existed against the weird menace magazines and, by extension, their authors. Even though Burks, Schachner, and Zagat were active in science fiction on a regular basis, their work in magazines such as

Dime Mystery, *Spicy Mystery*, *Horror Stories*, and so on was ignored by collectors and anthologists alike. Robert Jones's masterful book *The Shudder Pulps* (1975) went a long way in rectifying this situation, but anthologists who might have been interested were faced with another problem: since early SF fans hadn't collected the weird menace pulps, they were hard to come by and very expensive.

Let's face it, anthologists do not, as a general rule, earn a lot for what usually amounts to an awful lot of work. Adding the extra wrinkle of having to spend a lot of money out of pocket to acquire an obscure pulp magazine to acquire *one* story for an anthology is far more trouble than most are willing to go to. We probably wouldn't have access to any of Wyatt Blassingame's work today had it not been for Robert Weinberg publishing a series of pulp reprints in the 1970s and Sheldon Jaffery issuing two anthologies of material from the weird menace pulps in the late 1980s. Wyatt Blassingame still has yet to catch the eye of anthologists, but the last couple of years have seen several volumes of his best work collected, so it may well be that in the next few years we'll be able to drop the "Forgotten" from his title!

Notes on Contributors

Jason V Brock is an award-winning writer, filmmaker, composer, and artist, and has been published in *Butcher Knives & Body Counts*, *The Devil's Coattails*, *Calliope*, *The Bleeding Edge*, *Black Wings II*, and many others. He was art director/managing editor for *Dark Discoveries* magazine for more than three years, and has a new magazine out called *[NameL3ss]*. As a filmmaker, his work includes the documentaries *Charles Beaumont: The Short Life of Twilight Zone's Magic Man*, *The AckerMonster Chronicles!*, and *Image, Reflection, Shadow: Artists of the Fantastic*.

Michael Cisco is the author of the novels *The Divinity Student* (Buzzcity Press, 1999; winner of the International Horror Guild Award for best first novel), *The Tyrant* (Prime, 2004), *The San Veneficio Canon* (Prime, 2005), *The Traitor* (Prime, 2007), *The Narrator* (Civil Coping Mechanisms, 2010), *The Great Lover* (Chomu Press, 2011), and *Celebrant* (Chomu Press, 2012). His short story collection, *Secret Hours*, was published by Mythos Books in 2007.

Phillip A. Ellis is a freelance critic, poet, and scholar. His chapbooks, *The Flayed Man* (Gothic Press, 2008) and *Symptoms Positive and Negative* (Picaro Press, 2011), are available. He is working on a collection for Diminuendo Press. Another has been accepted by Hippocampus Press. He is the editor of *Melaleuca*.

Michael Fantina has had hundreds of poems published in North America, the United Kingdom, and Australia. He estimates that just about 97% of his poetry falls into the categories of fantasy/horror/supernatural. He has had horror fiction published in the U.S., U.K., and recently a Cthulhu Mythos tale in the Japanese horror magazine *Nightland*.

Tom Fletcher was born in 1984. He is a husband and father, and currently lives in Manchester, England. He is the author of two novels—*The Leaping* (Quercus, 2010) and *The Thing on the Shore* (Quercus, 2011)—and numerous short stories.

Sam Gafford has been active in weird fiction criticism since the 1990s. His work has appeared in *Lovecraft Studies*, *Studies in Weird Fiction*, *Crypt of Cthulhu*, *TAPS Magazine*, and other periodicals. In "Writing Backwards: The Novels of William Hope Hodgson," he provided proof that

Hodgson's novels had been written in virtually the opposite order of publication which changed many preconceptions about Hodgson. He has co-compiled a Hodgson bibliography with S. T. Joshi and is currently working on a book-length critical study of Hodgson.

Stuart Galbraith IV is the author of seven books, including *The Emperor and the Wolf* and *Japanese Cinema*. His audio commentaries include *Tora-san* and *Musashi Miyamoto*, he reviews DVDs and Blu-ray at DVD Talk.com, and he lives in Kyoto, Japan, with his wife and daughter.

Wade German's poems have received nominations for the Pushcart Prize and Rhysling Award, as well as honorable mentions in Ellen Datlow's *Best Horror of the Year* anthologies. Some of his latest work can be found in recent and forthcoming issues of *Abyss and Apex*, *Dreams and Nightmares*, *Nameless*, and *Space and Time*. He currently lives in Prague, Czech Republic.

James Goho is an education researcher and planner working mostly with colleges. He has published many research articles in such academic journals as *Medical Teacher* and the book *Assessment and Evaluation in Higher Education*. His mainstream short fiction has appeared in *Descant*, *Grain*, and others. With a keen interest in the American Gothic, he has published literary criticism on Lovecraft. He divides his time among Winnipeg, Phoenix, and Boston.

H.W. Janson (1913–1982) was an American scholar of art history best known for his *History of Art*, which was first published in 1962 and has sold more than two million copies in fifteen languages. He taught at Washington University in St Louis from 1941 to 1949, in which year he joined the faculty of New York University, where he built the undergraduate arts department and taught at the graduate Institute of Fine Arts. He was recognized with an honorary degree in 1981 and died on a train between Zurich and Milan in 1982 at the age of 68.

Charles Lovecraft has written fantasy verse since 1975. He established P'rea Press in 2007 to publish weird and fantastic poetry, literary criticism, and bibliography. Forthcoming in 2012 is *Avatars of Wizardry*, a contemporary collection inspired by the poetry of George Sterling and Clark Ashton Smith. He promotes reading, writing, and performance of fantastic poetry by conducting panels and workshops at conventions.

Charles has edited twelve books, including *Metabolism* (2012), a members' anthology of Australian Poetry Ltd.

Danel Olson lives in The Woodlands, Texas, with his family. He has edited new essays on the Gothic (*21st Century Gothic: Great Gothic Novels Since 2000*, Scarecrow Press) and movies (*The Exorcist: Studies in the Horror Film*, Centipede Press), and continues to gather new stories for a literary franchise called *Exotic Gothic* (a fifth volume appears in January 2013 from PS Publishing, and Danel hopes to pilot ten of them). He is most interested in contemporary master horrorists across media—in graphic novels, cinema, and fiction—who reinvent the genre as they create involving and fundamentally human yet surreal nightmares.

John Pelan has recently assembled and introduced some twenty volumes of collections from the weird menace pulps and obscure British supernatural thrillers for Dancing Tuatara Press at www.ramblehouse.com.

W. H. Pugmire has been writing Lovecraftian weird fiction since the mid-1970s. His newest books include *Uncommon Places* (Hippocampus Press, 2012) and *The Strange Dark One: Tales of Nyarlathotep* (Miskatonic River Press, 2012). His next book, written in collaboration with Jeffrey Thomas, will be *Encounters with Enoch Coffin* (Dark Regions Press, 2013). He is at work on a new book, *Bohemians of Sesqua Valley* (Arcane Wisdom), that will debut at the NecronomiCon in Providence, Rhode Island, in 2013.

Joseph S. Pulver, Sr. is the author of the novel *The Orphan Palace* (Chomu Press, 2011) and three collections from Hippocampus Press, *Blood Will Have Its Season* (2009), *SIN & ashes* (2010), and *Portraits of Ruin* (2012). His work has appeared in such venues as *Phantamagorium*, Ellen Datlow's *Best Horror of the Year*, and *The Book of Cthulhu*.

Ann K. Schwader's most recent book, *Twisted in Dream: The Collected Weird Poetry of Ann K. Schwader*, was published by Hippocampus Press in 2011. *Wild Hunt of the Stars* (Sam's Dot, 2010), a collection of dark SF verse, was a Bram Stoker Award finalist. She lives and writes in Westminster, Colorado.

Darrell Schweitzer is the author of three novels, *The White Isle*, *The Shattered Goddess*, and *The Mask of the Sorcerer*, and about 300 short stories. He has been nominated four times for the World Fantasy Award and won it once, for *Weird Tales*, of which he was coeditor for nineteen years. He has also edited or coedited anthologies, including *The Secret History of Vampires*, *Cthulhu's Reign*, *Full Moon City*, and *That Is Not Dead* (forthcoming from PS Publishing in 2013).

Bradley H. Sinor has seen his work appear in numerous science fiction, fantasy, and horror anthologies such as *The Improbable Adventures of Sherlock Holmes*, *Tales of the Shadowmen*, *The Grantville Gazette* and *Ring of Fire 2 and 3*. Three collections of his short fiction have been released by Yard Dog Press, *Dark and Stormy Nights*, *In the Shadows*, and *Playing with Secrets* (along with stories by his wife, Sue Sinor). His newest collections are *Echoes from the Darkness* (Arctic Wolf Press) and *Where the Shadows Began* (Merry Blacksmith Press).

Jonathan Thomas is a native of Providence, Rhode Island, whose story collections include *Stories from the Big Black House* (Radio Void Press, 1992), *Midnight Call and Other Stories* (Hippocampus Press, 2008), and *Tempting Providence and Other Stories* (Hippocampus Press, 2010). Arcane Wisdom has published his novel, *The Color Over Occam*, and more recent short stories have appeared in *Black Wings I* and *Black Wings II* (both from PS Publishing), *A Mountain Walked* (Centipede Press), and *Nameless* (Cycatrix Press).

Richard Thomas was the winner of the "Enter the World of *Filaria*" contest at ChiZine. He has published more than sixty stories in such venues as *Shivers VI* (Cemetery Dance), *Speedloader* (Snubnose Press), *Gargoyle*, *PANK*, *Pear Noir!*, and *Opium*. His debut novel, *Transubstantiate* (Otherworld Publications), was released in 2010.

Robert H. Waugh is the author of *The Monster in the Mirror: Looking for H. P. Lovecraft* (Hippocampus Press, 2005) and *A Monster of Voices: Speaking for H. P. Lovecraft* (Hippocampus Press, 2011), as well as the author of two collections of poems, *Shorewards, Tidewards* (Codhill Press, 2007) and *Thumbtacks, Glass, Pennies* (Codhill Press, 2009).

The Weird Fiction Review
Issue number 3
Fall 2012

Published by Centipede Press
2565 Teller Court, Lakewood, Colorado 80214

ISBN 978-1-61347-040-4 (ppb.: alk. paper)

Printed and bound in the United States.

www.centipedepress.com